Acknowledgements

Many thanks to my wife Mary and my sister Helen for editorial advice and encouragement

Barcelona Vendetta

9th September 2018

MIKE

As I carefully positioned the wooden crate the thought crossed my mind that nobody keeps their car in the garage anymore. Glancing around at the tumble dryer, lawnmower, fertiliser, workbench, anti-freeze, an assortment of offcuts and tools – certainly no room for a car! 'Keep your mind on the job in hand Mike', I thought to myself, 'Unlike everything else in my life, I can't muck this up'. I sling the rope over a beam, grab the decorator's steps and tie a knot immediately under the beam, then pull firmly to ensure no slippage. Thus effecting an efficient hangman's noose. I'd always had an eye for detail and wouldn't leave anything to chance. I had no doubts that this was the only way out of the mess I'd gotten into. How had it come to this? Alcoholic fog didn't prevent the litany of faults flashing through my brain. I'd gambled, drunk excessively, lied, got into debt and ruined just about every relationship I'd ever had! This was the easiest way out, no more shouting, no more creditors banging on the door, no more no more anything. Peace.

Chapter 1 – New Beginnings

16th March 2018,

MIKE

I could never please my father. He found fault in everything I did and I grew up thinking I wasn't good enough and would never live up to much. I steered clear of him and lived most of my early years in solitude in my bedroom cramming my head full of pointless facts from the internet. My mother loved me I'm sure but was too weak to stand up to my domineering father so as soon as I was able I left home and haven't had any contact with either of them since. I was bright and easily got a job in IT, enjoyed pub quiz nights and gambled away a fair share of my earnings. I was finally diagnosed with autism at the ripe old age of 30. It explained a few things, my inability to interact socially, my lack of communication and my repetitive habits.

So you can imagine it was a big step for myself and Connie moving in to the newly purchased two-bedroom apartment in Bermondsey, London. We had met at work, a large government office block, just over a year ago, at the coffee machine as it happens, sharing a few thoughts about the weather, work, you know the usual. This went on for a few weeks until I plucked up courage to ask her out for a few drinks. Where I found we had quite a lot in common, theatre, TV and a love of reading. And quite a lot that we didn't have in common, Connie was a triathlete and excelled at judo, whereas I enjoyed online gambling, however these differences made us 'interesting'. We seemed to get on pretty well and one evening in the wine bar I suggested, half-jokingly, that we move in together. Much to my surprise Connie didn't scoff at the idea. As we discussed it, our enthusiasm grew and we decided to take the plunge! Obtaining a mortgage was fairly straight forward as we were both on good salaries.

The apartment is a modest two bedroom on the second floor of a three-storey block with separate lock-up garages. There are some small green spaces outside with an occasional Judas Tree dotted around. It gave me a feeling of satisfaction to hold the paperwork confirming Michael Dean and Connie Crawley as the owners of number 21, representing a major commitment to each other. Just then Connie's voice broke through my thoughts, 'Come on Mike, stop dawdling!'
'Sorry Connie', I replied as I struggled with a particularly large box up the stairs. No lift in this building. Connie, being a lot fitter than I will ever be, seemed to be taking it all in her stride. Anyway, between us we made good progress and by 4 o'clock we had deposited all the boxes in the flat. I didn't need to worry about the rental white van as I'd be returning it the following morning.
'Ready for a brew Connie?', I said knowing that we had most of the unpacking still to do.

'I thought you'd never ask', Connie replied as she hugged me from behind and kissed my neck.

We both sank down into our comfortable pale green chairs. The décor of the living room was fairly nondescript, being mostly beige. However it didn't matter as, given time, we would put our own mark on the place. Connie, being a Project Manager by trade, is impatient to get everything done to her exacting standards as soon as possible, whereas I tend to follow in her wake!

CONNIE

I had the happiest of childhoods, an only spoilt child growing up in a house full of love and laughter. Daddy was sports mad and encouraged me to take up running, cycling and swimming which I loved. He insisted I take up Judo just in case I needed to defend myself in the future. It turned out I was pretty good at everything, not that I'm blowing my own trumpet! Mummy on the other hand ensured I kept up with my academic work and I excelled at IT too. We weren't well off but I never felt I missed out on anything. Tragically I lost both of my beloved parents to cancer within two years of each other. I was away at university and I found myself having to grow up very quickly. My sport was everything and I threw myself into it wholeheartedly. I was lucky enough to get a well paid job in a government office and a flat share with two other girls.

Now I can't believe I've committed to a relationship with another person. My whole life up to now has been getting fit for my triathlons and that has meant being focused. Yet here I am moving in with Mike. I think it's love. We met at work, he was the IT whiz kid everyone went to and I had to get his advice a few times. He's quite good looking I suppose, could do with losing a few pounds but mostly he makes me laugh. He has a repertoire of "dad" jokes and his dancing isn't much better! My best friend Sarah tried to warn me off but that's because she has my best interests at heart. Mike and I are so different. He drinks far too much for a start and is bit of a lazy bastard but somehow it works. He has a head full of useless information which he loves to share with anyone who'll listen but sometimes that comes across as boring. I have to kick him under the table to shut him up at times. Don't get him onto the subject of IT or you'll be there all night. Mind you he probably thinks I'm obsessed with my fitness and he's right. We haven't discussed having children yet but it's early days. I've got quite a few more years before my biological clock runs out. There's no way I'm giving up my triathlons yet!

7th April 2018

MIKE

We've been living in the flat for three weeks now and are mostly ship-shape and Bristol fashion – a saying from the nineteenth century apparently in reference to ships going in and out of Bristol harbour, a very important city in those days. I'm a mine of useless information as Connie will tell you. To be honest I've done most of the work, painting and decorating, putting up shelves, hanging pictures. Connie keeps the work schedule updated and then goes off training for her next big triathlon!

CONNIE

Mike has surprised me. He's really worked hard on the flat. He makes me laugh too with his little snippets of information. Perhaps this will work after all?

15th April 2018

MIKE

Connie is out training again and I'm so bored, but I've found this great online casino website and having a flutter. It certainly gets the adrenaline going!

CONNIE

Mike is so patient with me. I'm out running and training every day but he's so sweet about it. I've got the Bermuda triathlon approaching so I'll be away again, but he doesn't seem to mind.

26th April 2018

MIKE

Connie is away for just over a week, she has flown out to Bermuda for a triathlon. I'm at a bit of a loose end. In fact, I don't seem to see much of her at all during the week, especially as she often has to work late or is working away. At the weekend and early mornings, she is usually training either swimming, cycling or running.

6th May 2018

MIKE

Connie flew back from Bermuda on Friday and seems to have recovered quickly from the jetlag, so she has arranged for us to have Sunday lunch at the local pub with her best friend Sarah. She lives in her own apartment set amongst four others in a rambling Georgian building about 20 minutes away. It is a 10-minute walk to the Dog and Pheasant for us and Sarah is already seated at the table, but gets to her feet as we approach. She looks gorgeous as usual. If I wasn't with Connie and she wasn't her best friend who knows? Don't get me wrong, Connie is pretty but she's not one for make-up and floaty dresses. She's mostly in joggers or jeans which show off her gorgeous long legs and pert backside so I'm not complaining.

'Hello Connie, hello Mike, lovely to see you both', followed by a couple of air-kisses.
'Lovely to see you too Sarah', Connie gushes.

'You two sit-down while I get the drinks. What's your poison?' I ask.

'Oooh, mine's a glass of Prosecco please', Sarah replies.

'And I'll have the same please Mike', said Connie.

At the bar I order a bottle of Prosecco, a bottle of Merlot and three glasses. Then return to the table with the menus. I pour the wine for all of us, 'Cheers', we all say and clink the glasses. Connie has been telling Sarah all about the Bermuda triathlon, while I study the menu. We are ready to order, Connie chooses an appropriately high-carb pasta dish. Sarah, melon slices followed by a Caesar salad, obviously watching her figure! For myself whitebait then duck à l'orange – the house speciality!

The small talk continues and we are onto our mains. 'More Prosecco ladies?', I ask.

'Oh not for me thanks Mike, as I am in training for my next triathlon', Connie says with a smile.

Sarah smiling broadly, 'Yes please Mike'.

I top-up my fourth glass.

We all decide to skip dessert and order coffees. Time to sit back and relax.

Unexpectedly Sarah lowers her voice, 'You know, I think my apartment is haunted!' I struggle to suppress a laugh, 'What do you mean?' I ask.

'Strange things keep happening'

'Like what?', Connie interjects.

'Well, the other day I came in from work to find one of the rings on the hob was switched on!'

'There must be some logical explanation', I respond, 'Perhaps you left it on at breakfast time?'

Sarah defensively, 'No, I'm sure I didn't. But anyway there are other happenings.'

"Such as?" I lean forward attentively.

"Objects move around, they are not where I put them. Also there are strange noises, rustling and knocking sounds in the night."

Somewhat scornfully I say, 'You must be mistaken, perhaps a little too much Prosecco? Anyway there are always odd noises in old houses.'

Connie jumps in, 'Mike! Don't be so rude! I'm sure Sarah knows what she's seen and heard.'

I counter, 'There are no such things as ghosts. If there were, then we'd be seeing them all the time. There would be a serious overcrowding problem given the billions of people that have died since the dawn of time. Not to mention the billions of animals too!'

'Oh shut up Mike!' Connie's raised voice immediately taking on a calmer, lighter tone. 'Sorry Sarah. Let's change the subject'

'There she goes again', I thought, 'Connie bending over backwards to avoid any angst'

Connie changing the subject asks Sarah how her job as an Estate Agent was going? I finished my coffee and made my excuses. Once back home I open another bottle of wine and log onto the casino website.

CONNIE

I'm feeling quite good about myself. I did a personal best with my running, swim was okay but got a puncture on the bike so that knocked me back a bit. Still I'm chuffed and Sarah at least was interested. Mike was drinking too much and was a bit of an arsehole. Poor Sarah thinks her place is haunted and of course Mike had to go off on one and poo-poo the idea. I don't know what to think. It's not like Sarah to be spooked so there must be something going on, but what?

12th May 2018

MIKE

Saturday lunchtime Connie comes in from training, 'You're very late', I say.

'Yes', Connie explained, 'Sarah is still very worried that her apartment may be haunted. So I suggested she see a priest to discuss it. In fact I've arranged for her local priest to go round next week'

'You what!' I exclaimed, then laughingly, 'Now I've heard it all. The church is great at all this hocus-pocus, it's part of how they have managed to keep themselves in jobs over all these years!'

'Mike that's not fair! You know I'm not a big church goer myself, I'm just there to support Sarah.'

'Connie all you're doing is helping prop up an ageing dinosaur, one that is overdue for extinction!'

'The church does a lot of good things in the community. Lots of people still believe you know.'

No longer laughing I say, 'They do lots of not so good things too, such as fiddling with choir boys and causing wars'. I was really getting my teeth into this argument.

Exasperated, Connie said, 'Mike you really are the limit. Everything has to be black and white for you! You're so big headed at times. Just because you don't believe in ghosts or other people's religions you had to have a go at me. I'm just supporting Sarah when she needs me. Perhaps we're not so compatible after all!' Connie leaves the room, slamming the door behind her.

13th May 2018

MIKE

Connie joined me for a late breakfast. 'Coffee or tea?', I ask. 'Coffee please', replied Connie nimbly positioning her 5' 11" athletic frame on the dining chair. Her close-cropped chestnut brown hair still damp from an early morning swim at the local indoor pool. I poured the coffee from the cafetiere, black no sugar just how she likes it. While she busied herself with cereal, I sip my hot tea and ponder. 'Connie', I say, 'Seriously, this ghost exorcism thing, don't you think it's going a bit far?'

'No I don't.' Connie continued, 'Even if there aren't any such thing as ghosts, then at least it will provide some reassurance for Sarah. I mean, it could all be in her mind. If she believes in the exorcism, then maybe she will also believe that the ghost has been banished.'

I respond, 'Yes, I suppose so, I guess it all comes down to 'faith'. If you so badly want to believe in something, even when there is no substantive evidence, then you will do. Prime examples are the Flat Earth Society and those people who don't believe that man ever landed on the moon!'

'We all need to believe in something Mike! I do believe in God or at least that there is something that oversees everything'.

'Oh come off it Connie. Throughout mans' thousands of years of existence he has always needed to invent a god or gods. It all stems from his non-acceptance that death is final. He has to believe that there is an afterlife! Modern science has proved that all we are is a carbon-based lifeform. A collection of molecules that interact with each other to form an advanced organism. When we die, finito, that's it!'

'You want evidence Mike, then what about Noah's Ark, and there are the miracles such as Jesus feeding the five thousand?'

'Fairy stories. Stories handed down by word of mouth for generations and exaggerated in the retelling. Similar to the old battlefield joke, "Send reinforcements we are going to advance." Passed on from messenger to messenger and finally arrives at the general's ear as "Send three and fourpence we are going to a dance!"'

'Bloody hell Mike, you have an answer for everything!'

'And you know what Connie, all the religions in the world come down to one thing, control. Name any religion you like Islam, Buddhism, Hinduism, Christianity, it all comes down to rules, rules that control the lives of the devotees. Of course the trouble is the written text is so large that there are many contradictions, leading to all sorts of confusion. Like wars, for example, 24th August 1572 French Catholics slaughtered between 5,000 and 10,000 French Protestants in the St Bartholomew's Day Massacre. Fellow Christians, I ask you!' I said my head was full of useless facts didn't I?

Connie moodily retorted, 'You just can't let it drop can you? You're like an old scratched vinyl record, repeating the same old stuff again and again. Well I have my faith and I'm sticking with it!'.

Realising I wasn't going to shift Connie's view, I disparagingly threw out, 'Good for you!'

CONNIE

Mike really annoyed me today with his know-it-all attitude. He's spending a lot of time on his laptop too. I think he's gambling too much but he assures me he's careful and sticks to a budget. I suppose I can't complain as I'm always out training and he doesn't seem to mind. The Leeds triathlon is coming up and I really want to do well.

19th May 2018

MIKE

Thank goodness another week of work is over! I feel absolutely knackered! Dragged from pillar to post! Everyone wants their particular problem dealt with first! There are some nice people at work, but the obnoxious ones can really be awful. There is one particular guy, a high-level manager, who really thinks he is dynamic, results driven and always right, when in reality he is a complete twat! We've all come across them haven't we? Still it's the weekend now and a chance for me to relax and unwind. A typical Saturday morning ritual for me is to study the football fixtures, including all the gossip and latest news. Then I place my bets, an accumulator is my favourite. To make it worthwhile I usually put on around £100 pounds, and it really pays off, once I won £3,056! Of course Connie frowns at this, says it's a complete waste of money, but I get a real buzz out of it! So now I try to avoid Connie being around when I'm gambling, anything for an easy life! Anyway my luck's in today as Connie and Sarah have gone up town to see the show 'Wicked'. As the saying goes, 'While the cat's away, the mice can play!'

CONNIE

Having grabbed a coffee, Sarah and I jumped on the tube at Bermondsey. We are going to have a look around the shops, eat at a good restaurant and experience the musical 'Wicked'! It feels like a special girls day out! Not to mention a bit of a break from Mike who has been getting on my nerves recently.

'Sarah, how have you found Mike recently? I hope his 'put downs' didn't upset you too much'

'No, not at all. He did mention that he has had a few issues at work recently. It probably is the stress of it all getting to him'

'Yes it could be, but it still doesn't give him an excuse to be rude to you'

'Well no, but most of the time it's just water off a duck's back for me'

'I hope it is just a phase that he is going through, otherwise moving in together will have been a big mistake!'

'Oh I'm sure that it will work out okay. He's a good-looking bloke and he can be very witty at times. Some of the one-liners that he comes out with, well!'

'Yes, I hope you're right. Do you know the other day he started lecturing me about religion! No regard for my own views, which I'm just as entitled to hold, as he is to hold his!'

'That doesn't sound like Mike to me, it could be another sign that work is getting on top of him perhaps?'

'Yes you could well be right. Changing the subject, I do like your boots. Where did you get them from?'

'Oh, thank you, NEXT and they weren't that expensive either'

'Well they look very good on you'

'Thanks', she smiles, obviously pleased with the compliment

'So what else do we know is going on with the world today?'

'Prince Harry is marrying Meghan Markle in St George's Chapel at Windsor Castle', Sarah announced

'Yes of course, I'd quite forgotten. I do hope that they find happiness together'

'Yes, they seem like a well-suited couple. I suppose Meghan will give up acting?'

'I don't know, but yes, I suppose she will'

'I do admire the royal family, they are so hard working and boost the economy through tourism income'

'Yes, I expect your right. I tell you what, we could visit the Tower of London to see the Crown Jewels, if you fancy it?'

'Ooh yes we must, I've never been before. Yes let's go there first!'

'That's the trouble with London', Connie chuckled, 'There's so much to see!'

'The V&A, stunning costume designs'

'Madame Tussauds'

'The National Gallery'

'The London Dungeon', Sarah sniggered

'Not forgetting the Jack the Ripper Museum!', Connie was laughing now

'Enough, enough, enough!', Sarah exclaimed, almost doubling up with laughter!

We sipped our coffee, taking a moment or two to recover our composure.

'Sarah we could do the V&A first and then the Crown Jewels, as they are only a short tube journey apart. What do you think?'

'Sounds good to me! OK, what else is there to see at the Tower of London?'

'The building itself, including Traitor's Gate where they brought the prisoners in by boat before execution'

'Gruesome!'

'Then there's the Beefeaters who guard it and the ravens'

'Isn't there some legend associated with the ravens?'

'Yes, it is said that the kingdom and the Tower of London will fall if the six resident ravens ever leave the fortress. Charles II is thought to have been the first to insist that the ravens of the Tower be protected after he was warned that the crown and the Tower itself would fall if they left'

'Are there six ravens living there even today?'

'Yes, I expect we will see them'.

Aagh I'm beginning to sound more like Mike every day! He's forever filling my head with all these facts and figures!

We had decided to take the tube all the way to South Kensington before taking in some of the sights and sounds of London. After spending a couple of hours at the V&A we walked past Buckingham Palace, then caught the tube at St James Park to Tower Hill. The Crown Jewels most certainly lived up to our expectations. When we exited the Tower we walked over Tower Bridge onto the south bank side of the Thames because I knew a number of good eateries in that area. Sarah laconically piped up, 'I'm hungry and my feet hurt!' 'Yes, okay', I looked around and spotted a pub sign, 'Ah! Look the Dean Swift. Mike has often eaten here and says the food is good'. He was right, it's a small pub full of character and the food was excellent. 'Are you feeling better now?', I asked Sarah.

'Yes thank you', she replied. I couldn't help noticing that she had kicked her boots off too!

'Good, well it's probably time for us to make a move if we are going to be on time for the matinee performance. It's only a short walk back to Tower Hill, from there we can catch the Tube to Victoria. The theatre is very close by'

'Ok, if I must', Sarah said resignedly.

It was an easy journey, so we made it in plenty of time.

'Wicked' was fabulous! We both really enjoyed it. Elated, we left the theatre singing the catchy songs! We headed across the road to Cardinal Walk where there is a good selection of

23

restaurants and opted for Wagamama. We then indulged in a couple of margarita's and a bottle of wine, oh yes, with some food too! Then we wobbled back onto the tube before arriving safely back in Bermondsey!

MIKE

What a shit day! First my laptop gives up the ghost, so I decide to take it down to the local computer repair shop, but my car won't start!!! So I have to walk! They're too busy to look at it today, so I've left it with them. Next I go to the bookies close by and put a few bets on and play the bandits. A small win then nothing, I've lost the lot today! So I decide to visit the nearest pub, after all I do need to eat something, mindful that Connie is out all day enjoying herself!

About three hours later I stagger out and make my way back home. I look up at our apartment window, the lights on, which means Connie's back. It's gone 9:30pm and in the twilight I trip over the step, falling and banging my knee hard. 'This day just gets better and better!', I mutter to myself ironically. I pick myself up and enter the building. In front of our apartment door I search my pockets for my key, all to no avail. Oh well, I'll just have to ring the bell. I knock the door for good measure. A minute later Connie opens the door, she doesn't look too pleased!

'Mike what on earth is all this racket about?'

'Er, I don't know', I slur

'You're drunk!', she shouts, giving me one of her filthy looks

'No need for that, the shouting'

'Whose shouting?', she replies loudly. I respond with a smirk that a naughty schoolboy would be proud of. 'Get in here right now, I'm not going to debate this with you on the doorstep!' I shuffle in. 'Just look at you, what a state you're in. You've even torn your trousers'. I glance down and notice the rip with blood seeping through. 'Oh Mike, you are the limit!'. She disappears into the kitchen, returning with a bowl of warm water, a cloth and a towel. 'Take your trousers off', she commands. I grin up at her saying, 'That's a good idea', as I struggle to take them off.

'Don't be so stupid Mike. Now sit still, so I can clean you up'. Sluggishly I do as I'm told. She proceeds to cleanse the gash with water with a dash of Dettol in it. I think it should sting but the alcohol has numbed the pain. She gently dries the area before applying a large dressing. 'You are an idiot Mike. There, you'll do!' She stands, hand on hips and states in a matter of fact way, 'You're to sleep on the sofa tonight. There is no way I'm having you in bed with me in that state!'. Thoroughly deflated I hobble through to the lounge and collapse onto the sofa. I think, 'I wonder if there is any sport on the TV tonight?' Fumbling with the remote I've found the FA Cup final between Chelsea and Manchester United on catch-up. Hurrah! At that moment Connie comes into the lounge with a mug of coffee for me and places it carefully on the table coaster. 'Aren't you going to ask me if I've had a nice time?', she says without smiling.

'Have you had a nice time Connie?', I repeat parrot fashion

'Yes, no thanks to you!'

I look at her, no point arguing, no point saying anything.

'Well if all you're going to do is sit glued to the tele, then I'm off to bed!', and with that final barbed remark she disappears in the direction of the bathroom.

CONNIE

Mike is the limit! I've been reading my book for over an hour and I can still hear him snoring loudly. That's with the tele blaring away! I'm feeling very tired myself and ready to get some sleep, but I'll just turn the TV off before I turn in. That done, I put the light out and bury myself under the duvet, whilst hoping for a fresh start tomorrow!

23rd May 2018

CONNIE

Things aren't any better between myself and Mike. He certainly knows how to wind me up. This in turn causes me to bite back at him, which I regret almost as soon as the words have left my mouth. He is grumpy most of the time, but maybe that is partly down to the fact that he is still sleeping on the sofa. Currently we have the second bedroom set up as an office, but I'm seriously considering putting a bed in there!

Chapter 2 – Los Ghouls

It was around midnight when the stillness of the night was shattered by the sound of broken glass exploding onto the pavement of Passeig de Gràcia in Barcelona. A grey Nissan Navara rammed the jewellers front door, the alarms having been deactivated earlier. Four men dressed all in black, wearing balaclavas jumped out, two had pistols tucked under their belts. 'Hurry, hurry', the first urged in rasping Catalan. They rushed into the store and broke open the locked cabinets, quickly removing trays of Rolex watches and diamond jewellery, which they emptied unceremoniously into army issue Petate Militar (military duffle bags). The whole heist only took about three minutes.

'Quick! We must leave now!', the leader urged and without another word, they exited the shop, as one well drilled unit. They raced towards the Navara, however as the leader had his hand on the door handle, he stopped for a split second. The sound of police boots clattering towards them reached his ears, he spun round, his worse fears confirmed, it was a member of Mossos d'Esquadra. 'Merda', he cursed under his breath and in one swift movement he had the gun in his hand and aimed at the onrushing individual. A single shot rang out and the policeman stumbled forward for two more steps, his momentum throwing him into the pavement. Already a crimson stream of blood appearing to pool about his head. 'In the truck now!', commanded the gang leader. They needed no second bidding, they jumped into the vehicle and with a screech of tyres were on their way.

Sometime later the police found a stolen Navara, burnt out, any possible fingerprints totally destroyed. Another successful smash and grab by the brothers, Kylo and Carlos Garcia, founders of the notorious Los Ghouls gang. They had, quite literally, just got away with murder!

Chapter 3 – Sarah

9th June 2018

MIKE

8pm, I'm at home when the phone rings, 'Hello?'

'Hi Mike, it's Sarah could I speak to Connie please'

'I'm sorry Sarah but Connie is away in Leeds competing'

'Oh gosh, I forgot. I'm sorry but I'm in a bit of a state. Well actually more than a bit'.

'What on earth's wrong Sarah?'

'I can hear weird noises again and this is despite the exorcism ten days ago! I'm really scared!' Sarah's voice quavers.

I think to myself, 'It's probably just the plumbing but it is Connie's best friend, and she certainly can't call the emergency services!'. So I say, 'Sarah you are obviously upset, so I'll pop round and see if I can help in anyway. Then at least you won't be on your own.'

'Oh that would be great, thank you so much Mike.'

'Okay, I'll see you in about twenty minutes. Bye for now'.

'Bye'.

I gather my box of plumbing tools and I'm on my way. 'Bloody nuisance', I think, 'I was just about to play the online casino.'

Sarah opens the door, her blond hair and sparkling blue eyes standing out from a very fetching dressing gown. 'Hi Mike'

'Hi Sarah'

'Thank you so much for coming round'

'That's OK, glad to be of service'

'Would you like a tea or coffee'

'I'd prefer something stronger if you've got it. A glass of red possibly?'

'Yes of course. Take a seat and I'll get it.'

I sit on the sofa and a few minutes later Sarah is back with two glasses and the bottle.

'Now then, what is this all about? Strange noises you say?'

'Yes, knocking sounds, rattles, swishing and....', she hesitates

'Yes?'

'You'll probably think I'm nuts but I'm sure I heard someone sobbing!'

'Well some of those noises could be the plumbing, but definitely not the sobbing – how odd! Anyway I'll check round the house for any airlocks in the central heating system'.

'Thanks Mike, I really do appreciate it'

I go around the house bleeding all the radiators, then run all the taps hard to flush out any airlocks. Returning to sit next to Sarah on the sofa I say, 'I've done what I can with the plumbing, but I can stay a while and listen out for any more noises if you'd like that?'.

'Yes please and thanks Mike, I've been a bag of nerves here on my own. I thought the exorcism would 'cleanse' the place but it doesn't seem to have worked. It must be a very powerful spirit'.

I almost laughed at this, but realised Sarah was being deadly serious. Oh well, tea and sympathy needed I suppose. 'Sarah, why are you so sure that the place is haunted?'.

'It's the noises, they aren't all day long, they only start-up after dark, mostly late at night. I can never get a good night's sleep. Then sometimes I'm sure my ornaments get moved around. Oh dear! You must think me so silly!'

'Not at all', I say putting my arm around her for comfort, 'Please don't worry I'm here now. I'll sit up all night if necessary just so you can get some sleep'.

Sarah turns her head to look directly into my eyes. 'You are kind Mike, I can't thank you enough'.

Strangely I'm drawn to this beautiful, vulnerable creature. For a moment time stands still and we look into each other's eyes. Then with almost imperceptible movement our lips slowly move together. A brief kiss, quickly followed by a full embrace. Passion overtakes me, a long lingering kiss while I caress her back. Sarah is responding, I can feel her nails firmly gripping my back. One thing leads to another and Sarah, taking my hand, steers me to the bedroom and a bout of frantic love making.

As we lay there spent, Sarah gently caresses my cheek and whispers, 'Stay the night Mike, I feel so much safer with you beside me'.

Drawing her to me and running my fingers down her spine, 'Of course' I reply.

SARAH

I'd only told Connie the flat was haunted to windup Mike and Connie, knowing she'd tell Mike and he'd poo-poo the idea and they'd have a row. To be honest I quite fancied Mike and wanted to split them up. It was jealousy really as Connie doesn't have so much time for me anymore. Our trip out last month was great although even Connie is sounding more like Mike these days with her facts and figures. We used to have so much fun but now she's with Mike when she's not doing her triathlons and can hardly fit me in these days. I didn't expect Connie to take it so seriously that she would send a priest round. How embarrassing! Then Mike turned up to sort my plumbing out if you know what I mean! I certainly didn't expect to end up in bed with him and now I'm feeling guilty as hell. Connic mustn't find out. I'd better come clean to Mike at least. He looks so cute asleep.

10th June 2018

MIKE

Upon waking I realise that I've slept soundly, Sarah has just arrived back in the bedroom with a cup of coffee.
'Good morning Mike', she says coyly.

Not quite knowing the right thing to say, 'Morning Sarah, did you sleep OK?'

'Only when you let me', she replied coquettishly, with a slight smile. Getting back into bed, 'Actually that's the best nights sleep I've had in months. Mike, I'm sorry I have a confession to make, I exaggerated the story of ghostly noises and objects moving around, in the hope Connie would send you round to investigate. I've fancied you for ages'.

What a bombshell! For a moment I'm speechless. Thoughts race through my mind, but one thought dominates, 'What have we done?'. Connie is my partner. Sarah is Connie's best friend. Instead of dealing with reality, I side-step with, 'Gosh, you are so beautiful Sarah'.

Sarah flutters her eyelashes and replies, 'You're not so bad yourself Mike!'.

We are soon making passionate love again.

Later as I leave Sarah's apartment and begin the walk home along wet pavements, my head is in turmoil, 'Oh god, life has just got a bit more complicated. What do I do? Do I tell Connie? No, she'll kick me out and I still love her. Will Sarah confess to Connie? I don't think so. Will the three of us be able to face each other when we go out together? Or will the embarrassment find us out? Will I see Sarah again? She certainly hasn't put me off. It wasn't just me, she enjoyed herself too! Didn't she say she had fancied me all this time?

How will all this end? It's all too much, No, I won't go straight home, I'll have a few pints at the pub instead!'

Feeling better in myself after several pints and a delicious roast beef dinner, I unsteadily weave my way back home.

11th June 2018

MIKE

Monday evening at home, Connie is back from Leeds, arrived mid-morning, got changed and then went straight into work and staying late to catch-up. There's nothing decent on TV, so I go onto the online casino. I start off well, slightly ahead after an hour, encouraged I make some larger bets and now I'm a few thousand down. I can make it back though, 'it's just an unlucky streak' I think to myself. I have another drink and play again, this time I win! There you are! I'll just double up my bet as my luck has turned!

Another hour goes by and I've hit my credit limit, I can't believe that I'm £20,000 down! Oh Christ! I open another bottle of wine.

CONNIE

I did quite well in Leeds but nowhere near my best. Mike thinks it's because I'm trying to do too much with work and everything. When I got in tonight feeling absolutely shattered he was acting a bit strange. He drinks far too much, has dark rings under his eyes and is getting a bit of a paunch. I'll have to get him to go running with me.

15th June 2018

MIKE

Connie suggests that we eat out tonight at the Dog and Pheasant as it's Friday. 'I'll call Sarah and see if she wants to join us' she says brightly.

'Err, OK', I reply.

Arriving at the pub, I spot Sarah ordering a cocktail at the bar. 'Hi Sarah', I say with a smile. 'Hi Mike, Hi Connie', she replies. 'Hi Sarah, you are looking well, even your cheeks are a tad flushed', Connie grinned.

'Are they? It must be the warmth in here', Sarah responds. Connie dictates, 'Mike you grab a table, I'm just popping to the ladies', and makes her way through the crowd.

I speak in almost a whisper, 'Sarah I really like you, and well, we had a marvellous time last weekend, but Connie mustn't know, OK?'

'Ok Mike, our little secret', Sarah smiles and winks at me.

We sit down and peruse the menu, and Connie re-joins us. The meal proceeds much as last time, Connie full of her Leeds triathlon exploits and Sarah, this time, making no mention of ghosts! I'm prepared to take a backseat and simply ensure that the conversation stays on safe ground. Time marches on and Connie asks for the bill, 'Mike will you do the honours please'. I present my credit card and the waiter types in £142.55. I enter my pin, then almost immediately, the waiter says apologetically, 'I'm sorry sir, your card has been declined'. Just then I remember that I used it for the online casino. How embarrassing! I take out another card and this time, thankfully, the transaction goes through. Connie, somewhat shocked, says, 'Mike you haven't blown your limit, have you?' I smile and reply, 'No, it must be a glitch. Never trust a computer!'

CONNIE

Mike and Sarah looked a bit too cosy when I came out of the Ladies at the pub. Mike said he'd managed to cure the noises at her flat with some plumbing techniques and Sarah didn't mention she'd had any more trouble.

It was slightly embarrassing when Mike's card was declined when he went to pay for the meal. I hope he's not lying to me about his gambling.

16th June 2018

MIKE

Saturday morning and Connie is out for a long early morning run, I'm still in bed and losing badly on the online gambling. I try to transfer some money from my bank account into my online casino account but "Insufficient Funds" is displayed. 'Oh shit!', I exclaim, I hadn't realised quite how much I'd drawn on my reserves. That's it then, I've actually used up all my liquid assets! Usually I can have a losing run but then start winning again to recoup at least some of my losses. Oh I so need a big win right now! I really must get back online ASAP, I need some funds, I daren't ask Connie, I know what she will say!

Hurriedly I get dressed, skip breakfast and soon on my way round to see Sarah. Two sharp knocks and Sarah, in her dressing gown, somewhat tentatively opens the door. 'Good morning Mike', smiling she continues, 'I didn't expect to see you this early. Do come in.' She turns and leads me down the hall, 'Coffee?'.

'Yes please, it's just what I need!' I sink onto the settee in the lounge while Sarah busies herself in the kitchen.

Sarah returns with two steaming mugs. 'Thanks Sarah, the coffee smells great!', I say.

'To what do I owe this honour Mike?', Sarah impishly asks.

'I just had to see you and thank you for not saying anything to Connie'.

'That's OK Mike, it was fun though wasn't it?'

'It certainly was Sarah, you are one sexy lady!'

'Do you think so Mike?', Sarah allows her dressing gown to loosen, exposing a bit more cleavage and her thigh.

'Now then Sarah, you are making my blood pressure rise', I smile in return.

'Nothing else on the rise then Mikey?', Sarah teases.

'Now you mention it', I respond, putting an arm around Sarah's shoulders and gently pulling her in towards me until our lips lock in a passionate embrace.

In the next moment I'm being led by the hand towards the bedroom. This isn't what I'd planned!

Later, I'm lying in bed sated, Sarah too. 'Why did you come round?', Sarah asks.

'I'm having problems with the car', I lied, 'I urgently need another vehicle while mine is in for repairs, which I don't know how long they will take. The thing is, I'm a bit short of funds just at the moment and wondered if you might be able to help me out'.

Sarah hesitates before replying, 'Can't you ask Connie for a sub?'

' 'Fraid not, you see Connie and I have had a big row and we're not speaking'.

'Sorry to hear that. What about your car, is it major then?'.

'Yes, the garage said it sounds like the big-ends and that is an engine rebuild. There is value in the car, but I'll only get a reasonable price once it's back on the road'.

'So how much do you need?', asked Sarah, no longer smiling.

'Well five grand should get me something reliable'.

'How much are you putting towards it?'

'About three', I said putting on my best little boy lost expression.

'I don't have much in the way of savings Mike, but I suppose I could lend you two grand on the strict understanding that this is a short-term loan.'

'Oh thank you so much Sarah, I can't tell you how much this means to me', and I lean in to kiss her on the lips.

'OK Mike, I'll transfer the money this morning if you write down your bank details'.

'You're a real star Sarah. Thank you'.

SARAH

Mike came round again and I'm ashamed to say I flirted with him outrageously. We ended up in bed again. I don't know why I did it. Boredom perhaps. He asked for money after and I stupidly agreed. Should I have done that? He said it was to fix his car but I know Connie has told me he has money issues. If Connie finds out about any of this I could lose my best friend. Is he worth it, I just don't know.

MIKE

On the way back home I pop into the corner shop for a Scratchcard, newspaper and croissants in order to satisfy Connie's curiosity as much as anything else. I win nothing on the Scratchcard. Sometime later I get the opportunity to sneak away for another adrenaline rush on the online casino. However my mood darkens as I lose the two grand Sarah lent me. Things are beginning to really get on top of me now, but somehow I must keep all the plates spinning!

17th June 2018

MIKE

I'm desperate for some cash. I can't ask Connie but I figure it out, I sell my car. I put it on Auto Trader for £6,950. I tell Connie that I don't need a car and I'll manage with public transport just fine and anyway she has her car. Connie snaps, 'Well don't expect to borrow mine at the drop of a hat!' I ignore her remark and continue reading the newspaper.

CONNIE

I don't know what's going on but Mike has decided he can do without a car and is selling his. Well if he thinks he can use mine he can think again!

30th June 2018

MIKE

I've sold the car! This morning a chap came over for a final inspection, going through the service history, MOT etc and paid the full asking price. Cash flow crisis averted! Hurrah! I'm off to make a bank deposit and repay Sarah her two grand.

It's a sunny afternoon, dappled light shines through the leaves of the trees that are interspersed down Sarah's road. I'm feeling pleased with myself, I've rescued the situation. I knock on Sarah's door, noting for the first time the rather twee cross-hatching of lead stripes on the double-glazed windows. The door opens and smiling, Sarah greets me, 'Come on in Mike, what a pleasant surprise.'

'I just had to see you again', I wink, 'But, more importantly, I'm returning the two grand you lent me'.

'Oh, that's great. Thanks Mike. Would you like a coffee?'

'Yes please', and I take a seat.

A few minutes later Sarah returns with our coffees, 'Mind, it's very hot', and carefully places them on the coffee table coasters.

'Thanks Sarah. What have you been up to this week then?'

'Oh just the usual, Estate Agent property viewings and paperwork.'

'Well it's certainly nice weather for it'

'It's always nice weather for it', Sarah replies with a wink, and smiling, flutters her eyelashes.

I chuckle, 'Stop it, you are making me all hot under the collar'

'Is that the only place?', Sarah teases, and then, 'Too bad I have another viewing in about an hour'.

'Too bad, but that gives me more to look forward to next time!', I continue, 'Connie is going away 23rd August for the Chicago Triathlon on 26th. So I might just call round if you're free'

'I'll make sure I'm not washing my hair then', Sarah jokes.

'Great. Oh before I forget, here's your money, thanks.', I say passing an envelope across.

'Thanks Mike. Now if you'll excuse me I must ready myself for the viewing. Let yourself out when you have finished your coffee.', says Sarah disappearing in the direction of the bathroom. I'm so tempted to follow but resist and head off home.

SARAH

Well that was a surprise. Mike came round and paid me back my two grand. Shame I had to leave to show a client round a house but I can't afford to lose business much as I fancied Mike again. He said Connie is away at the end of August so we should have some more fun then. If only I didn't feel such a bitch, Connie's my bestie for god's sake.

2nd July 2018

MIKE

Back to the daily grind! I have put myself forward for regular overtime to boost my income. Unfortunately when I'm not working I'm gambling, and still losing money. Never mind, I'm sure my luck will soon change for the better.

27th July 2018

MIKE

Thank goodness it's the end of the month payday! I've gambled away most of the funds realised by the car sale. I'm getting quite desperate now, and I think Connie is beginning to get a bit suspicious, what with my drinking and my cancelling the Sky contract. I have however managed to pay my half of the mortgage on the apartment.

CONNIE

I don't know what's going on but Mike has not only sold his car but has cancelled our Sky contract. Not that I'm too bothered about that as he's the only one using it. I'm too busy getting fit for the Chicago triathlon. I do wonder if he has money troubles but he's paid his half of the mortgage so maybe I'm wrong. If only he'd stop drinking so much and go to the gym occasionally.

29th July 2018

MIKE

Connie is back from her early morning run, the beads of perspiration evidence of her exertions. She does look sexy in that figure-hugging Lycra! She's growing her hair as she knows I like long hair although it's usually tied back in a ponytail most of the time.

'Mike, you lazy so and so, you are still in bed!', Connie rants.

'Christ Connie, aren't I even allowed a Sunday morning lie-in?', I counter.

'Not when the apartment is in such a mess! Empty wine bottles everywhere, the whole place stinks!'

'Well I don't see you doing much about it. Anyway you are always out training so why should you care?'

'They're your wine bottles Mike! You should have cleaned up last night before you went to bed. It's a pigsty, it's a bloody disgrace!', Connie raises her voice by several decibels.

'Anyhow isn't cleaning what we pay the cleaner for?', I shout back.

'Mike don't you remember? You let her go, said it was an "unnecessary expense", remember?'

My brain is a bit slow, the effect of last night's binge. Oh shit, she's right!, I realise. I reply disgruntledly, 'Okay, okay, I'll do it when I get up'.

'Thank you!', Connie says tersely with undue emphasis, grabs her towel and heads towards the shower.

I need a good strong coffee, I think as I pull the quilt back over my head for just a little bit longer.

CONNIE

Mike really pissed me off today. I got in from a ten-mile run and he was still in bed. The air stank of stale booze and the place was a bloody mess. He's even let the cleaner go as he said it was an unnecessary expense as he could do her job for nothing. I'm beginning to wonder why we ever got together!

4th August 2018

MIKE

Connie has had lunch with a group of her friends. She is now sitting comfortably with a coffee and Saturday's paper in our lounge. I've been 'busy' gambling online and had another big loss. Now the realisation has hit me that I'm broke and won't be paid again until the end of the month. I pour myself a large glass of red and summon up the courage to ask Connie to sub me. Desperate times, call for desperate measures and Connie appears to be in a good mood.

'Connie, darling', I start, immediately interrupted by Connie's, 'Do you want something Mike?' No flies on her! She saw straight through my attempt to smooth talk her.

'Well, actually yes, unfortunately I'm temporarily short of funds this month I was hoping you would help me out until next pay day please.'

'Honestly, I don't know what you do with your money Mike, you have only just been paid!'

'It was the large garage bill for fixing up the car in order for me to sell it', I lie.

'But Mike you sold your car, so you must have plenty of cash'.

'I did, but I took out an investment bond with the money', I lie again.

'I don't believe you Mike, show me proof', Connie replies.

My heart stops, she has finally seen through my lies. I hate to do this, but I'm going to appeal to her better nature and come 'clean', well almost! 'Connie I've been a fool, I've lost a bit gambling online, please help me out'.

Connie responds, 'A bit? Just how much is a bit?'

'Just a little over six grand', I say, trying to minimise the impact of it, my voice several octaves higher.

'Six grand! You have got to be joking!', a visibly shocked Connie continues, 'That isn't a trivial amount. Don't try and tell me that your online gambling is "just a bit of fun". That is a serious amount of money to lose. Mike, I think you have a real problem'.

I'm down but not out, I'll make it her problem too. 'Connie I'm at my wits end, I can't think straight, I can't see a way ahead. What do you think I should do?'

'Well, it seems obvious to me, you're addicted to betting. You need professional help and counselling. Have you tried contacting Gamblers Anonymous?'

'No, but I'm willing to give it a go'.

'Mike, I don't think you are taking this seriously enough. So here's the deal. You provide weekly evidence that you're having counselling and I'll pay your living expenses each week. How does that sound?'

Sanctimonious or what, but she's got me over a barrel. 'I can live with that. Thanks Connie, you have got me out of a hole, I won't let you down'.

'You'd better not Mike', Connie mutters and goes back to reading the paper.

CONNIE

Well my fears were realised today. Mike admitted he has a gambling problem and is in huge financial trouble. He has to contact Gamblers Anonymous, give up gambling, get counselling and in return I'll help him with his finances. Otherwise it's over between us. My patience is almost totally exhausted!

6th August 2018

MIKE

I contacted Gamblers Anonymous and they referred me to a counsellor. I have a phone appointment for later this week.

11th August 2018

MIKE

Connie is being stubbornly true to her word and only paying for my living expenses! I desperately need some dosh. Fortunately I've inherited my grandmothers diamond brooch and I'm going down town to pawn it this afternoon.

I got three grand for the brooch, I'd never imagined that it was worth that much. Massively looking forward to playing online as soon as Connie is out of the way!

CONNIE

I think Mike is keeping to our deal. He did contact a counsellor and seems to be drinking less. There may be hope for us yet. I really need to concentrate on my training and could do without having to worry about what Mike is getting up to. I've been neglecting Sarah too.

I can't remember the last time we had a girls night out. As soon as I get back from Chicago I'm going to have a break from training, catch up with her and give more time to Mike. Perhaps I have been a bit hard on him?

20th August 2018

MIKE

I am not in Connie's good books! I had one or two successes gambling and overtime pay from work but unfortunately I celebrated over exuberantly and came back to the apartment rather the worse for wear! As a consequence I'm in the doghouse and Connie's not speaking to me again.

CONNIE

I don't believe it! Mike's gambling again and came home drunk as he'd won this time. I just don't know what to think. How could he do this when I'm just about to fly out to Chicago. We're going to have to have a serious conversation when I get back but in the meantime I won't be speaking to him.

23rd August 2018

MIKE

I bump into Sarah at the local supermarket and she invites me back to her place for coffee. 'So how's it going Mike?', Sarah asks once we've settled down on the sofa.

'Well, not too good if I'm honest. Connie and I aren't speaking again. She's away in Chicago so I'm waiting to see what mood she comes back in.'

'Oh, sorry to hear that. Hopefully nothing too serious?'

'Yes and no. We argued over a few things but Connie just isn't able to see my point of view. Also she's always off training or competing somewhere, so what am I supposed to do with myself when she's away? I'm fearful that our relationship is over'.

'Gosh, I didn't realise that things between you had deteriorated to that extent. You poor thing'. Sarah extends her arm and gently draws her fingers down Mike's cheek in a fond caress.

'Thank you for being so understanding Sarah. And, how are things with you?'

'About the same as always, still waiting for mister right to come along', she laughs.

I say rather cheekily, 'In the meantime, will I do?'

Sarah, smiling broadly, 'Well, I suppose you'll have to' and she leans in for a kiss. Our lips lock together, bodies press together and our arms encircle each other in a tight embrace.

Once again Sarah asserts herself and we head towards the bedroom.

SARAH

Honestly I tried to resist but Mike came round and one thing led to another. How can I live with myself knowing that he should be with Connie and not cheating on her. He said he thinks their relationship is over but does Connie think that too? Is there a chance me and Mike could end up together after all. Would I want him then or is it because it's exciting having an affair. I don't know what to think anymore.

28th August 2018

MIKE

Connie came back from Chicago in a better mood as she'd done really well.

'I'm really sorry Connie, I've been an idiot. If you'll forgive me I'll try really hard to control my gambling and drinking'

'I hope you mean that Mike', she responded, 'because I want this to work. I'm sorry too for neglecting you so I'm going to cut down a bit on the triathlons. In fact I must contact Sarah too and have a catch up with her. I guess I've been pretty selfish so forgive me too.'

With that we made it up in the bedroom, if you get my drift!

CONNIE

Mike and I have made it up and we've both decided to try harder. Chicago was great but I'm going to slow down a bit and spend more time with him. I must get in touch with Sarah. It's ages since we had a girly night out, just the two of us. I've not been much of a friend and hope she can forgive me.

Chapter 4 – Maria López in Barcelona

MARIA

'I grew up in a very poor district of Barcelona known as the Ciutat Vella or Old City. Back then there were many slums and I lived in one. It was a difficult time for my parents, just about surviving under the suppression of the Catalan culture by Franco's fascist regime. It forced people to get involved in illegal activities just to survive in that environment. Thankfully that regime collapsed after the death of Franco in 1975. However the die was cast and borderline criminal activities had become the norm for many families. Even at ten years old I was involved as a runner, collecting and delivering notes in a clandestine manner. I soon gained an insight into how these gangs operated. Then, about a year later, a greater disaster befell me, my parents were killed in a road crash. As an orphan my very sparse prospects diminished further. At the time the Garcia family were close neighbours and señorita Marta took pity on me, informally adopting me. Marta was very kind to me, I was fed, clothed and encouraged to go to school. In return I did household chores, cleaning, washing and continued my courier duties. Marta's husband had died two years previously in a gangland shooting, so Marta ruled the roost and kept 'business' operations running smoothly. She had two sons that lived there too, Kylo and Carlos.

Kylo was about six years older than me and Carlos four years older. Even then they thought themselves much better than everyone else!

Although I went to school much of my education came from being close to Marta. I learnt everything about the business from her. Unfortunately the boys resented my relationship with their mother, they were always making digs or snide remarks at my expense. However Marta kept control of the situation, until that is, she suddenly had a massive heart attack and died! I was only thirteen at the time. Things went downhill rapidly from there. The two brothers were horrible to me, bullying and treating me as their skivvy. With the death of Marta the business started to suffer, the boys didn't have the same aptitude as their mother. Unable to deal effectively with the pressure Kylo started drinking and then he would become abusive towards me, verbally and physically. It all came to a head when one night he arrived home drunk. No sooner had he got through the door than he slurred, in our native Catalan, 'Get my dinner bitch!'

I replied, 'It's keeping warm in the oven'.

'What good is it there?', he slurred, 'Fetch it here!'

I'd already started to bring it to the table, so I continued and placed it on the table. 'Here it is you ungrateful oaf!', I said firmly. Kylo momentarily froze before placing one hand on the back of the dining chair to steady himself, then with his eyes popping out of his head, 'What did you say bitch!' He lunged towards me, his flailing arm whacking me across the head. I cried out in pain and fell to the floor. Simultaneously Kylo had blundered into the table and knocked it over, his dinner crashed to the floor, the plate shattering.

'You, you bastard!', I exclaimed as blood started to ooze from the side of my head where his rings had caught me. Enraged, Kylo loomed above me like the oaf he was, 'I'll teach you a lesson you won't forget bitch!' and he punched me full in the face. At that point I lost consciousness. Much later, when I woke up I discovered I was locked in the cellar. My head was throbbing like a tractor engine, the blood had congealed and matted in my hair. My clothes were dishevelled, and much to my consternation, my panties were lying on the floor a metre away. I tried to rise, but pain shot through my limbs. The enormity of what had happened was only just beginning to hit me. Had I been raped? I didn't know, I certainly was very sore. Had a very drunk Kylo even been capable? I started to check myself out, most certainly I had sustained severe bruising. I managed to sit up and gather my thoughts. I can't stay here, I must go to the police. No, I daren't, some of the police are corrupt and in the pay of the gangs. I will have to get away from here and find a refuge. I just about managed to stand and patted down my clothes, I felt awful! Oh, my head ached so! I looked around the cellar, there was nothing of any comfort, no tap for a wash, not even a glass of water. Gingerly I made my way to the door, I tried the handle, this confirmed that the door was locked. I felt so low! I have to admit at that point I felt completely defeated and fell to the floor sobbing. Sometime later I woke to discover that I had slept again. My head wasn't throbbing quite as much, but my body felt as sore as ever. However the biggest change was my mental attitude, I resolved to escape these circumstances and wreak revenge on Kylo, however long that took and at whatever cost! Once again the die is cast!'

Chapter 5 – Amadou in Mali

AMADOU

'My life started on a small farm on the outskirts of Sorobasso, 30km from Koutiala in Mali. I was one of the lucky ones as my parents sent me to school from age seven. I don't have any brothers and sisters but there were other children my age in Sorobasso. We used to play football on the dusty streets, occasionally having to move goats off our 'pitch'! Once in a while my father and I would drive the donkey and cart to Koutiala, taking produce to market. We always tried to make the trip coincide with when Étoile Filante de Koutiala football team were playing. This was indeed a rare treat! Mali has a very good national team. Mohamed Sissoko is one of my hero's, a defensive midfielder, he has played for Liverpool, Juventus, Paris Saint-Germain and has been capped 34 times for Mali.

Back home there was plenty to do, I'd help with the crops and with chores in the kitchen. Assisting with preparation of Maafé (peanut stew) or Jollof rice, my favourite! I quite enjoyed washing up too, as long as I could listen to the BBC World Service on the radio and learn to speak some English.

Although we are quite poor by western standards, we were happy. However about three years ago things changed, regular raids on outlying farms were being made by tribes from the north, with banditry and animal theft becoming commonplace. My parents insisted I was back home by the time it got dark. My father was very concerned and kept an old shotgun by his bed. If a noise outside disturbed him then he would go to the door, shouting a warning that he was armed with a gun and not afraid to use it!

Almost two years ago my whole world came crashing down around my ears. It was dusk and I was late going home. This close to the equator the transition from light to dark is very swift. As I approached the house I could just make out a group of men rushing around our yard. Some of them were herding our goats! I ducked down behind a bush. Two men arrived at our door just as father appeared with his shotgun. One man punched father hard in the face while the other grabbed the shotgun. Whilst father wrestled for control of the gun, I could see something glinting in the hand of the other raider – it was a knife. In a flash the knife was embedded in my father's chest and he dropped to the ground. I put my hand to my mouth to stifle the inner wail that was rising in my chest. I could see father lying there in the dust, with blood trickling out of his mouth. I felt sick, but before I could grasp the full implications, the robber had entered our house. I heard mother screaming and then a shot rang out from father's gun. Then complete silence, a sense of doom sweeping over me. The men busied themselves gathering up anything of value and loading it onto our donkey cart. They then set fire to the house and hastily disappeared into the blackness of the night. Fortunately they never spotted me, I was rooted to the spot, shaking violently before retching. A cold, clamminess swept my body as I thought, 'What do I do now?"

Chapter 6 – The End?

8th September 2018

MIKE

Connie noisily enters the apartment, having consumed a glass or two of wine over Sunday lunch at the Dog and Pheasant with Sarah. She storms into the lounge where I am seated.

'Mike, what the hell are you playing at? How dare you discuss our private relationship with Sarah!'

My mouth drops open, but I manage to stutter a response, 'C-Connie, all I said was that we were having some "difficulties".'

'From what Sarah told me, you said a lot more than that'

'I didn't, honest I didn't'

'Don't lie to me Mike. I know you too well, I know you are lying. What were you doing round at Sarah's anyway? I'm beginning to get the impression that you seem to be seeing quite a lot of her.'

'Of course I speak to her occasionally, after all she is your friend as well'

'Don't make excuses Mike, I know something's going on'

'No, nothing's going on, please believe me!'

'In that case, why then is Sarah wearing your grandmother's diamond brooch?'

I'm stunned, what a bomb shell! I'd retrieved the brooch from the pawn shop just before I'd met Sarah. She had admired it and asked if she could borrow it for a friend's wedding next week. I had absolutely no inkling that she would wear it out to a Sunday lunch! I answer, 'I said she could borrow it for a friend's wedding'

'I'm sorry Mike I don't believe you, there is more to it than that. Sarah must be a VERY good friend indeed for someone as selfish as you to do something like that!' Connie responded angrily. 'In fact you tell me lie, after lie. You're having an affair, admit it!'

'Alright, it's true Sarah and I did have a fling, but it didn't mean anything!'

'That's the bloody limit! Do you think I'm stupid or something! Get out! Get out right now!', Connie losing it completely, throws a cup that just misses my head. I decide to leave immediately and won't return until she cools off a bit!

CONNIE

Mike admitted to having a 'fling' with Sarah my supposedly best friend. I threw him out. After he'd gone I realised I wasn't as broken hearted as I should have been. He and my best friend had betrayed me so why wasn't I crying my eyes out? Then it hit me. I loved Mike but more like a good friend than a lover. He was too much trouble, high maintenance. Sarah can have him if that's what she wants!

MIKE

I make my way to the pub and order up a pint plus a whisky chaser. Sitting on my own, I contemplate where my life is heading. I've badly hurt the person I love, I've lied, cheated and been reckless with money. I'm feeling sorry for myself, so better have another drink. Several drinks later the world isn't looking any better. I muse, 'How the hell do I get out of this situation?' I don't have any answers, except to have another couple of drinks. My head is in my hands, a strand of spittle dribbles from my mouth onto the table top. I'm pissed! The landlord comes over, 'It's about time you went home matey'. He gently guides me to the door, I stagger out, bumping into the door frame as I go. What now?

I head round to Sarah's and knock the door. I'm unsteady on my feet, Sarah taking one glance at my dishevelled state and bleary eyes, 'What do you want Mike?'
'Can I come in? I'd like to talk to you. Connie knows', I slur the words.
'No, I don't think so. Not in your current condition. You're a mess Mike, get yourself sorted out'. Sarah shuts the door on me.
'Yes, thank you, you are so nice', I mutter at the door and erratically walk away. I glance at my phone. It's gone midnight. My head is banging, I need another drink.

SARAH

I've just turned Mike away. He was pissed. Really pissed. I think he said Connie knows! Well as they say 'the shit has hit the fan' if that's the case. Now I have to see if I've lost Connie or Mike or both.

MIKE

I head back towards the apartment, stopping at the 24-hour service station to buy a bottle of whisky. I walk on, taking swigs of whisky and contemplating my complete failure at life! I feel awful, confused, useless. What do I do next? There is no way out of this, is there? I'm approaching the apartment and my gaze falls upon the door of our lockup garage. Suddenly a thought crystallises in my sedated brain. I know now what I must do.

I enter the garage, the ill-fitting door screams as I open and close it behind me. Rather haphazardly in my befuddled state I grab the rope and make good the hangman's noose. I am determined to go ahead, there is no alternative!

Connie has been my rock. She has provided everything a man could wish for. Why then did I betray her? Let her down? Even when my gambling debts had come to light she had stuck by me, but then I couldn't leave the bottle alone and began a long spiral of descent to the deepest depths, the dark place where I am right now. 'Damn it!', I exclaim, throwing the empty whisky bottle at the wall, where it shatters into a myriad of pieces that spray across the concrete garage floor. It has to end. I slowly step onto the crate and tentatively place the noose around my neck, carefully steadying myself with one hand firmly holding the rope just above the noose. Preparing to kick the crate away, 'No mistakes now Mike, I chide myself'.

I kick the crate away, and feel the rope tightly constrict my airway. Panic and pain combine in my head as the bells of doom reverberate inside. Is this how it ends? Almost simultaneously the garage door squeals again. Lit from behind by the streetlight, Connie's silhouetted figure dark in the doorway, stunned, frozen for a split second while she takes in the shocking scene. Then, rushing forward, 'What the bloody hell Mike, you fucking idiot!' Deftly she recovers the crate and places it under my feet, grabs a pair of shears off the wall and with one quick action cuts the rope. I collapse in a heap on the floor, twisting my foot in the process.
'Mike, let's get you inside', she helps me to stand and supporting one arm we limp back to the apartment.

Connie makes me comfortable and provides a pack of frozen peas for my swollen ankle. My neck has been abraded by the rope and feels a bit sore, but otherwise I'm unhurt. Connie thrusts a strong black coffee into my shaking hands in an effort to sober me up.

Sometime later we have a heart-to-heart. Connie tells me that she understands the reasons for my attempt at taking my own life. That lots of people love me, including her and that I must think about the hurt and distress that I would cause to those people. She emphasised that things are never as bad as they seem, and that with her help, I'll be able to put my life back together again. We agree that I'll have counselling, and that although we are no longer an 'item', I can continue to stay in the apartment, at least for the time being. The following day I see the doctor, who prescribes Prozac and I get signed off work for the next four weeks.

CONNIE

I'm still shaking. Mike tried to take his own life in the early hours of this morning. Awaiting Mike's return I was lying awake when I heard noises coming from the direction of the garages. Looking out of the window I saw a light coming from under the door of our garage and went to investigate. The bloody idiot was trying to strangle himself. Thank goodness for all my training as I had the strength to get him down. We had a good talk after I'd sobered him up with coffee and I've agreed to support him but the relationship is over. He can stay here in the meantime until he sorts himself out.

29th September 2018

MIKE

Counselling is going well and things are settling down again. I've stopped drinking and gambling. A weekly Scratchcard doesn't count as gambling does it? I think the shock of what I've done has really hit home hard. I'm determined to become a better person. I'm still living in the apartment, although Connie and I are now just good friends. She is being very supportive, I can't thank her enough. Also I have spoken to Sarah and apologised for my poor behaviour.

CONNIE

Despite what I said I'm throwing myself into training again as Barcelona is coming up. Mike is sticking to his recovery programme and is more like the Mike I fell in love with. Although that boat sailed a long-time ago. We can only be friends from now on but he's good company and helps with the bills.

Chapter 7 – Moving On

SARAH

Mike came round about a week ago and apologised for his poor behaviour. We had a heart to heart talk. He said that him and Connie are over, but I'm not sure that I believe him, he has told so many lies. What he divulged next shocked me to the core. He told me how he had tried to end his life and Connie had saved him at the last minute! Of course I was very sympathetic but also reluctant to get too close to him again. He is carrying so much emotional baggage I'm a bit scared that he will do something else a bit manic. Anyway I think we've both moved on, so I hugged him, wished him well and sent him on his way.

Afterwards I sat on the sofa for ages just thinking it all through. Mike and I, we have been very close. However the money I loaned him, that saga was all rather odd. Then there is his heavy drinking, which set alarm bells ringing. But I genuinely liked him, a lot! So he's not with Connie anymore. Do I want an ongoing relationship with him? We did get on well together, but then he lied to Connie and didn't treat her fairly. Might not he do the same to me? Oh! My head is in such a whirl! Now is probably the wrong time, so I'll let the dust settle. Maybe my thoughts will clarify over the next few weeks! I just need some excitement in my life and maybe a man of my own.

1st October 2018

SARAH

It's Monday and back to work, I have a very important client viewing a large, gated property at 3pm this afternoon. His name is Bradley Wilson-Smythe, he is a stockbroker and is very wealthy! I chose one of my favourite outfits, a white silk blouse, short black skirt, black stockings, black high heeled shoes and a white short coat blazer suit jacket. The 'look' finished off with silver earrings set with black stones. I chose my favourite perfume, I need to look and smell my best!

After lunch I pick up the keys plus the gate code from the office and drive twelve miles to the semi-rural location. Once in the property I walk around the rooms checking everything is in good order, happily it is. Although currently vacant, it is furnished in a thoroughly modern style, hopefully just what my client is looking for!

At precisely ten past three the gate buzzer sounds, 'Who is it please?', I ask on the intercom. 'Wilson-Smythe, I am expected'

'Thank you', and I open the gates remotely. There is a crunch on the gravel drive and a black Porsche Cayenne comes to a halt on a spot opposite the front portico. Out steps a self-assured, dark haired, well-built, handsome man in his late forties I'm guessing. I open the door to greet him, 'Good afternoon Mr Wilson-Smythe'

'Oh, please call me Bradley. You must be Sarah Lovage'

'Yes, very pleased to meet you Bradley', we shake hands.

'Follow me please', we enter into a spacious hallway with a sweeping staircase. 'Did you manage to find us alright?'

'Yes thanks. Damn traffic was a bit thick you know'

'Sorry to hear that. Now, what would you like to view first? The reception rooms perhaps?'

'Yes please, but no particular preference, just lead on'

'Right. This is the first reception room. It has a very comfortable, homely feel about it. Don't you agree?'

'Yes, I do like leather Chesterfields'

'I hope you don't mind me asking, but do you have any children?'

'Oh lord no! I don't even have a Mrs Wilson-Smythe!', he chuckles

Inadvertently my eyes widen slightly and I smile sweetly back at him. We move on to the next reception room and then the kitchen. I point out all the main features, which he duly takes in before we move into the spacious lounge. There is a half-grand piano in one corner. 'I shan't be needing that', he laughs, 'Can't play a single note!'

I smile and say, 'We can arrange the removal of any items that are not required'

'Splendid!'

'Now you must see the garden', I operate the electric blinds that reveal a wall of bi-fold doors and a stunning view of a mature and expansive garden.

'Wow! That is wonderful! It looks a great place to relax once we are into some warmer weather'

'Yes, I thought you might like it'. We carried on moving through the property, five bedrooms, three with en suites, a large wet-room and office. Finally we arrived back at the lounge and made ourselves comfortable.

'Well Bradley, what do you think?'

'On the whole very good. I like the large double garage. Big enough for three cars'

'Is motoring a particular hobby of yours?'

'Oh yes. I even participate in motor racing at club level. Time permitting of course!'

'What do you race?'

'A Caterham 7 at circuits all over England. It's great fun!'

'That sounds amazing'

'It is, you should come and see it'

'Yes I'd like to'

Bradley warms to his subject, 'It is very exciting. Certainly gets the old adrenaline racing through one's veins!' Adopting a serious tone, he continues, 'Really need some excitement, life can be so damn dull at times. Especially when one is on one's own. Do you find that?'

'Yes, although I do make time to socialise whenever possible. Of course overseas holidays are the highpoint of the year, as they are for many people'

'Take today for example, as dull as ditch water! Dark clouds overhead, wet roads, damn traffic! Not much to look forward to, until I saw you of course!'

I blush and momentarily look down at the floor, then looking directly at Bradley, 'That's nice of you to say. You aren't so bad looking yourself', I giggle.

Bradley holds my gaze and says, 'Sarah are you up for some fun?'

'It all depends what you have in mind'

Bradley leans forward and speaks with intensity, 'I have some Blow if you want to share it?'

Rather naively I ask, 'What's Blow?'

Bradley looks surprised and laughs, 'You haven't heard of that expression? Dust, Snow, Nose Candy, commonly known as cocaine'

Flustered and feeling slightly stupid, I reply, 'Yes, of course I have'

'Well then, how about it?'

Although I've never taken cocaine before, I hate being belittled, so against my better judgement, I hear myself saying, 'Alright then'. After all wasn't I craving some excitement?

Bradley delves into the pocket of his leather jacket and extracts a small bag of white powder. He carefully arranges this in a line on the coffee table with the aid of an American Express card. With one finger he closes one nostril and lowers the other nostril to within touching distance of the line of Coke.

71

He sucks air and powder up his nostril, leans back and indicates that it is my turn. I'm slightly shaking, I hope he doesn't notice. I mimic Bradley's actions. Wow! A feeling of euphoria sweeps over me. Bradley smiles and suggests, 'Shall we go upstairs?'

'Oh yes!', I reply, 'I feel so alive! I could run a marathon! This is amazing! I've never felt this good before. Let's have some fun!' A fleeting thought crossed my mind, 'What on earth am I wittering on about?' Instantly dismissed as I raced up the stairs two at a time!

That was how Bradley became my dealer, but he never did buy that property. However I did sell it the following week and earned myself a healthy commission in the process. Over the course of the next few months I found that I had to increase the amount of cocaine to obtain the same effect. I'd arrange to meet Bradley at one of the properties, that way avoiding the suspicions of my nosey neighbours.

Chapter 8 – Trauma

3rd October 2018

MIKE

I'm driving Connie to the airport today, she is flying to Barcelona in preparation for the triathlon weekend 6th/7th. Upon arrival I help her with her bags and wish her luck. Connie reciprocates and reminds me to look after myself, kissing me on the cheek. I stop to buy a Scratchcard on the way home and can't believe my luck when four bells means I've won £10,000. I ring the company and it's confirmed. The money will be in my bank account within a few days. I also ring my counsellor to tell her as I need support right now not to gamble it all away.

4th October 2018

CONNIE

Since flying in yesterday I've been enjoying my stay at the Hotel Majestic and all of its facilities. After lunch I decide to be 'the tourist' and visit Antoni Gaudi's stunning Sagrada Familia basilica and soak up the fabulous architecture. I see posters advertising La Mercè Festival and tonight is the night of Correfoc where devils dance in the streets. Intrigued, I decide there and then to venture out tonight to see what it is all about. So I make my way back to the hotel to shower and change my clothes. Upon reaching the hotel I go to Reception to ask for my room key, 'Buenas tardes señor. My room key please, Connie Crawford', I say with a smile. 'Certainly Miss Crawford', the receptionist replies in faultless English. I take the key and ask, 'Do you know much about the Correfoc? I intend to see it tonight'.

'Yes I do, it is a famous event. Correfoc literally means 'Fire Run' in Catalan', and he hands me a leaflet before continuing, 'But please be careful Miss Crawford, it can be dangerous if you aren't dressed correctly'.

'What on earth do you mean?', I ask puzzled.

'Well there are a lot of pyrotechnics, bangers and fireworks. There are even fire-breathing dragons!' He says with a wink. 'Seriously though you must wear a hat or a hoodie, protective glasses and a thick, long sleeved non-flammable top.' I must have look rather shocked because he responded, 'Do not be alarmed, you can safely stand back and watch'.

'Thank you', I reply, 'You have been most helpful señor'. With that I take the lift to my room and prepare myself for whatever eventualities the night has in store for me.

It's after dusk as I leave the hotel suitably attired. Approximately fifteen minutes later I'm approaching Via Laietana where all the action takes place. Already the bustling crowds have gathered, many in strange garbs, and I continue by walking towards the raucous noise. There is a buzz of excitement about the place, punctuated by flashes and loud bangs as fireworks are set off. I walk deeper into the crowd, I see devils dancing in the street, then suddenly a large dragon looms at me through the smoke and it is breathing fire! Sparks shower down on me, the smell of acrid smoke and singed clothing permeates the air. The crowd surges and I'm swept along, my feet barely touching the ground. In the confusion I'm afraid that I will lose my footing and be trampled! Then just as suddenly as they took off, the crowd stops. There, directly in front of me is a huge man dressed in a garish bright red and black costume, his face adorned with a ghoulish mask and corded dreadlocks that hang down to his waist. He is armed with a pyrotechnic lance and performing a violent, macabre dance. Another loud bang and more sparks reign down on us. The 'ghoul' suddenly stops dancing, I've caught his eye. He stares at me, his cold dark eyes boring deep into mine. I don't understand, he looks so angry, he looks as though he wants to kill me! I think he is about to launch himself at me and for a split second, complete stillness and a deep silence, it is as though time stood still. The moment passes. The noise, the explosions, the flashes, the sparks resume and the crowd surges forward past this chilling scene. I have no choice in the matter but to go where this sea of people dictates.

A short while later the ebb and flow of the crowd subsides and I manage to find a seat in a less busy spot. I catch my breath, a chance to reflect upon the chilling and somewhat puzzling experience I've just encountered. I decide that I have had enough excitement for one night and start making my way back to the hotel. However, and this is quite spooky, I have the strangest feeling that I am being followed. Every now and then I look over my shoulder to check, but always no one is apparent. Shaken and feeling drained, I am very much looking forward to a decent night's sleep in the hotel bed!

5th October 2018

CONNIE

Tomorrow I plan to visit both Park Güell and Casa Milà (La Pedrera), especially keen to see the amazing chimney pots on the roof of the latter. Today I'm on a training run, starting from the hotel and taking in some of the sights too. The first being the Arc de Triomf, then meandering across town to the beach of Platja de la Mar Bella, before working my way back along the seafront. From there through Parc de la Ciutadella, then onto Avenue del Marquès de l'Argentera before taking a right turn into Carrer Antic de Sant Joan. I'm jogging along quite steadily, thinking I hope Mike is doing okay without my support, when suddenly a moped runs onto the pavement right in front of me! Simultaneously a grey saloon car screeches to a halt and to my surprise two men with balaclavas run towards me. Before I know it one of them grabs both my arms and holds them firmly behind my back, the other man approaches from the front and I manage to give him a good hard kick right where it hurts! His face screws up in pain, he lunges forward and forces a pad of material across my mouth and nose. The stench is unbearable – chloroform, and then total blackness descends upon me!

I wake up, drowsily, in a dingy cellar lit only by a single bare bulb, my wrists handcuffed together. 'Oh shit, surely this can't be happening?' My thoughts slowly crystallising. 'What on earth am I doing here? Why am I in my running gear?' Slowly it comes back to me, I was out running, the moped, the car, my assailants! 'But why, oh why? I've been kidnapped, but why would anyone want to do this to me? It doesn't make any sense!'

MIKE

Friday night and I decide to have an early night, 10pm and sound asleep before 11. I'm woken by my mobile ringing, it's 12:05 a.m. I don't recognise the number. Sleepily, I say, 'Mike Dean, who's calling please?' A foreign sounding voice replies, 'Hello, this is Pablo Martin, Inspector from the Cuerpo Nacional de Policía, Barcelona.' Suddenly all vestiges of sleep fall away, I am listening intently. Inspector Martin continues, 'Do you know a Connie Crawford?' My thoughts are racing, what on earth has happened? 'Yes, I'm Mike Dean and I live with Connie Crawford'.
'Good. Mr Dean, do you mind if I call you Mike?'

'No, that's fine'.

'Mike, please prepare yourself for some bad news. I'm sorry but we believe Ms Crawford has been kidnapped'.

'What? How?'

'She was out on a training run this evening when a car pulled up alongside her and two men bundled her inside and drove off at speed. This, according to bystanders'.

'Oh my god!'

'This is a rare occurrence in our beautiful city. I am sorry to be the bearer of bad news'.

'Surely it can't be Connie. Why would anyone want to kidnap her? Are you sure it is her?'

'We are sure, she dropped a bank card and hotel key card in the scuffle. We double-checked with the Hotel Majestic, but of course she hadn't returned there. However we established that she was on her own and her passport held in reception provided your contact details. It would help with our enquiries if you would come out to Barcelona as soon as possible. Are you able to do this?'

'Yes, yes, of course, I will come out on the next available flight'.

'Thank you. I will text you my location and contact details. Please let me know as soon as you have arrived'.

'Of course Inspector Martin'.

'One other thing, please bring a recent photograph of Connie with you'.

'Yes, I have several on my phone'.

'Good, thank you for your co-operation. I know it's a lot to take in, so I'll leave you to your thoughts until we talk again. Good night Mike'.

6th October 2018

CONNIE

I've had a very disturbed night, snatching what sleep I could on a paillasse, with just one blanket for cover. At least the handcuffs were removed, however it's uncomfortable and every time I've woken thoughts of my predicament start racing through my head. Just then the door swings open and down the steps comes a diminutive Spaniard, his heavily tattooed arms bearing a breakfast tray. 'Buenos días señorita!', he cheerily greets me, 'Breakfast', placing the tray on a small wooden table in the corner. I glare back at him. His smile replaced by an injured look, 'Señorita be nice, Juan brings you nice breakfast'.

'Juan let me out of here!', I demand.

'Perdón señorita, I can't do that'.

'Well then you aren't any use to me!'

'Please don't be like that señorita. Poor Juan is only following orders'.

'Poor Juan, poor Juan. What about poor Connie?'

'It is not good, Juan is sorry'. On that note, Juan turns on his heel and ascends the steps muttering under his breath, 'Juan haz esto, Juan haz aquello. ¡No tengo nada que decir al respect!'

I am left alone again, and in the circumstances, strangely feel hungry. On the tray is a bottle of orange juice, pan con tomato and a black coffee. My train of thought causes me to glance around the drab cellar, my eyes rest upon a chamber pot in the other corner, which answers that question!

The hours pass very slowly, the same questions go round and round in my head. Why have I been taken? Where am I? How long will I remain in this goddamn awful cellar? What are my captors' intentions?'

MIKE

I manage to book a British Airways evening flight from Heathrow to Barcelona and I'm soon on my way. Once in the air, my mind keeps returning to the same questions. Can this really be happening? Why would anyone want to kidnap Connie? What sort of person would do this? What are the police doing about it? What can the police do about it? Christ, what a nightmare!

My flight arrives on schedule, just after 10pm local time. I jump in a taxi, 'Flor Parks hotel Ramblas por favor'. The taxi driver replies, 'Sí, señor'. Twenty-two minutes later we arrive at the three-star hotel amid the hustle and bustle of Las Ramblas.

My room is clean and perfectly serviceable, I sit on the bed and text my details to Inspector Pablo Martin. A few minutes later I receive a reply asking me to attend the police station at 9:30 a.m. Suddenly I'm feeling very tired and decide to turn in.

7th October 2018

MIKE

I wake, shower and breakfast in the hotel restaurant before a 35-minute walk to the Policía Nacional for 9:30. Arriving 5 minutes early I tell the desk officer that I am here to see Inspector Pablo Martin. He shows me to a small interview room and asks me to wait there. A few minutes later Inspector Martin enters the room greeting me, 'Buenos días Mike, and thank you for coming in today. As I'm sure you appreciate, this is all in Connie's best interests. Before we start would you like a coffee or a glass of water?'

'Yes please, a glass of water'

Inspector Martin fetches a glass from the water cooler and takes a seat opposite me. He states, 'I'll get straight to the point, I'm afraid I haven't got any news regarding Connie's whereabouts. Do you have any urgent questions for me?'

'I'm totally confused. Who would do this? What would their motive be? Is this a common occurrence in Barcelona?'

'I understand your immediate concerns Mike, and I'll do my best to provide some answers, even if they are rather limited'.

'Thank you Inspector Martin'

'Mike did you bring the photos of Connie with you?'

'Yes, they are on my phone', I say quickly finding the images.

Inspector Martin scrutinises the pictures, 'Oh Dios mío, sí!'

'What is it?'

'Apologies Mike, it is a big surprise. Connie is an exact double of Maria López, the leader of one of the biggest gangs in the region. I strongly suspect that Connie has been mistaken for Maria, and possibly taken by a rival gang!'

I am speechless for a moment, as this shocking news sinks in.

Inspector Martin continues, 'Maria López's gang is notorious, they have interests in all sorts of criminal activities as long as it makes them money. The gang is known as *Los Silenciosos*, the Silent Ones in English, as they work stealthily, almost invisibly you might say'.

Regaining my composure, 'But Connie's been taken by a rival gang, what of them?'

'That is where I am at a loss for the moment as we don't know which gang has taken her. In fact we haven't had this confirmed as yet. I must stress Mike that the police are doing everything in our power to ensure Connie's safe return. We are conducting house to house enquiries as well as exploring other avenues of investigation'.

'Progress seems desperately slow, Connie must be found!', my angst surfacing.

'I understand your concerns Mike, but I don't have anything else to tell you except to restate that my team are working hard and this is the police department's number one priority job'.

'OK, thanks Inspector Martin. Well I guess I had better be going so you can focus all your efforts where they are needed'.

'Thank you Mike. I will of course contact you as soon as we have any news. In the meantime please allow me copies of Connie's photograph'.

'I'll email a couple over straight away'

'Thanks again Mike and let me see you out'.

'By the way Inspector Martin your English is very good'.

'Thank you Mike, that is because I studied Psychology at Royal Holloway in Surrey'.

'Impressive!'

'Here we are back at the entrance, so I will leave you now. Buenos días'.

I have a lot to think about as I make my way back towards the hotel. Where is Connie? Is she hurt? Is she really in the hands of a gangster?

CONNIE

'Christ it's bloody boring shut up in here', I think as I pace up and down in this small space. I have been doing exercises to keep in shape. I have also been wracking my brain for a way to get out of here, so far nothing has seemed credible. Suddenly there is a knock on the cellar door and the door swings open. It's Juan, I guess he didn't want to catch me indisposed.

'Buenas tardes señorita! Juan has brought you lovely lunch, comida', he enthuses as he comes down the steps carrying a tray and places it on the table. 'How is señorita today?'

'I'm fine, what do you think?', I reply sarcastically.

This goes straight over his head. 'Juan doesn't know, that is why Juan asks'.

'Never mind. When am I going to get out of this place?'

'Sorry señorita, Juan doesn't know, Juan just following orders. Juan only servant'.

'Juan, where are we?'

'Barcelona señorita'

'But where in Barcelona? What street?'

'Oh, sorry señorita, Juan cannot say. Juan must go now'. And with no further ado Juan gives a slight bow and retreats up the stairs. Leaving me to contemplate his culinary delights!

MIKE

Back at the hotel room, I'm worried sick. I can't stop thinking about other missing persons that you read about in the newspapers. Often they are discovered too late, that is, dead. Connie is such a good person, she doesn't deserve this. I realise now that I love her very much, but not in the soul-mate-for-life way, but more like a brother because she has stood by me and supported me through my difficult times.

I'm not feeling very hungry but I suppose I should find something to eat. I get up from the chair and as I walk towards the door I spot a note that has been pushed under it. It reads, 'Meet me at 17:00 at L'Ovella Negra Ramblas. Look for the lady in black. Don't inform the police if you want to see your friend alive'. I am taken aback, I don't know what to think. On the one hand it seems ridiculous, but on the other hand it appears well informed and I daren't ignore it. How on earth did anyone find me? I must go. I have around two hours to wait, but I can't sit still, so I decide to walk the streets to kill some time.

Seventeen hundred hours and the tapas bar L'Ovella Negra has just opened. I am watching from across the street, and see a stylish lady in black approaching the bar. 'Good god, it's Connie!', Oh no, it can't be, that's impossible and she, she is different. Her hair is a bit longer for a start, and the tan darker and Connie would never choose that particular outfit. My mind is buzzing, could this be the mysterious gang leader, Maria López, who Inspector Martin told me about? Only one way to find out! I enter the bar and immediately spot her sitting in a discrete corner. Otherwise the bar is empty. As I approach she glances up and smiles, 'Señor Mike Dean?' I nod. She continues, 'Please take a seat. I am Maria López, I am pleased to meet you'.

I take the proffered hand, 'Mike Dean', and tersely, 'Now what on earth is all this cloak and dagger stuff about?'.

'Mike, may I call you Mike?' Again I nod approval. 'Mike, I know why you are here, your girlfriend is missing, I have inside information and know that she looks very similar to myself. I believe that Connie has been mistaken for me and has been kidnapped by my bitter rival, Kylo Garcia, who leads the Los Ghouls gang. He will be feeling very angry and stupid knowing he has the wrong person and I guess won't know what to do with her. I know that this is a lot to take in'. She looks at me expectantly.

'The police had guessed as much, but why haven't you gone to the police with this information?'

'I would have thought that was obvious Mike. Let's just say that the police don't look upon my business very kindly and leave it at that. However I want to help you find Connie, which is why I invited you here'.

'OK, I'm listening', I reluctantly reply, not wanting any involvement with a gang.

Maria continues, 'I have been given the name of an informant. Sorry, I can't meet them myself, it would put both our lives at risk. So I want you to meet them, very discretely you understand?'

I answer hesitantly, 'Yes I understand, but it sounds dangerous. Why does it have to be me?'

'Because you are the only person I can trust in this situation. One more thing, if you agree to do this, then I need to have your word that not a word gets back to the police. If it did it could put Connie's life in peril, more than it already is'.

It is an impossible situation, I quickly weigh it up, this may be the only way to get Connie back alive. 'Right, you have my word. What happens next?'

'I will arrange a rendezvous and contact you with the details. Remember, not a word to anyone, Connie's life depends upon it'. With that Maria stands up, shakes my hand and leaves the bar, leaving me to contemplate the many unknowns, not least my fear for my own safety!'

8th October 2018

CONNIE

Having endured another uncomfortable, sleepless night, I am almost glad to hear the cheerful voice of Juan, 'Buenos días señorita! Breakfast'

'Buenos días Juan'

'Juan has for you present', and with that he hands me an English edition of Charles Dickens' A Tale of Two Cities'.

I laugh out loud, oh the irony of myself being given a book based on imprisonment, when I am imprisoned too!

Juan looks puzzled and hurt, so I quickly reassure him, 'Juan that is very kind, muchas gracias'. I think, what a nice gesture, especially helpful as the boredom is killing me.

Juan smiles, again the slight bow, before turning and ascending the steps. Leaving me to my thoughts and the book.

MIKE

It is a warm and sunny morning, I've had breakfast and now sitting in my Flor Park room reading the paper and mulling things over. I raise my head to a rustling sound; my eyes switch to the door and the note that has been pushed under it. I throw the paper down and rush to the door and out into the corridor. I look up and down the corridor, but nobody is there. Back in my room, the note reads, 'Meet 14:00 hrs Park Güell, The Greek Theatre. Follow the man with the Times rolled-up under his arm, but do not approach him, keep your distance and follow'.

I'm not very hungry, my nerves on edge with trepidation, so just after 12 noon, I ensconce myself in the bar, order a bocadillo and fresh orange juice, followed by a black coffee. Later I purchase a ticket for the Metro de Barcelona from Liceu to Vallcarca, followed by the short walk to Park Güell. I purchase a ticket for Park Güell with timed entry at 2pm, perfect!

I slowly make my way to the appointed rendezvous, Teatre grec del Parc Güell (The Greek Theatre). There are plenty of tourists in this area, so I feel inconspicuous. Nervously I look around for my contact, black flamenco waistcoat, black suede shoes and carrying a rolled-up newspaper. Ahh! There he is nonchalantly leaning against the masonry. I approach hesitantly and the man speaks, 'Señor Mike?'

'Yes, and you are?'

'Just call me Hugo. Let us walk.'

We move off down one of the paths. Hugo, if that is his real name, continues, 'I have good news, your pareja is unharmed. It is difficult, a dangerous situation.'

'I am relieved that she is unharmed, but what do I need to do to get her back?'

'It is not simple. You need to pay me €10,000. Phone me when you have the money.' Hugo said, pushing a written number towards me.

My jaw dropped, for a moment I didn't know what to say, then 'Wait, how do I know that you are genuine?'

'You don't!' came the blunt reply. 'Adiós for now Señor Mike'. With that he turned on his heels and briskly walked away.

As I walk back, I ponder, 'Can I trust this man? Probably not. Should I go to the police? No, it might endanger Connie's life. I really have no option but do what Hugo wants me to do.' I make my way to the bank. To me, €10,000 is a lot of money and would wipe out my bank account but Connie's life is at stake, I have to do this!

Later, having collected the cash from the bank I phoned Hugo's number. He instructs me to leave a package at my hotel's reception desk for him to collect, this duly I do. Hugo assures me that he will contact me again as soon as he has more news.

CONNIE

Once again Juan appears, this time with lunch. I have a plan, I can't just sit around doing nothing. 'Juan, just look at me, I feel so dirty and my hair is a mess'. Juan smiles exposing his imperfect teeth, 'Señorita bello'.

'Juan please help me. I need a hairbrush and a mirror. Would you do this for me please?', I say in the sweetest voice I can muster.

'Si señorita, Juan will try.', and with that he retreated back through the door.

That evening Juan reappears with supper on a tray and, to my delight, a hairbrush and mirror. 'Thank you so much Juan', I gush.

'Juan happy for señorita. Have nice evening.', and with an extravagant wave of his arm he sweeps out of the door.

9th October 2018

CONNIE

I'm awake early and after utilising the piss-pot in rather an ungainly manner, I set to work. First, I place the mirror on the ground and then carefully apply pressure with my foot until it breaks into several long shards of glass. Then I tear a strip off of the blanket, using the sharp edge of the glass to sever any stubborn threads. Next, I take the longest shard and cautiously wind the blanket strip around the wider end to form a makeshift handle and dagger. I am ready.

About half-an-hour passes before I hear Juan fumbling with the lock. From my seat on the paillasse I studiously watch his every move. Juan issues a cheery, 'Buenos días señorita!' and, breakfast tray in hand, shuffles towards the table. As he places the tray on the table his back is completely turned. Seizing the moment I leap to my feet and in one swift movement, put my left arm tightly around his throat, jerking his whole body backwards. He is completely taken by surprise; his eyes widen in abject fear as he sees the makeshift dagger in my right-hand. The shard glinting with malice in the subdued light of the windowless cellar. 'Señorita no!', he gasps his half-strangled response.
'Do exactly as I say Juan,' I sternly reply, 'and no harm will come to you.'
'Sí'
'Now answer my questions and don't try anything stupid!'
'Sí'

'Who are you working for?'

'Los Ghouls señorita'

'What is that?'

'Pandilla – a gang. Juan knows this from American movies'

'Why am I being held?'

'Juan not know, no one tells him'

'You are about as much use as a chocolate teapot!'

'Qué?'

'Never mind. Juan, I am about to walk out of the door and you won't stop me. Do you understand?'

'Sí señorita'

The exchange over, I quickly advance to the door. Fortunately the key is still in the lock. I lock the door behind me, make my way up the stairs and out of the front door. Unaccustomed to daylight, I shield my eyes from the early morning sun and look round to get my bearings. I don't recognise anything in this back street, but can't hang about here, so decide to move off to my right. I soon arrive at a junction with a commercial street, tourist shops, bars and cafés proliferate. I enter a café and order an expresso. I must catch my breath and think what I need to do next.

MIKE

I've been worried sick all morning over Connie's disappearance. Pacing up and down my hotel room the time has really dragged. It's midday when my mobile rings, my hand is shaking as I grab the handset. The dulcet tones of Hugo crackle through the receiver, 'I have some bad news Señor Mike.'

'What's happened?', I interject.

'I'm sorry, but your pareja has disappeared. She has escaped from where she was being held. I can do no more to help you.'

'Oh my God!', I exclaim as the reality hits home. 'What should I do now? What about my money?'

'Your money has been paid over. Sorry I can't help. Do not contact me again.' The line goes dead. Frantically I redial the number Hugo gave me but all I hear is a continuous tone, that particular phone is no longer in service!

What on earth do I do now? I decide another conversation with the police is my only option.

CONNIE

I beckon the bartender over and ask if I can use his phone and thankfully he agrees. I call the police station and briefly explain my situation to the duty officer who immediately puts me through to an Inspector Martin. 'Señorita Crawford please allow me to introduce myself, I am Inspector Pablo Martin. Your partner Señor Mike Dean has told me much about you and I have a team assigned to the investigation into your disappearance.' Reassuringly he continues, 'It is great news that you are able to talk to me now. Where are you right now? Oh, and please call me Pablo.'

'Thank you Pablo, and please call me Connie. I have just escaped from where I was being held and calling from a nearby café'

'Are you hurt Señorita Connie?'

'No, thankfully'

'What is the name of the café?'

'ARTiSA Barcelona'

'I know it! Stay right there, I will dispatch a car to pick you up immediately and bring you back here. Then you can tell me your story in full.'

'Thank you Pablo and please can you bring money to pay for my coffee'

'Certainly I will and I look forward to meeting you very soon Señorita Connie.'

MIKE

'Is that the Cuerpo Nacional de Policía? Great. Please put me through to Inspector Pablo Martin, it is in connection with the missing Connie Crawford'

'Who is calling please?', comes the reply.

'Mike Dean'

'Ah, just a moment please Señor Dean', and the line goes quiet for a few minutes before the duty officer continues,

'Inspector Martin requests that you make your way here as soon as possible please. Señorita Crawford is here'

'What! How?'

'Sorry I don't have any details. Inspector Martin will be able to update you'

'Well that is a relief, Connie being safe that is. Yes, I'm on my way!'

'Thank you Señor Dean'

I grab my wallet and jacket, dash out of the hotel and hail a cab.

'Cuerpo Nacional de Policía por favor'

'Sí señor'

Ten minutes later I have arrived.

The duty officer ushers me into a room where Inspector Martin sits in a comfortable chair behind a large desk. He rises to offer his hand, but before we can shake hands Connie is out of the chair opposite, dashes across the room and wraps her arms around me in a big hug. I reciprocate. Joyously she exclaims, 'Oh, Mike I am so pleased to see you, you won't believe what I've been through. At one point I thought I might never see you again!'

'Connie, I am so relieved to see you too!'

I hold the embrace until a polite 'Er hm' from Inspector Martin causes us to reluctantly disengage.

Inspector Martin's proffered hand indicates a chair, 'Take a seat Mike and I'll bring you up-to-date.', Inspector Martin continues, 'I'm also pleased and relieved that Connie is unharmed.', he smiles, 'From what Connie has described, I think her jailer is perhaps more shocked, although he can consider himself fortunate that he got off so lightly!' Inspector Martin had already explained to Connie that it was the Los Ghouls gang that had mistaken her for Maria López, the leader of the rival Los Silenciosos gang.

Connie enquires, 'What happens now Inspector?'

'Well, obviously we are trying to find the people responsible. Unfortunately that may take some time due to the clandestine manner in which these gangs operate. As you know I have recorded our interview and a statement will be prepared. In the meantime I suggest that you both retire to your hotel and unwind from what must have been a very stressful time for you.'

An upbeat and relieved Connie responds, 'Thank you Inspector. Yes, I'm really looking forward to a shower and clean clothes, followed by a decent meal!'

'I'll be in touch shortly. So for now I'll see you out and bid you Buenos días.'

As we walk out of the door, Connie turns to me and says, 'Mike, would you mind coming over to my hotel in about two hours' time please? I don't want to be on my own just at the moment. We could have dinner together'

'That would be lovely Connie. We have so much to catch up on. I have things to tell you that I couldn't say in front of the Inspector'

'What?', Connie exclaimed, a puzzled look flashing across her face.

'Don't worry, I'll explain everything later', I say with a reassuring smile. 'In the meantime I'll share a cab with you to your hotel, before going on to mine to freshen up. If that's ok?'

'That's perfect, thanks Mike'.

CONNIE

Around 8pm Mike arrived at my hotel, I met him in Reception and we went into the restaurant together for dinner. Over dinner I told Mike about Juan and the conditions that I'd been held in. Mike reciprocated with details about his meeting with Maria López and the subsequent meeting with Hugo, one of Los Ghouls' henchmen. That Mike had paid €10,000 for my safe return, the plan being thwarted by my escape. After my ordeal the dinner tasted like the best meal ever and finally I relaxed over a coffee. Suddenly a wave of tiredness washed over me, the adrenaline from today's excitement finally dissipated. So, after agreeing to meet Mike in the morning, I excused myself as I desperately needed to hit the sack.

MIKE

I get back to my hotel at around ten past eleven and go straight to my room, where I find another note has been shoved under my door. It states, "You and Connie are in danger. Both meet me at 09:30 in the Citizen Café, Plaça d'Urquinaona. The lady in black". Momentarily dazed, I sit on the bed and reread the note several times. 'The lady in black', well that must be Maria. I don't want to disturb Connie but this is so important that I must. I pick up the phone and dial the number Connie provided. Frustratingly it goes straight to voicemail, so I leave a message, 'Connie, I've had a note from Maria. She says we are in danger and to meet her at 09:30 Citizen Café, Plaça d'Urquinaona. I'll see you there at about 9. Any problem, then let me know'.

After my usual ablutions, I go to bed but unable to sleep as the questions whizz around my head, 'What danger are we in? Aren't we free of this mess? Why is Maria still involved? Should I contact the police?' I have no answers and eventually doze off.

10th October 2018

CONNIE

After a fitful night's sleep I wake at about 7 a.m, which is somewhat surprising after what I have experienced over the last few days! I see I have a missed call and voicemail. I listen attentively to Mike's message, puzzled and surprised. A quick call to Mike establishes that he can't shed any more light on the matter, except to say that the Citizen Café is about 15 minutes walk away for both of us. With some trepidation I agree to meet him there at 9.

A shower revitalises me and a fresh set of clothes enables me to face the day, whatever it may bring!

MIKE

I arrive at the Citizen Café at just after 9, Connie had arrived a few minutes before me and greets me with a warm smile.

'Good morning Mike, or at least I hope it is going to be good!'

'Same here. Good morning Connie. Did you sleep well?'

'Yes thanks Mike, although I woke once or twice and then you know how it is, thoughts start racing through your head'

'Me too. Look, that's a comfortable sofa, let's sit there'

We sit down and order coffee that arrives a few minutes later.

'This place looks very trendy, but with a certain rustic charm' Connie remarks.

'Yes, and the coffee is good too'

'Mike do you have any idea what this is about?'

'Not a clue. Your guess is as good as mine'

A few minutes later in walks the lady in black, Maria. For a moment Connie's jaw drops, wham, it hits her like a thunderbolt out of the blue, the resemblance isn't superficial, they are identical! It seems to cause Maria to draw breath too, as she hesitates before greeting us, 'Buenos días Mike and Connie', as she takes a seat.

'Buenos días Maria', Connie and I reply simultaneously.

Connie enthusiastically, 'We are so alike Maria. I can hardly believe my eyes'

'Yes Connie, we are and that is the nub of the problem. That is precisely why you are in much danger'. She clicks her fingers and the waiter comes over, 'Buenos días'.

'Buenos días señorita'

'Un espresso por favor'

'Sí señorita', and he bustles away.

Addressing Connie and I, Maria continues, 'Los Ghouls is a threat to us all. Their leader, Kylo Garcia, has a vendetta against me. His kidnapping you Connie, thinking you were me, has caused him to lose face amongst his peers. I've heard on the grapevine that he intends to, er, eliminate the problem and that is very bad news for both of us'.

The colour is noticeably draining from Connie's face. I'm starting to sweat profusely. The adrenaline starts to kick in and excitedly I suggest, 'Connie and I had better head for the airport and get the first flight back to England, don't you think?'

Maria, adopting a very serious tone, responds, 'No, you are not safe anywhere. Think how easily I found you in your hotel. Kylo has contacts or associates internationally, he will find you'

Connie queries, 'Well, what on earth do you suggest we do?'

'I was coming to that', Maria replies, 'We must work together to destroy Los Ghouls for once and for all'

Connie incredulously, 'What! You can't be serious! We should go straight to the police!'

'That is the last thing you should do', Maria snaps, 'The Spanish police haven't managed to nullify Los Ghouls for all these years. Also, I don't think the British police are any better. With all the red-tape involved it would take months to set up protection for you, by which time…,' and Maria signals a throat cutting motion with her hand.

Connie gasps, 'Oh my God!'

I interject, 'Well what do you propose then Maria? Do you have a plan?'

'The first thing is we have to get you out of Barcelona immediately. It just isn't safe here in light of the events of the past few days. Then we need to lure Kylo to follow us to a place where we can clearly see him, where he and his gang don't have the advantage of surprise. Connie, do you think you could find the place where you were held?'

'Yes, yes, I think so'

'Good. Then I have a plan, we will leak to Los Ghouls that we are expecting a large consignment of heroine. This news will get back to Kylo, he won't be able to resist the twin attractions of the drugs and the chance to put me out of business – permanently'

I strike a cautious note, 'This all sounds very dangerous to me'

Maria impatiently retorts, 'If you are too scared Mike go home, take your chance. You maybe safe, but it is Connie and myself where the real threat is aimed at.'

'I'm sure you are right, but I will stay around for Connie's sake', I reply trying to assert myself in the face of two strong women.

'OK we are all agreed then? We go with my plan?'

Somewhat reluctantly I respond, 'Yes okay'

'Yes, it appears to be the only option' Connie replied.

Maria retorted, 'Good, I'm sure it's for the best. I will go through a few more details, then I need to make some phone calls and other arrangements. We meet back here at 12, yes?'

'Yes', we say in unison.

'Adiós por ahora, or goodbye for now, as you English would say', and with that she makes a swift exit.

Connie looked at me, 'I can't believe what just happened, we have agreed to a gangster's plan to thwart another mob!'

'I know, I'm feeling shell-shocked too. But do we really have a choice?'

'There's always a choice Mike, but the challenge is choosing the right one!'

'So is this the right one?'

'Only time will tell, but one thing for sure is that we need to get fully behind Maria's plan for it to stand any chance of working'

'If you say so'

'Mike you don't sound very convinced. Either you are in this one hundred percent or you're on the next flight home. Which is it?'

I shift my eyes towards the floor, hesitate, then look Connie directly in the eyes and say, 'Okay Connie, I'm in. One hundred percent'.

'Good. In that case I suggest we both get some rest and then meet back here at 12'

'Right you are. I'll see you later then'.

Chapter 9 – Maria's Plan

MIKE

We reconvene at the Citizen Café at the appointed time. Maria says brightly, 'I am pleased that you are here. I thought that you might have had second thoughts'

Connie replies, 'No, we are fully committed. Aren't we Mike?'

I respond earnestly, 'Yes, of course', but inside I have a sense of impending doom.

'Good. We don't have much time, so I suggest we go immediately'

'Where to?', Connie asks.

Maria looking directly at Connie, 'You must take me to the place where you were held captive'

'Okay follow me', and with that we all make our way out of the café.

It takes about twenty minutes for Maria to show Connie and I the way to the ARTiSA café. From there Connie was able to take us directly to the place where she was held. Maria boldly knocks on the door. In a few moments the door is cautiously opened by Juan, whose jaw has just hit the floor! He stands there for a moment speechless, before hastily trying to shut the door. Too late. Maria has a foot inside and bundles Juan backwards, and before he can react she has snapped on handcuffs. Maria barks, 'Siéntate y cállate y no te pasará nada malo'. Juan, glaring at Maria, sits down on the floor. I ask, 'What did you say to him?'

'To shut up and he won't be hurt', Maria smiles and continues, 'Now search this place for anything useful, perhaps some clue as to why Connie was held here'

'But...', I start to say.

Connie interrupts, 'Just do it Mike!'

The search is fruitless, the place is fairly bare and easy to search. We finish up in a small room, Juan is just out of sight.

'I've found nothing', Connie says. 'Me too', I agree.

'Disappointing', Maria said quietly and winks, 'OK, just to recap, the merchandise must be moved tonight, I will pick you up outside the Hotel Majestic at 19:30'. OK?'

'OK', reply Connie and I

'Good, we leave now'. Maria leads the way out of the room, stopping only to retrieve the handcuffs from a frightened and puzzled looking Juan. As soon as Maria is out in the street she says loudly, '19:30 Hotel Majestic, don't forget', she turns and winks. As the last one out I shut the door behind me.

As our trio makes away Maria explains, 'I think that even that stupid man will have got the message. I expect that we will have company tonight! In the meantime I want you to keep out of sight in your hotel. I don't want you to take any unnecessary risks. I will be outside in my car at 19:30. I'll meet you then'.

'OK, see you later', I respond

'Yes, see you then', chimes in Connie.

19:30 came round very quickly. I met Connie in Reception and together we stepped out of the hotel into the gathering dusk. Maria's black Mercedes-Benz AMG GT 4dr Coupe was waiting, the window down, she shouted 'Hurry' and beckoned us forward. Seated next to her was a rough-shaven, burly man, who she introduced as Raúl. Connie and I slipped into the luxurious rear seats. Maria teased the motor into life and a satisfying growl emanated from the exhaust as the Merc eased forward into the traffic. 'Where are we going?', Connie asked. Maria replied, 'I will explain all. We are going to Montserrat. Have you heard of it? No? It means "serrated mountain". It is remote, about an hour's drive, but also easy to find. I have arranged a rendezvous with some people from Italy, in order to hand over the merchandise.'

'What merchandise?', Connie asked, for a moment fearing that we are to be the merchandise. 'Drugs, we have a large consignment'

Connie and I exchanged worried looks. I blurted out, 'We didn't realise you really were carrying drugs. Then why are we going with you? We don't wish to be involved in drug running!' Maria, somewhat coldly replied, 'It is necessary. It is also bait, something to tempt Los Ghouls out of their enclave. They control drug trafficking in Barcelona. I have intruded on their territory. If my plan is working, even now they are following us'. Right then it hit me square in the chest, the realisation that

we had embarked upon an extremely dangerous mission. Worse still, there could be no turning back! Small beads of perspiration exuded across my brow. Again I looked across to Connie and she looked just as much in shock as I felt. By this time the Merc had reached the C-58 dual carriageway and we were making good progress. The conversation had died out, leaving Connie and I to our thoughts, these mostly being 'black'! How was all this going to end? The big V8 Merc was eating up the miles and as it stretched its legs across the countryside the traffic became much lighter. However I noticed that Maria kept glancing into the rear-view mirror. So I asked, 'What is it Maria? You seem to be looking behind a lot'
'Yes, I think we are being followed. As I predicted. This is good'.
Connie and I both looked back, but in the darkness could only make out car headlights. Sure enough, the headlights were maintaining a constant distance behind the Merc.

A good forty minutes had passed since we left Barcelona and we left the C-58 for a short stretch on the C-55, then onto the BP-1121. The latter was a narrow, mountain road with a series of sharp bends as we climbed higher and higher. To describe it as a 'switchback' would be a fair comparison. The unique serrated mountain tops towered above us, while at the roadside there was a dramatic drop to the gorge below making for an unsettling ride. Maria spoke tersely, 'Their car it is gaining on us. I will drive faster'. With that she urged the Merc forwards furiously, the tyres protesting around the chicanes. To no avail, the car behind was steadily gaining on us. Within another thousand metres it had caught us. Suddenly there was a loud bang, our heads jerked and Maria exclaimed, 'Mierda!'. 'Oh shit!', Connie echoed the sentiment. 'We've been rammed!', cried Maria. The other car was coming alongside now. Another loud bang as it deliberately drove into us! Maria skilfully corrected the steering. The other car now had its nose ahead. Then Maria did the unexpected, she jerked the steering wheel hard to the left, immediately back again and braking hard. The other car spun, still moving forward, hit a large sloping rock that acted as a ramp flipping the car onto its roof, a trail of sparks showered down the road before it came to a grinding standstill. Maria gingerly drove past, we observed some movement inside. Maria carried on, however there were some unhealthy noises coming from our ripped bodywork dragging along the road. Fortunately the car park was in view and within just a few minutes we were parked up. No sooner had we got out of the car and taken a deep breath of the cool mountain air, than two men jumped out of a parked Maserati and quickly made towards us. 'Hola Señorita López, you have the merchandise?', said a swarthy Italian with a neat moustache. Maria testily replied, 'Yes of course. Now hurry, we have company not far behind'. Just then there was a loud explosion. We all looked back down the road where smoke and flames were gushing from the other car. We could also just about make out the silhouette of two figures against the orange backdrop who were hurrying up the road towards us! So with no further prompt needed the merchandise was transferred from the boot of the Merc into the Maserati. 'Adiós Señorita López, it has been a pleasure doing business with you'. With that the Italians jumped back into the Maserati and with a throaty roar disappeared back down the road. The air was still, not a cloud in the sky, just starlight and the pale lights from the abbey shining out. 'Well, what next?', I asked directing my gaze at Maria. Suddenly before she could answer, the stinging whistle of a bullet flew close to our heads. 'Run!', shouted Maria. We ran, as fast as we could away from the two armed assailants! We ran past the Benedictine monastery and kept running. There in front of us were steps leading further up into the mountains. 'This way quick, rápida!', Maria directed. Oh so many steps, I was puffing and panting. Thank goodness Connie had persuaded me to go to the gym again. Super-fit Connie was doing much better. Maria and Raúl appeared to be familiar with the path and we were soon amongst the distinctive shapes of the saw-tooth like mountain tops. Maria raised her hand and called a halt, then whispering, 'This is what we will do. This place is suitable for an ambush.' My eyes opened wide, this is madness I thought, but only managed to say, 'Surely you don't expect to ambush these thugs? They're armed!' Maria smiled,

'And so are we'. Her hand went inside her jacket and withdrew a gun. 'My dependable Glock 26', she whispered. Raúl followed Maria's lead by producing a Glock 17, with a big smile, his gold tooth glinting in the subdued light. I recoiled in horror, so far out of my depth now! Maria sensed my unease, 'Don't worry we are professionals, we know what needs to be done', she said ominously. I looked at Connie, who shrugged her shoulders as if to say, 'we just have to get on with it'. Maria told us where to stand, sheltered behind the rocks. Then we waited. It wasn't long before we heard them, puffing away, shoes clattering on the stone. 'Ssshhh! Bastant!', the leader said in a hushed voice. That was Maria's cue, 'Atureu-vos, us tinc cobert', she commanded in Catalan. The two men ducked behind the nearest rocks and fired a couple of shots in our direction that harmlessly ricocheted away. Maria raised her voice again, 'Us esteu fent les coses més difícils per a vosaltres mateixos. Rendir-se!' (You are making things harder for yourselves. Surrender!) 'No, mai!', came the stern reply, followed by two more shots.

'Ximples, en patireu les conseqüències!' (Fools, you will suffer the consequences!). Maria returned fire. This drew a hail of bullets in her direction. Meanwhile Raúl had been carefully working his way around the flank. He took careful aim and fired, a single bullet spiralled into the right arm of one of the thugs, whose gun clattered to the ground as he shrieked out in pain. His buddy fired off a shot at Raúl, who had already ducked behind a large boulder. For several minutes it went very quiet, followed by some whispering. Unexpectedly their leader shouted, 'Ens rendim!' Maria explained, 'He said "We surrender"'. Sure enough the pair emerged from their cover, the leader helping to support his wounded partner by the arm. It was all over, so I stepped forward, but in a flash the leader had grabbed me, spun me round and I could feel the cold muzzle of his firearm hard in my back! The leader snarled, 'Baixeu les armes ara!' (Put your guns down now!) Before Maria or anyone else could react, Connie who had been emerging from a slightly higher vantage point, leapt down onto the back of the thugs leader. She took him down onto the floor, his gun going flying and a scuffle ensued. Maria and Raúl's guns were useless in this situation, they couldn't risk hitting Connie! Just as it looked like the thug was winning Connie used her judo techniques to throw him off and then pinned him to the ground, immobilised. Raúl took the opportunity to grab the thug and press his gun hard into his back. The beaten thug responded weakly, 'Em rendeixo'. 'He surrenders', Maria translated.

Connie ripped off the shirt sleeve of the wounded thug and tied it tightly around his arm to stem the bleeding. The six of us slowly made our way back down to the carpark, all the while Maria kept her gun ready in case of any more funny business. At the carpark Raúl gave some attention to the Merc, folding the damaged bodywork up so it wasn't dragging

111

on the ground. He also found out two pairs of handcuffs from the boot and used these to secure the two thugs to a metal pole. Maria told them not to worry, the police would be here very soon! The four of us piled back into the Merc and soon passed the burnt out remains of the thugs car. Just before we joined the C-55, Maria called the police and informed them where they could find two suspicious characters handcuffed to a pole! After all this excitement the journey back to Barcelona was, I am pleased to say, uneventful!

Chapter 10 – Flight or Fight?

11th October 2018

SARAH

I had another property viewing at 10 a.m, so arranged for Bradley to come here at 11:30 a.m. Slightly late as usual, with a slight squeal of rubber he pulled up outside, before making his way to the front door. 'Hello again Bradley', I said with a broad smile. He replied, 'The lovely Sarah. How are you today?'

'Very well thank you. Do come in'. Actually I had been feeling a bit off colour, some dizziness and restlessness, but I don't want to bother Bradley with those details.

Bradley follows me into the lounge, 'The weather's better today, I managed over 90mph down the dual carriageway!'

'Oh, you just be careful you don't get stopped, especially when in possession!'

'Nothing to worry about there dear girl', he grinned like a naughty schoolboy caught smoking behind the bike sheds.

Suddenly I felt his condescension getting under my skin, 'Well, if you get caught, just ensure you don't bring my name into it', I snapped irritably. Somewhat surprised, Bradley looked at me a moment before answering, 'Of course not dear girl, wouldn't dream of it'

'As long as we are clear on that point', I said firmly

'Don't you worry your pretty little head about it'

'Shut the fuck up Bradley! I don't need this crap at the moment', I exploded, a bit surprised by how suddenly my feelings had risen to the surface. Bradley looked very taken aback, 'Terribly sorry my dear, didn't mean to offend you. No hard feelings?'

'No, sorry, I don't know what came over me'

'Down to business then', he said drawing a packet of white powder out of his jacket pocket. 'I assume you want to sample the goods first?', he grinned

'Yes please'. I wanted to say 'No', but somehow couldn't bring myself to say it. So we commenced the ritual. Afterwards I purchased three small packets from him, paying cash of course. We parted company once more friends. I had intended going back to work but I felt the dizziness returning, this time accompanied by nausea, so phoned in sick and took the afternoon off.

MIKE

I met Connie for breakfast at a convenient pavement café, the sun was shining and the coffee was great. Connie looked tired but was otherwise in good spirits. 'What an eventful night! Well that's twice I've saved your life Mike', she grinned.

'Alright, no need to rub it in', I replied feigning hurt feelings. Connie sipped her coffee and I continued 'We are still in danger aren't we Connie?'

'Yes I think we are', Connie studiously responded.

'We could talk to Maria for her advice?', I ask

Connie sits up straight, 'I don't think any further dealings with Maria and Los Silenciosos are advisable. We risk getting caught up in their illegal activities. We already know that they are involved in drugs and carry guns. I'm sure the police will take a very dim view of our associating with them'

'I'm sure you're right Connie, but I can't see another way forward'

'I agree it's a difficult situation all round. Perhaps we would be safer returning to England, although Maria cautioned against this. I'll just grab my phone and look up the return flights. Connie moves to look under the table and exclaims, 'Oh my god! Mike, my – my bag is gone. It's been stolen!' Connie's shocked expression is mirrored by my own. Helplessly I look round. Not a sign of anybody running away'

'Oh Christ Connie! What do we do now? What was in your bag?'

'My smartphone, a tourist guide, a purse with Euros. Lucklly my passport is being held by the hotel. Oh yes, the hotel key was in the bag too'.

I signal for the waiter to come over, explain the situation and ask for his advice.

'I am very sorry, señor and señorita. This is not uncommon in tourist hotspots. Please report to the police. I am very sorry'.

'OK, we'll do that. Gracios señor'.

We pay the bill and head towards the police station.

At the police station we complete the usual formalities and Connie decides to head to her hotel to report the missing hotel key and smartphone. Luckily she had a small pocket wallet of payment cards on her person. I accompany her, and upon reaching the hotel, sink into a comfy chair in the entrance lobby. Meanwhile Connie converses with the receptionist, and is soon issued with a replacement electronic key card before going up to her room.

CONNIE

Out of the lift on the 3rd floor, I reach my door. Insert the key card, but at first it doesn't seem to work, then it does. There follows a loud click as I turn the handle and push the door open. Unusually the lights don't go on immediately, so I'm slightly disorientated. Then as I step further into the room in order to find the light switches, someone shoves me hard out of their way. With a gasp of surprise I stumble and fall onto the floor. Twisting round I look back towards the door. I get a fleeting glimpse of a man dressed in black disappearing out of the door. Breathing rapidly as the adrenaline kicks in, I get up to find the master light switch and flood the room with light. I try to gather my thoughts, 'Is anything missing?' I look round and to my surprise see my bag in the corner, 'So the intruder is the same person who stole my bag. This means it was a targeted attack!' I check my bag and discover nothing missing, even my smartphone is still there!

I go back down to report this to Reception and update an incredulous Mike.

Mike stares at me and for a moment is lost for words, then, 'Connie we should check your room thoroughly there must be something missing'

'You're right Mike. Come on then'

We make our way up to the room and search everywhere, including under the bed. Finally Mike asks, 'Well Connie, do you think anything is missing?'

'Not as far as I can tell Mike', I answer. 'I wonder what they were after. Perhaps I disturbed them just in time'. Little did I know but the intruder had planted a listening device and even now was sitting in a van across the road listening to every word we were saying!

A few moments later the phone rings and I answer. It is a woman's voice, 'Buenos días Señorita Connie. It is Maria. I had to warn you, you are still in danger. I have inside information, Kylo Garcia and Los Ghouls are still after all of us. He means us harm!'

I recount this morning's events and a shocked Maria exclaims, 'It is worse than I thought. You must get out of there pronto!'

'But where should we go?'

'Anywhere. For now find another hotel'

Maria continues, 'For Los Ghouls it is business, big business and maybe they suspect that you know more than you actually do. They see you as a threat. Threatening their entire enterprise. Why only this morning did I learn that they are bringing a plane full of illegal immigrants in to Aeródromo Barcelona – Bages, tonight, midnight'

'I'll go to the police'

'No! That would sign your own death warrant. They have insiders working there too. Also the police are unlikely to take you seriously. You are just tourists!', Maria paused for breath. I for once, didn't know what to say. A thousand thoughts whirling around in my head. Maria continued, 'Go, get out now. I will try and contact you again later'

'OK, thankyou for the warning. We'll leave this hotel now. Gracios Maria'.

'Oh yes, if you need to contact me again, leave a note at the ARTiSA café. There is a click as the phone goes dead. 'Mike we need to leave now. Go and checkout of your hotel and I'll meet you in reception in one hour'.

'Right you are Connie', Mike replied as he had been able to overhear most of the conversation.

One hour later Mike walks into Reception with his two suitcases. I rise to meet him. 'Mike we need to discuss this. Leave your luggage with the concierge and then we can go for lunch'. Mike follows my advice and not long after we are seated in a quiet restaurant a few blocks away. I state my main concerns, 'Mike the police didn't want to know about the theft of my bag. They just aren't interested in routine stuff. I don't want to get involved with Maria, well not any more involved than we are already. However as she said, we are seriously at risk. We don't know how far Los Ghouls will go'

'I agree Connie, but what else can we do? I'm feeling very shaken by what's happened', Mike groaned.

'Yes me too, but I've been thinking, what if we were able to ensure that all Los Ghouls were picked up by the police, the whole gang?'

'That sounds great, but how on earth would you ensure that?'

'I have a plan. We contact Inspector Martin. He knows us and I feel sure we can trust him. We tell him about the arrival of the illegal immigrants, that is surely a big deal. However we keep Maria's name completely out of it. Of course we don't know how reliable Maria's information is, so that is another risk.'

'Hmm, I'm not too sure about this'

'Well have you got any better ideas?'

'No, and I agree we do need to do something. Before something ugly happens to us!'

'That's agreed then. I'll make a quick call to Inspector Martin's office and get an appointment'. I dial the number, from the other end a voice answers. 'Hello, this is Connie Crawford. I'm speaking on behalf of myself and Mike Dean. We need to see

Inspector Martin urgently. We have important information about my kidnapping'. I'm asked to hold the line, it goes quiet. Then I wait for what seems like an eternity, but in reality is only a few minutes before the voice comes back on the line, 'Sí, Señorita Crawford, Inspector Martin will see you as soon as you can get over here'. 'We are on our way', I reply.

A taxi drops us off at the Policía Nacional. Mike and I are shown to a small interview room and a few minutes later Inspector Pablo Martin enters the room, 'Buenos días Señor Mike and Señorita Connie'.
'Buenos días Inspector Martin', I reply and Mike echoes.
'Please call me Pablo and would you like a coffee?'
'No thanks', Mike responds
'Ok, now please tell me what this is about'
So with no further ado, Mike and I tell Inspector Martin about the snatched bag, my encounter with the unknown man in my darkened hotel room. The tip-off via a mysterious phone call about illegal immigrants being flown in to Aeródromo Barcelona – Bages at midnight tonight. When we'd finished Inspector Martin looked thoughtfully down at his hands clasped together on the desk. You could have heard a pin drop. Slowly his eyes came up to meet mine and he spoke deliberately slowly as though he was still thinking things through, 'I appreciate your coming here with this information. Of course we don't know how reliable it is, but if it is correct,

then it may be just the opportunity we need to stop these illegal activities and catch the ringleaders. So I have decided to move against them'. He pauses, Mike and I exchange glances but say nothing. Inspector Martin continues, 'This is my plan. I take a few of my most experienced officers to the aeródromo with the intent to capture the gang, seize the plane and their transport. I assume they will have transport arranged for the illegal immigrants, probably a minibus. I may need your help with the minibus because dressed as civilians you won't raise suspicions. There may be an element of danger to yourselves, but my men will be armed and they will keep you safe. What do you say?'

Again Mike and I exchange looks. I feel that we have come this far and want to see it through to the end. I gently nod my agreement at Mike, who reciprocates. We both turn our gaze back to Inspector Martin, who waits in silent anticipation. 'Yes, we will help', and Mike nods his head too.

'Good. Thank you', Inspector Martin smiles and continues, 'Please return here at 9 pm for a full briefing and dress in some warm clothes as we may have to sit around for quite a while'. With that he shook our hands and then showed us out.

Mike and I stood outside on the pavement. Mike said frowning, 'I didn't expect to be asked along for the ride'. 'Nor me', I replied, 'but if it leads to a successful conclusion, then that will be a massive relief.

'It will certainly be a weight off my mind!', exclaimed Mike. 'I do worry about the risks though'

'Don't Mike, as Inspector Martin said, he has experienced men and they will be armed'

'Yes, of course you are right. So what now?'

'I suggest we get something to eat, then collect our luggage and find another hotel. By the time we have done all that it will nearly be time to meet the Inspector again'

'Sounds like a plan, I'll hail a taxi then'.

MIKE

Connie and I arrive back at the Policía Nacional offices at 20:45 hours. The duty officer is expecting us and issues us with temporary passes. Inspector Martin arrives a few minutes later and greets us warmly, 'Buenas noches. Would you like a coffee or water before we start?'

'Buenas noches inspector', I reply, 'No thanks'. Connie responds, 'Buenas noches inspector. No thank you, we've just had coffee'

'In that case I'll take you straight into the briefing room, my men are already there'.

We enter a large, well lit room with a number of desks, chairs and a dry-wipe board, probably doubling as a training room. Four men and one woman officer looked in our direction with curiosity, it being very unusual to involve civilians in an operation. Inspector Martin and his team were kitted up like commandoes, full bullet-proof jackets and an assortment of weapons. 'This is my team', Inspector Martin indicated with his hand, 'Team, I'd like to introduce you to Connie and Mike'. He then proceeded to run through the plan in detail. Connie and my role, potentially, being to drive the transport to gather the immigrants from the aircraft. 'You'll need to wear these under your outer garments so that they can't be seen', Inspector Martin pointed at two bullet-proof vests on one of the tables. He continued, 'We plan to sit quietly in our vehicles, out of sight, until we see the gang arrive. Any earlier might give the game away'. He then moved away to continue briefing his team in Spanish.

Connie and I donned the bullet-proof vests, slightly uncomfortable, but you do get used to them we were assured. Inspector Martin came over, 'We are taking two cars, you will come with me. The aeródromo is about an hour away. This way please'. He showed us out via a back door to where the unmarked cars were parked. Connie and I sat in the back. Inspector Martin turned the ignition key and the engine burst into life with a deep-throated growl that held the promise of power yet to be unleashed. Then we were off, heading for Saltamos Village and Aeródromo Barcelona – Bages!

We arrive at the airfield at about ten o'clock, the two cars are parked discretely with good visibility of the hangers. We turn the lights off, sit in darkness and wait. We don't have to wait too long before a car and minibus arrive, parking outside one of the hangers. Two men get out of the car and two more jump out of the minibus, slamming the doors behind them. They don't appear at all concerned about the noise and talk loudly amongst themselves. The lead man opens the hangar door and enters, the others follow, leaving the hangar door ajar.

Inspector Martin instructs, 'Connie, Mike, you stay here until I say it is safe. My men will come with me'. With that Martin and his five operatives quietly got out of the car, kitted up with weapons and night-vision, before stealthily made their way towards the hangar. At the opening they halted and I could just about make out that they were retrieving small devices from their pouches, thunder flashes and smoke grenades! The next moment they burst into action, throwing the devices into the hanger with accompanying bangs and flashes. Immediately bursting through the doorway and fanning out with firearms at the ready. There was a sharp exchange of gunfire, but this only lasted a few seconds before muffled shouts could be heard as the gang surrendered. Inspector Martin reappeared at the hanger door and beckoned Connie and I over. It was relatively quiet when we entered the hanger, through the drifting smoke we could make out the four thugs handcuffed and sitting on the floor looking very sorry for themselves. I could see that one had taken a bullet in the leg and one of Martin's men was attending to it. The smell of explosives hung heavy in the air and the lighting bore witness to the residual smoke, but otherwise everything appeared quite peaceful! Inspector Martin came over, 'Mike, Connie, when the plane lands I want you to drive the minibus to wherever it stops and pick up the passengers. I want them all safely onboard the minibus before my men move in. Whatever happens I don't want them caught in the crossfire. My men will deal with the pilot and co-pilot. Just act causally. Don't worry, we will have you covered. Is that clear?'

'Won't the crew be suspicious?', I asked.

'No they shouldn't be, you are dressed as civilians and there won't be any talking above the aircraft's engine noise.'

'OK, thanks', said Connie, not looking very convinced!

Connie and I checked over the minibus, luckily the keys were in the ignition. I climbed into the driving seat and Connie into the passenger seat. We waited and we waited, for what seemed like an eternity. However at about fifteen minutes to midnight we heard the approaching sound of a small plane. Inspector Martin and his men gathered around close by, 'It won't be long now, we are tracking the plane. We know the type, a PZL Mielec M28, manufactured in Poland and it has the ability to land just about anywhere, no airstrip needed. Short take-off and landing. Ideal for this purpose.' Martin winked and smiled.

My nerves jangled, despite his cheeriness I didn't feel at all confident. I looked across at Connie, who smiled back. 'Yes', I thought, 'you always were the one looking for adventure and worldly wise!'

12th October 2018

MIKE

The plane sounded a lot closer now. Inspector Martin commanded, 'Start the engine. I need you to be ready and move quickly once the plane comes to a halt'. I nodded affirmative, started the engine and drove the minibus nearer to the airstrip. The M28's twin engines much louder now as it approached the airstrip, my heart thumping in my chest. Then it was down, trundling along the airstrip. I engaged first gear and we were off, heading towards where the M28 would stop. I pulled up at the rear of the plane. It looked so large for a 'light' aircraft, it struck me then, just how powerful Los Ghouls must be to operate on this scale! The rear door opened followed by steps being lowered. Connie jumped out of the minibus and opened the sliding door, before moving over to the M28 and beckoning the first of the migrants towards the minibus. The migrants looked worried, confused even, but they starting boarding the minibus amongst the swirling noise of the M28's engines. I counted fourteen in all. I shouted to Connie to check that we had them all, but she couldn't hear me, so I jumped down and moved closer to her. At that moment I could see the two police cars speeding towards the plane. The crew must have spotted them too, as one stood in the front doorway and opened fire. Not wanting to be caught in the crossfire I made for the rear door of the M28, Connie followed me too. Within just a few strides we were inside the aircraft, the gunfire loud in our ears! Connie mouthed, 'What the hell Mike?' I shrugged my shoulders. Suddenly the M28's engines were roaring, the external doors being closed by a thickset thug and we, we were moving! 'Oh Christ we're trapped!', I thought as my pulse raced and adrenaline coursed wildly around my veins. In a few moments the M28 was airborne. It was a steep ascent, Connie and I only just able to hang on to whatever we could. The M28 swung around and into a more level flight. As it did so the thug reappeared, grinning and pointing his gun at us. 'Quieres un viaje gratis?', he grunted. Connie and I returned blank looks. This seemed to annoy him because he repeated more loudly now, 'Quieres un viaje gratis?' I attempted, 'English. We don't understand you'. He snarled, 'Cerdo inglés sí', moving to hit me with his pistol. He advanced quickly, but Connie moved faster, her athleticism paying off. She swung her foot hard behind his leg and pulled it towards her in one deft movement. The thug, completely off balance, fell backwards with a crash, his pistol knocked from his grasp. Connie jumped up, grabbed the pistol and shouted, 'Tie him up Mike!' I looked around and saw several parachutes. Working diligently I unpacked one and requisitioned the cords. Our would-be combatant was soon tightly bound. 'What now?', I asked Connie.

'I've had some time to think', she continued, 'You know I have done several freefall parachute jumps.' Full of confidence she smiled, 'Well I think it will be the only safe way out of this mess'. She looked at me, 'Well what do you say?'

'You, you mean', I stammered, 'You want me to jump out of the aircraft?'. My heart was already in my mouth

'Precisely! It's a far better option than being captured by this gang. Who knows what our fate would be in their hands'

Glumly I replied, 'Yes I suppose so'

'Oh come on Mike. I'll show you precisely what to do. After all what could possibly go wrong!', she laughed. Connie seized a life-jacket and parachute, helping me on with both, she then put her own on. 'Mike, all you need to do is pull this cord when you see me release my chute, and of course, don't forget to jump out of the plane!' She laughed again and then more seriously continued, 'It is very important that you jump at the same time as me, or as close as possible. Otherwise we could land miles apart! Have you got that?'

'Yes got it', I nodded. Connie opened the rear door, 'Quickly now', she said, well aware that a warning light would have gone on in the cockpit. We moved to the rear exit, the wind buffeted us madly. First grabbing my arm, Connie jumped and terrified I followed her move. The world stood still. I struggled to catch my breath, the cold penetrated every part of my body as we 'floated' down. Peering through the darkness I could just about make out water below. 'It must be the Med', I thought. Reassuringly there was Connie, only a few metres away, indicating the correct posture with arms and legs spread out. She maneuvered herself to link hands with me, reassuringly we made eye contact. We fell for what seemed ages, but in reality was only half a minute or so, then Connie, with a hand movement to her chest indicated that she was going to pull her ripcord. I returned a thumbs-up signal and she pulled her ripcord. I did likewise and the wind noise lessened as the water beckoned. Splash! For a moment I was under the water, moonlight and bubbles above me. Then, as if in slow-motion, I slowly surfaced and gasped in a lungful of air. We were down! Connie immediately taking command again, indicated the toggle to pull for the lifejacket to inflate. Then she maneuvered herself over to me and cut away the parachute. 'What ever next?', was just one of many disturbing thoughts that cascaded through my head.

The still quietness of the night was only broken by the gentle lapping of the water as Connie and I floated under a starlit night. The lifejacket had a small light attached which added to the surreal, dreamlike quality of our predicament. The seconds ticked by, the seconds ran into minutes, the minutes into hours and finally dawn beckoned. I was beginning to give up any hope of our being found when I heard the distant chug-chug of a marine diesel engine. Slowly it drew closer, I could now see that it was a fishing boat. It came closer still, I shouted and waved furiously, while Connie sensibly blew on the whistle attached to the lifejacket. The boat veered in our direction, my heart pounded, they had seen us! Soon we were being helped on board, my whole body shaking with cold, my limbs stiff and refusing to work, I hadn't realised just how serious our situation had been. However a sense of relief washed over me. The fishing boat was heading back to port with its cargo destined for the early morning fish market. I was assisted in wrapping myself in a large towel. The fisherman poured hot, dark coffee from a vacuum flask, which was most gratefully received.

The boat chugged into harbour where our reception committee awaited us, the fisherman having radioed ahead. An ambulance whisked us away to the local hospital, with a police car escort. In the hospital we were fully checked over and found to be suffering from mild hyperthermia. Connie and I were supplied with warm dressing gowns, while our clothes were taken away to be washed and dried. A policeman questioned us about recent events and then left saying that he would contact Inspector Martin with an update.

Later that day a police car picked us up from the hospital and within a couple of hours we found ourselves, once again, sitting in Inspector Martin's office. He said, 'I am so sorry that you have had such an awful experience. Thankfully no real harm has been done. How do you feel now?'

Connie, smiling, replied, 'I would have preferred not to have had this particular experience, but as you say no harm done'

Still feeling a bit shaken I answered, 'I just feel really, really tired. I'm looking forward to a good night's sleep'

Martin nodded, 'I'm sure you'll get that, you certainly deserve it!'

Connie chimed in, 'What about the gang? What happened? Did you capture them all?'

Martin smiled, 'Well thanks to your efforts we captured the gang members at the aeródromo. Simultaneously my other team raided the gang's premises and apprehended four people there. Unfortunately the aircraft disappeared off of our radar, also Los Ghouls leader, Kylo Garcia is still at large too'

'So what happens now? Are we out of danger? Can we go home?', Connie articulating the questions on my mind.

Martin, looking and sounding very serious, replied, 'We are going to continue hunting down the gang members. The part you have played is over and I sincerely thank you for everything that you have done in this respect. The gang's business has been severely disrupted if not completely destroyed. Are you out of danger?' he paused and then continued, 'I think so. I certainly hope so. All things considered, I think it will be best if you go home and put this experience firmly behind you.'

Connie smiled 'Thank you Inspector Martin. I think I speak for both of us, when I say, that is very welcome advice'. She looked across at me and nodding I replied, 'Yes, much as I love Barcelona, I can't wait to get back home!'

Martin put his hand on my shoulder, 'I can understand that.' He frowned, 'However I must advise you that there is a risk, a fairly small risk, that Los Ghouls will seek revenge and try to interfere with your home lives. They may already have bribed a hotel clerk to disclose your home address from your passport.' Connie and I looked downcast. Martin continued, 'It may be an unfounded fear, but it is my duty to warn you. Please, hopefully it will come to nothing'

Connie glanced at me and spoke for both of us, 'We will bear that in mind. Thank you again Inspector'

Inspector Martin led us to the door, 'One final thing, I will contact the British authorities with a summary of events and to advise them that Kylo Garcia is a wanted man. That's all.'

'Thank you again Inspector Martin. We'll be on our way', I said. Connie enjoined, 'Yes many thanks. Buenos días'. I repeated, 'Buenos días'.

'Buenos días', Martin said as he shook hands, before showing us out.

Outside the police station we put our luggage into a taxi and instructed the driver to take us to the Yurbban Ramblas Boutique Hotel. Connie and I had agreed on sharing a twin-bedded room for the night. It was with much relief that, using the hotel Wi-Fi, we managed to book a flight home for the next day.

Chapter 11 – Making Amends

16th October 2018

MIKE

It's almost unbelievable, here we are back home and back to work on this Tuesday morning! Connie and my employer have been very understanding given the circumstances. Yesterday I saw my doctor, who signed me off as fit to work. I've been off for over five weeks! I'm still on Prozac, which isn't altogether surprising given what I've been through. Work has almost a surreal quality to it. As I move around the building some people are giving me strange looks, then I catch their eye and they look away. Others, who are aware that I have had mental health problems, ask how I am in a genuine way. I reassure them that I am feeling much better now, but decline to go into any detail.

Over the next three weeks I manage to get into a routine, work, attending counselling sessions and staying off the alcohol! Although there is no chance of Connie taking me back, recent events have brought us closer together than ever before. Connie is often out training or in the gym, but sometimes we watch a film together or just chat over a coffee. In many respects life has returned to normal.

CONNIE

I can't quite believe what Mike and I went through in Barcelona. I missed the triathlon of course but certainly had more than my fair share of excitement and exercise. Did that really happen? Mike is back at work and seems to be coping. He assures me he's not gambling and I believe him. He's good company again but that's all. No more romance for me.

23rd October 2018

SARAH

I went to see the doctor today. I feel out of sorts and having recurring bouts of dizziness and nausea. I'm becoming anxious that I have a serious underlying condition. The doctor gave me a thorough examination and then told me that I have high blood pressure (something that has never been evident before) and an increased heart rate. I sat there fidgeting uncomfortably as he asked me about my lifestyle and alcohol consumption. He insisted on a blood test and told me to come back in a month for a review. I feel annoyed that I haven't been given a prescription but I suppose he knows his job!

26th October 2018

SARAH

It's Friday, this morning I've done four viewings starting at eight o'clock. I hate being this busy, being rushed, I don't think the clients like it either. It doesn't help that I feel crap! Anyway I've finished for the day so decide to lunch at the Dog and Pheasant, maybe that will lighten my mood.

As I walk in I immediately notice Mike sitting alone at a table, Christ! I really don't need this right now! I can't avoid him, so I suppose I ought to go over and say hello. As I approach his table, Mike looks up, 'Hello stranger', he says. 'Hello Mike', I reply and manage a smile, 'How are you? I haven't seen you around lately'

'I'm fine, just been very busy'

That's not like Mike, he's usually very chatty about all his news. He must be 'off' me. 'Connie not with you today?'

'No, she is still at work. She has a big project that is nearing completion'

'She works too hard', I comment

'Yes, I think you are right', he pauses, 'How are you Sarah? You actually look very tired'

'I haven't been sleeping too well', I said, not wishing to give anything away

'Oh, who is he then?', asked Mike laughing.

'How dare you!', I raise my, voice and heads are turning to look at me. 'Just what are you insinuating?'

'N-nothing', Mike stammered, 'Sorry, it was only meant in jest!'

'Well it wasn't funny. In future please keep your smutty innuendo's to yourself', I snapped and stormed out. So much for a quiet, relaxed pub lunch. Mike can be such an arsehole! I make my way to the White Hart. As soon as I have found a table I order a double vodka and coke. Feeling calmer, I replay the conversation with Mike and although I still think he is a bit of an arsehole, I wonder why I lost my rag. Normally I am fairly chilled and can handle inappropriate comments with a quick putdown. I feel the need for some blow and head towards the ladies. On my return I feel revived and order my starter and main. The waiter is gorgeous! I start chatting him up, a torrent of small-talk pours out of my mouth and fills the void between us. The waiter looks slightly embarrassed and starts fingering the gold band on his ring finger with his other hand. I think he is subtlety indicating he is married. He smiles and retreats! Several double vodka's and coke later, I am feeling a bit woozy. I pay the bill and rather unsteadily get to my feet, nearly knocking the chair over. Wobbling I make my way back to my apartment, turn on the TV and sink into the sofa. Without meaning to I find myself dozing off, this is not how I planned to spend this Friday afternoon. Now I doubt if I'll be able to sleep tonight!

1st November 2018

SARAH

I've been called back in to see the doctor, he has the results of my blood tests. Doctor Jennings calls me into his consulting room, 'Good morning Miss Lovage, please take a seat'

'Good morning and thank you doctor'

'Now Miss Lovage, how are you feeling today?'

'Much the same doctor, nausea and dizzy spells'

'And how are you sleeping?'

'Not very well actually'

He clears his throat before proceeding, 'I have the results of your blood test here', he adopts a serious tone, 'and I'm afraid it is not good news'

My heart skips a beat and then my words come out in a rush, 'What is it doctor? Am I dying?'

'No you're not dying. The tests have found traces of cocaine in your blood. What can you tell me about that?'

'What! I've no idea what you are talking about!', I feign innocence

'There is no point in denial Miss Lovage, the evidence is clear, you are a user, aren't you?'

Confronted with the truth I blurt out, 'Alright, yes!', and burst into tears

'There, there Miss Lovage, I'm here to help you'

'But the police', I respond wiping away my tears

'No one else will find out from me, patient confidentiality is covered by the hypocratic oath'

 'Thank you doctor', a sense of relief sweeps through my body

'As a cocaine user you are displaying many of the early symptoms of addiction including nausea, dizzy spells and insomnia. Tell me do you find yourself short tempered in certain situations?'

'Yes'

'Well now, irritability is another symptom, as well as raised heart rate and high blood pressure. These we discovered during your last visit. There are other symptoms of course, but we needn't go through the complete list today', he said smiling

'Thank you doctor', I answered gratefully

'Adverse effects can include anxiety, crawling sensations on the skin, hallucinations and paranoia. Longer term effects include heart attack, heart disease and stroke. Do you understand what I'm saying?'

'Yes doctor. I need to come off it'

'Good. As I said earlier, I am here to help you. Unlike heroin, there aren't any alternative drugs to help wean you off. However there is therapy and self-help groups. I can also recommend Narcotics Anonymous in the UK. Take a look at their website and find the nearest meeting to you. The NHS website has lots of information and help too. In the meantime I'll prescribe some tablets to help with your insomnia and then I'll see you again in one month. How does that sound?'

'Thank you doctor that is very helpful', I replied brightly, standing up before leaving the consulting room, the prescription in my hand.

Back home I mull over what the doctor has told me. The more I think about it, the more I'm sure he's right in saying that most, if not all, of my symptoms are directly related to drug use. I check my diary and confirm that I have one viewing to attend to at 4pm. Unfortunately it is out of town, forty miles away! Never mind I have time for a hasty lunch and make myself a sandwich.

After lunch I sink into my sofa, cuddling a hot cup of coffee. I lean across to the table to grab my handbag, just to check my car keys are there. As I do so a white sachet of powder falls out on to the floor. 'Damn', I think, 'I'd forgotten that was there'. I pick up the sachet, intending to flush it down the sink, but instead hesitate. An internal battle of wills takes place, I know full well what I should do, but what harm can one last 'high' do? Anyway, it's expensive stuff, a shame to waste it. Carefully I arrange a line of powder on the table top, one long snort and its disappeared up my nose. I sink back into the sofa and absorb the full effect. A short while later I'm full of energy. Get up and go, that's me! I decide to leave for my appointment. Handbag, address, car keys and I'm ready to go. I slam the front door behind me and slide into the leather seats of my silver Audi TT Coupé. One turn of the key and the 2 litre TFSI engine bursts into life with a muffled roar. The wheels spin slightly as I take-off, oh, how I love driving this car! Having escaped the urban sprawl, Satnav is directing me down country roads with sweeping bends. The Audi takes these with ease, simply eating up the miles. My joy is short lived as a rather ominous black cloud appears ahead and it starts to rain. The Audi is exceptionally sure-footed and the automatic wipers are efficiently clearing the rain from the windscreen. 'My god!', I exclaim out loud, 'It's a deluge of biblical proportions!' Indeed the rain is now hammering down and there are torrents of water on the road. It is becoming harder to see properly, but I press on. Scarcely slowing I swoop around another bend to be immediately confronted by an expanse of standing water right across the road! I feel the Audi lose all traction as we aquaplane, but still coming out of the bend and sliding sideways! Everything happens so quickly, I press the brake pedal but this has no effect! Seemingly in slow-motion the car hits the low bank, and rolls over! Frighteningly we continue to roll over and over down an embankment. I hit my head as the roof is crushed and all my world goes black!

It's dark when I wake up still dazed. I wonder where I am and try to lift up my head to look around, 'Ouch! That hurts'. Without moving my head I manage to look around and quickly realise I am in hospital. A nurse arrives at my bedside, 'Where am I?', I ask. 'Snarefield Hospital', she replies.

'What happened?', I manage to ask through the brain fog

'You had an accident in your car and were brought in by ambulance unconscious'

It takes me a moment or two to phrase my next question, 'What injuries do I have?'

'Cracked ribs, extensive bruising, cuts to your head and hands. Oh, the neck brace is just a precaution. We will be closely monitoring your head injury'

I take a moment to consider this while my head clears. Suddenly a thumping headache erupts inside my head! I gasp, 'Nurse, I have such a headache, can you give me something please?'

'As you have only just regained consciousness I'll ask Mr Jenkins the consultant to come and see you first', and she paged him. He won't be long', she added reassuringly, adding, 'I'll just take a few obs – sorry, observations that is'

'Could I have a sip of water please'

'Of course, let me help you'. The nurse produced a beaker together with a flexible plastic straw. 'That's better', I said, 'Thank you nurse, nurse er?'

'Williamson, but you can call me Susan'

'Thank you Susan'. Nurse Williamson proceeded to record the obs and only a few minutes later Mr Jenkins appeared. 'Good evening young lady. How are you feeling?'

I retold how I felt, adding a few areas of soreness to the list as my senses recovered. Mr Jenkins listened intently and then asked, 'What is your name please?'

'Sarah Lovage'

'And where do you live Miss Lovage?'

'23 Lancaster Terrace'

'Very good. That checks out with your driving licence, the police recovered your handbag. It is in your bedside locker. Now I want you to follow my finger with your eyes please'. He moves his finger across my face from one side to another. Followed by pointing a light directly into each eye as he closely examined them one by one. He stood back and said, 'Very good Miss Lovage. Nothing amiss there. Well, we will need to keep you in under observation, at least for one night. I'll examine you again in the morning. In the meantime Nurse Williamson will give you something for your headache and then arrange for you to have a MRI scan on your head. OK?'

'Yes thank you'

Mr Jenkins smiled at me before turning to the nurse, 'Hourly obs please and if you see any changes then call me immediately'

'Certainly Mr Jenkins', Nurse Williamson replied.

With that Jenkins turned on his heel and busied himself off to see the next patient.

The next day I'm feeling much better. The MRI scan didn't reveal any cause for concern, my head has cleared, the neck brace has been removed and I've been given pain killers for my broken ribs. It only hurts when I laugh! Mr Jenkins came to see me late morning and is very happy with my progress, so much so that he says I can be discharged this afternoon! I am very relieved!

Chapter 12 – Inspector Biggins

9th November 2018

MIKE

3pm Friday and I've finished work early today, arriving back in the apartment before four. I'm making a cup of tea when the phone rings. The caller introduces himself, in a west country accent, as DCI Charlie Biggins. He proceeds, 'Mr Dean, Inspector Martin from the Cuerpo Nacional de Policía Barcelona has appraised me of your, and Ms Crawford's, involvement in recent events in Spain. As a result the UK border authorities have been maintaining a watch for a known criminal, one Kylo Garcia. Regrettably it is my duty to inform you that Garcia has entered the country via Heathrow Airport at approximately 9 a.m. this morning. I don't believe that either you or Ms Crawford are in any danger, but if you have any reason to believe that you are or if Garcia attempts to contact you, then please don't hesitate to get in touch. Do you have any questions?'

'Yes, I believe Connie and myself are in danger. Are you able to provide some degree of protection?'

'I understand your concerns but I don't have any direct evidence that you are being threatened. However I suggest I meet with you and Ms Crawford to listen to your concerns and provide some degree of assurance. How does that sound?'

I'm not altogether convinced, 'OK I think. I'm sure Connie will want to share her concerns too. When do you suggest we meet?

'Tomorrow morning 10 a.m. at your place, if that is convenient?'

'Yes that will suit me perfectly thank you. If Connie has any problem with this then I'll let you know'

'Great. I look forward to seeing you both at 10 a.m. Until then I wish you a good evening'

'Thank you and good evening', with that I put the phone down.

Sometime later Connie arrives home from work and I recount the conversation. Connie, understandably, is somewhat concerned.

10th November 2018

CONNIE

The doorbell rings as I'm just tidying my hair in front of the mirror. "Mike, can you get it please?' Mike goes to the door and shows DCI Biggins into the lounge. Biggins proffers his hand with a business-like handshake, 'DCI Charlie Biggins at your service. Pleased to meet you Ms Crawford'

'Pleased to meet you too DCI Biggins. Would you like a coffee? The pot is on'

'Yes please, milk and two sugars please'

Mike interjects, 'I'll get it. I was just doing ours anyway'. A couple of minutes later Mike reappears with the coffees. Biggins smilingly accepts the hot coffee, 'Grand. Now then, I'd like you to tell me in your own words, what went on in Barcelona please'

Over the course of the next half hour Mike and I go through our Barcelona experiences. When we are finished Biggins thoughtfully stroking his chin says, 'Hmm! Well, you certainly have been through the mill. Now I understand why you are both so concerned', he pauses and takes a sip of lukewarm coffee. Then, 'This is more serious than I thought. I'll circulate the photo we have of Garcia to all my colleagues and I'm going to post a man outside your home as a precaution'

'That's great. At least I'll be able to get some sleep tonight!' Turning to Mike I ask, 'What do you think Mike?'

'Yes, that does provide a degree of comfort'

Biggins intervened 'Well let's not get too carried away. You will both be going about your business as normal, work, shopping etcetera. I don't have the manpower to do any more, but we can review this arrangement whenever you like. I am just at the end of the phone', and he passed his business card to me and one to Mike.

I rose, 'Thank you DCI Biggins that has been most helpful. Let me show you out' 'Glad to have been of service Ms Crawford, Mr Dean'. With that he made his exit.

'Well what do you make of that?', I ask.

'I'm glad the police are taking it seriously, but still concerned that we have no protection as we go about our business'

'You're right of course Mike. I think we have two options, one is to stay at home and live like hermits, the other is to go about our daily business as usual. In the latter case I'd advise we keep in public areas, plus at night only venture where many people are about and the street lighting is very good. I'll carry a 'self-defence spray' too'.

'I don't want to live like a hermit, so I'll take my chance. You only get one crack at life and I'm determined to get the most out of it!'

'I agree. So that's settled, we carry on as normal, but also with a degree of caution'.

'Yes, so how about lunch at the Dog and Pheasant?'

'What a good idea. Back to normality!'

'Are you paying?'

'Not on your life! It's your idea so you pay!', I jest pushing him out of the door.

After only a ten-minute walk we enter the pub. It wasn't too busy and we select a table in the corner with comfortable chairs. Within half-an-hour we are tucking into our meals with two large glasses of red in front of us. At last it felt like we were home and I could properly relax. The pub door swung open, I briefly glanced up, but had to do a double-take. 'Mike',

I whispered, 'don't look now, it's Sarah!' Mike, of course, immediately looked towards the door and Sarah caught his eye. She hesitated for a moment, then strode forward, purposely in our direction. However I had noticed a slight limp. Sarah smiled and said, 'Hello Connie, hello Mike, I haven't seen you here for a long while'.

I answered, 'Hello Sarah. No we have been away, having adventures. Are you OK? I noticed a slight limp, and goodness me! Is that bruising?'

'Oh yes. Unfortunately I had a slight accident in my car. I'm still getting over it'

'I'm sorry to hear that. Well at least you are here to tell the tale!'

'Yes, nothing to worry about really. And you two, are you well?'

Mike, slightly embarrassed, 'Hello Sarah. Yes, I've been meaning to phone you. It's a long story'.

Sarah, indignantly, 'That's quite alright Mike, I didn't expect you to', more softly she continued, 'Look what happened, happened, we can't change the past, so I'd like to move on if you will allow it. Connie, I really value your friendship'. Sarah stops and looks directly into my eyes. With some reservations I reply, 'It's water under the bridge as far as I'm concerned, but just so you know, Mike and I are no longer an item'.

'Oh! I didn't know that'.

Mike explained, 'I'm still living at Connie's and had intended to move out but events took over. We've both been abroad, Barcelona, otherwise I would have told you. Sorry.'

Sarah digests this information and then, 'Oh I see. I had heard that you were ill Mike'.

'Yes that's true, I've had counselling and I'm feeling much better now' Mike responded.

Sarah smiled at him. 'I was worried about you. I'm glad that you are feeling better.'

'Thanks Sarah', Mike said brightly, 'Sarah I'd love to have a proper catch-up sometime soon, but we've just got back and have a few things to sort out'.

'Yes of course. I'll leave you to enjoy the rest of your meal. Good to see you both'.

'Nice to see you too Sarah' I replied 'We'll catch-up soon'. Sarah smiled and walked off.

For a few minutes silence ensued, then Mike spoke, 'I....', immediately interrupted by me, 'Do you still have feelings for Sarah Mike?' Mike hesitated, then, 'Yes and no. Yes I do still care about her and have regrets about how I treated both of you. No I don't intend to resurrect a closer relationship. I think we have both moved on. I wasn't in a good place back then, I am much better now. Also recent events have led me to take a different perspective on life'.

'Thanks for being honest with me. You are right about our experiences changing perspectives. Let's not dwell too much on past mistakes'. I raise my glass, 'To our good health and friendship'. Mike echoed, 'To our good health and friendship'.

Having finished our meals, we walk back to the apartment. As we approach the entrance I spot an unmarked dark blue van and turning to Mike, say, 'I think that must be the police observation point'. Mike replies, 'Most probably, it's not one of the regulars'. That afternoon we share the chores and then settle down, me with a book, Mike with the newspaper. Both enjoying a relaxing afternoon. At about 4.45pm it's getting dark so I walk to the window to draw the curtains. Down below, under the streetlamp, there is a well-built man in a black leatherjacket staring straight up at me. 'Mike come here quick!', I urge, but by the time Mike has reached the window the man has turned and is gone. In a concerned voice Mike asks, 'What is it? What did you see?' I reply, 'A man, staring up at me. Oh my god Mike, I think it might have been him!' Calmly Mike responds, 'If it was then the police will have clocked him. I don't think we should worry too much, but be on our guard all the same'.

'No, you're right Mike'

'Did you get a good look at him?'

'Not really the lamppost was behind him and cast shadows down his face'

'That's a pity. You look a bit shaken Connie, I'll make you a coffee'

'That would be nice, thanks Mike'.

MIKE

I'm glad Connie, Sarah and I have cleared the air. I've been an idiot really and now I've lost my chances with both girls but at least we can be friends again.

I hope Connie was mistaken about seeing Garcia outside our flat. We've had enough excitement to last a lifetime.

13th November 2018

CONNIE

I'm home from work late afternoon and decide to go for a run, it takes about an hour on my regular route. I enter Southwark Park by the sports centre and, within a few minutes, make my way past the Pavilion Café. I become aware of the sound of heavy footsteps behind me, I glance over my shoulder and my heart skips a beat. It's him, I'm sure of it, the same man that looked up at me from under the lamppost! No longer wearing the leather jacket, I can see he is well-muscled. He is only about 20 yards behind and gaining! As we pass the tennis courts I increase my pace to almost a sprint. I glance behind again and, thankfully, he is dropping back. I think to myself, 'Thank goodness I'm athletic!' Now passing the bandstand, I look back again, this time there is no sign of him, so I slacken my pace. My breathing eases, the adrenalin rush subsides.

Soon I'm approaching the apartment, and there's the parked blue van, fat lot of good it did me! Safely inside my apartment I call DCI Biggins and tell him what just happened. He assures me that they are doing all they can and 'pursuing their enquiries'. His response doesn't exactly fill me with confidence!

16th November 2018

SARAH

It's Friday, I had three viewings this morning and now I'm feeling pretty knackered! My Audi TT was a write-off, so I'm poodling around in a little hire car. Not really my style, but I'm afraid it will have to do. It's one thirty, so I decide to walk to the pub for a lazy lunch.

I'm sitting in the pub with a large glass of Pinot and about to order my food, when who do you think walks in? Only bloody Bradley Wilson-Smythe! He spots me straightaway and strides over purposely, grinning ear-to-ear like a giddy schoolboy!

'Sarah dear girl, so good to see you again'

'Hello Bradley', I respond with noticeably less enthusiasm

'Mind if I join you?', he asks presumptuously pulling out and sitting on a chair

Slightly taken aback, flustered I reply, 'No, of course not'

'How's tricks?', he asks

'Magic', I reply dourly. To which he responds with raucous laughter and, 'Very good, very good! I see you haven't lost your sense of humour!' He turns and signals for the waitress to come over, 'What's your poison dear girl?'

'I'm okay for now thanks'

Addressing the waitress Bradley says, 'A bottle of your finest Dom Pérignon and two glasses please'. 'Certainly sir', the waitress smiles sweetly, thinking about the rather large tip she hopes she will receive. Internally I'm fuming, I didn't want a drinking session right now and Bradley obviously expects me to share in his champagne. Once again Bradley attempts to engage in conversation, 'How's the estate agent business?'

'Oh okay, much the same as usual. Would be great except for some of the idiot punters I have to put up with!'

'Yes, but I'm sure that the monetary rewards are there to compensate'

'Of course, otherwise I wouldn't be doing the bloody job in the first place!'

Bradley a bit taken aback quickly changes the subject. 'Er right. Have you looked at the menu?'

'Yes thanks, I was about to order when you came in'

'Super', he looks away and scans the menu, 'Ah yes, the salmon en croute with lemon dill sauce, roasted broccoli, minted peas and herbed new potatoes is just the ticket'. He turns round to catch the waitress's eye.

As I enjoy my late lunch my mood improves. Bradley seems intent on cheering me up with his anecdotes and dubious jokes. I've even allowed myself a glass or two of the champers! 'Actually Bradley I've had a pretty shit month, the worst thing being that I wrote off my Audi TT'

'Oh dear girl, you poor old thing. How on earth did you manage that?' So I explain my accident and my injuries, while Bradley interjects with sympathetic noises at the appropriate moments. Then we are onto desserts and coffee. Finally we ask for the bill and Bradley offers to pay, which of course I accept. This day is getting better and better by the minute! Bradley helps me on with my coat and asks, 'Can I give you a lift home dear girl?' 'What the heck', I think and answer, 'Thank you, that's very good of you'. Back at my place I invite him in, I am not in the mood to be all alone in an empty apartment.

Bradley makes himself comfortable on the sofa, 'You have a very nice apartment Sarah'

'Thank you Bradley. Yes I like living here, it's secure and cosy'

'I do like your taste in furnishings too, the pictures and the objects d' art. I particularly like your coffee table centrepiece'. He picks up a heavily embossed silver pot, overflowing with an assortment of finely made gold charms. Each charm a delicate and intricate filigree work. 'Thank you', I reply, 'That is a traditional Nepalese ornament. It symbolises dignity, prosperity and the art of the country. I believe it is quite old.

These ornaments have played a significant part in ethnic and folk dances. Kumari dance, chanchar dance, chutka dance, Chyabrung Dance and Ghatu Dance being good examples.'

'That's very interesting. You certainly know your stuff', he carefully turns it round and looking at it intently says, 'It must be quite valuable I suppose?'

'I don't really know. It was handed down to me by my grandmother who lived in Nepal for many years. She used to tell me such wonderful tales about her time there'. Bradley carefully replaced the centrepiece upon the coffee table. 'I've been thinking', Bradley says brightly, 'Why don't you and I go down to London town for the weekend, see the sights, take in a show? What do you think?'

I hesitate, I don't have anything planned, but do I really want to spend the whole weekend with Bradley? 'What show do you have in mind?'

'Well I've read some amazing reviews about the new musical Six'

'Tell me more'

'The six wives of Henry VIII tell their story, and this is the unique angle, staged in the form of a pop concert. Each of the wives take turns in telling their story in order to settle who suffered the most'

'That's original! Yes I'm interested'

'Good, I'll see if I can get tickets'. 'In the meantime do you fancy some blow?'

Do I? I'm trying hard to break the habit. I really shouldn't, but just a little won't hurt, will it? 'Well I don't know, I am trying to kick the habit'

'Oh go on, just for old time's sake!'

Bradley waves a packet of white powder in front of my nose. It's just too much of a temptation, I capitulate! 'Alright, just this once, seeing it's you', I say with a cheesy smile. So we go through the ritual and then the hit. Almost oblivious to the ramifications, I'm leading Bradley to the bedroom.

Sometime later we are lying, sated, in my bed. 'Bradley', I pause, thinking is this wise?, 'Do you like me?' He laughs, 'Yes of course!'

'But do you really like me? You know, how much?'

'I like you an awful lot dear girl', he pauses and beams at me, then, 'I say, you are sounding very serious, you aren't going to propose to me or something equally mad are you?'

'No, no, it's just I was wondering…', I trail off

'Wondering what? Come on, spit it out!'

'Wondering if this weekend away makes us an item?' Bradley blushes, I think that provides my answer, but no he says, 'Of course you are my girlfriend, if that's what you want', and the big cheesy grin returns.

'Yes, of course it's what I want!', and once more I throw myself on top of him and engage in a passionate kiss.

17th November 2018

Having gone back to Bradley's for the night, the next day we are in his Porsche Cayenne on the M4 to London. Bradley is in a good mood and says, 'What would you like to do today?'

'I don't know, I haven't given it much thought really'

'Come on, you must have some idea about the places you'd like to visit?'

'Well yes, I've always wanted to visit Madame Tussauds'

'That's just perfect dear girl, as I booked tickets online that also includes the London Eye'

'Fabulous, you must have read my mind!'

'One of my many talents', he chuckled, 'Also we can take in London Zoo too if you'd like that'

'Oh yes please! I love animals'

'So that's why you like me!', Bradley roared with laughter at his own witticism

We parked at the Copthorne Tara Hotel London Kensington, where Bradley had booked an Executive Suite, no expense spared apparently! From there we took a twenty-minute cab ride to Madame Tussauds on the Marylebone Road. What a laugh we had, Bradley and I adopting funny poses with the Queen and various other celebrities!

After visiting Tussauds and London Zoo we caught the tube from Baker Street, Jubilee line, to Westminster, alighting opposite Big Ben. From there it was a short walk across

Westminster Bridge, then onto the South Bank and the London Eye. By this time I was feeling quite exhausted! 'Bradley', I said, 'I'm tired and hungry'

'Dear girl, don't you think I would have thought of that? I've a reservation at, what I consider the finest Italian restaurant in London. It's only about a ten-minute ride away' Without any further ado, he hailed a cab. In no time at all we were outside Osteria dell'Angolo. Bradley paid the cabby and we entered the restaurant. The staff were charming, immediately taking our coats and then showing us to our table. It transpired that Bradley was right, the service was first class and the food exquisite. I didn't want to leave! However it was now late afternoon so we jumped in a cab back to the Copthorne Tara Hotel. Our room was superb as you could imagine! Better still, was the champagne that Bradley ordered on room service! On top of the wine I'd had in the restaurant a couple of glasses of champers had made me decidedly light-headed. Before I was really aware of what was happening, Bradley was chasing a line of snow on the table top and invited me to do the same. I'm afraid I didn't hesitate and only much later suffered the consequences. The coke reinvigorated my energy levels and I found myself once again in a passionate embrace. We parted and rushed to the bedroom where we hastily tore off our clothes before leaping into bed. 'Oh Bradley', I sighed, 'I love you!', as I conferred love bites on his neck. A wild excitement coursed through my veins as Bradley explored my body with his soft hands. 'Sarah I've never met anyone who excites me as much as you do', as he held me closer in his tight embrace. Suddenly his face contorted and he grimaced with pain. An abrupt pain that shot through his chest like a bolt of lightning. 'Aaargh!', he exclaimed and relaxed his grip and fell backwards onto the bed. 'What is it? What's the matter?', I cried

'I d-d-don't know', he stuttered through clenched teeth, 'Call an ambulance. Quick!' I grabbed my mobile and dialled 999. 'Ambulance', I said. Then, 'Yes he is conscious, but his breathing is erratic. He has a severe pain in his chest. I think he's having a heart attack!' 'Yes' 'Copthorne Tara Hotel, room 627', 'No, I don't have any aspirin', 'Thank you'. Turning to Bradley I say, 'They're on their way', and clasping his clammy hand in mine, 'Please be alright!' Bradley had gone extremely pale. I moved the pillows to better support his head. The voice on the other end of the phone inquired how is the patient doing. I responded, adding that Bradley is very short of breath. I was advised to closely monitor Bradley's condition and to immediately mention any changes. I grabbed the hotel supplied dressing gowns, one for myself, the other I draped over Bradley's torso. A few minutes later there was a knock at the door and I let in two paramedics armed with their kit. They soon got to work, an injection (which I assume is adrenalin) and an electrocardiogram (ECG) to check the heart's rhythm, which proved to be quite erratic. Within a few minutes they had decided to evacuate him to St Thomas' Hospital, I said I would make my own way there as I needed to get dressed and pack a few things for Bradley too.

CONNIE

It's Saturday, Mike and I have decided to have a nice day out in London. There are so many sights to see, some we haven't seen for years and others we have never seen! Our first port of call is Madame Tussauds, there is always something or, more precisely, somebody new to see. Then we take the Circle Line tube from Baker Street to Tower Hill, with a short walk to Tower Bridge. The London Bridge experience is amazing, up the North Tower, along the high-level walkway, down to the incredible steam Engine Room, soaking up the history on the way. Then on to lunch at the Dean Swift, hidden away on Gainsford Street. After a light lunch we saunter to Bermondsey station, taking the tube to Canary Wharf, changing here for the DLR to Cutty Sark. We spend a fascinating couple of hours exploring the Cutty Sark, the last of the Tea Clippers as Mike informed me. We then decide we have just enough time to visit the Royal Observatory Greenwich. Situated in the middle of Greenwich Park, the Royal Observatory has an amazing Planetarium, telescopes and historic clocks that were developed, Mike explained, as essential aids to maritime navigation. 'I think that is quite enough for one day', Mike says as we leave the Royal

Observatory. 'What!', I exclaim with a smile, 'It was you who insisted that we come up here!' We walk down the grassy hill towards the Old Royal Naval College. We pass by the National Maritime Museum and through the college gardens. The old buildings are magnificent, such a contrast to the modern office blocks of Canary Wharf just across the Thames. Suddenly I feel that I'm being watched, a shiver runs through my body, I look around and there, skulking by the building is that man! He saw me looking and, trying not to be seen, turned away. 'Mike', I said, 'It's him!'

'Who?'

'The man who was under the lamppost'.

' We must get out of here. Quickly follow me' Mike urged, 'I think I know where we're going', as we walk briskly in the opposite direction. We are close by the Cutty Sark, where there is a small circular building with a glass domed roof, this is the entrance to the Greenwich Foot Tunnel dating back to 1902, it passes underneath the River Thames. Mike had been telling me about it earlier. We enter the building and rapidly descend the stairs. A long, cool tunnel covered in ceramic tiles stretches out before us. The frightening realisation then hit me that we must have been followed all over London, whoever it is, is waiting for the right opportunity! I break into a run with Mike close behind, our footsteps echoing eerily. At that moment another set of footsteps mingles with ours, a cold fear grips me, no-way out except forwards. Strangely the footsteps stop, but why? A bullet whistles through the air passing dangerously close to my head. Then another and Mike gives a shout, I stop and turn around, he is on the ground clutching the side of his head. I take a few paces back and kneel besides Mike. More footsteps, another two shots are fired, I look up and to my surprise see our assailant falling to the ground! Behind him is a police marksman. My attention goes back to Mike, although he's bleeding I can see the bullet has grazed the side of his head, thankfully there is no tell-tale entry point. 'You'll live', I say. He grins back at me, 'That was too close for comfort!' I find a clean tissue for him to hold against his head to stem the bleeding.

Extremely shaken, we slowly make our way back up the tunnel where the policeman is kneeling over the man. He stands up and issues instructions on his radio before turning his attention to us, 'Are you two OK?'

'Yes thanks, shaken up more than anything else', Mike manages to say whilst holding the tissue to the side of his face, 'And my head is rather sore'. The policeman fully in command, 'Here let me see. Hmmm. Just a flesh wound. I've asked for a paramedic to attend, they will be able to dress it properly'.

'Thanks', Mike responds. I chip in, 'Yes many thanks, you saved our lives', I continue, 'How did you know we were down here?'

'We've had this one under observation for a few days but didn't know quite what he was up to. Do you recognise him?'

'No, but it might be Kylo Garcia, who has a vendetta against us'.

'That's a name I'm familiar with from DCI Biggins' briefing'. Looking down he frowned then spoke seriously, 'Well he can't tell us anything now, I'm afraid he's dead'. Mike and I exchanged looks, but just then more footsteps and we could see the paramedic making his way towards us. When he reached us he looked briefly at Mike, 'Are you hurt anywhere else?', Mike shook his head, the paramedic continued, 'No. Good'. He then thoroughly checked the crumpled heap on the floor for vital signs, there weren't any. Standing up again the paramedic addressed the police officer, 'He's dead. Over to your boys to secure the crime scene and get forensics in'. To Mike he said, 'Ok let me take a look at your headwound.' Mike removes the tissue. The paramedic carefully inspects the wound and continues, 'I'll need to put a dressing on that', and dives into his kitbag for antiseptic spray and bandages. Once he'd finished the policeman said, 'You two look pretty dazed, but will you be able to get home from here without too much trouble?' Mike responded, 'Yes, I'm sure we can, it isn't very far'.

'And you madam?'

 'Yes, I'm fine thanks'

'Well in that case you can go, but you will need to visit the station on Monday to make a full statement. Is that convenient?'

'Yes', we replied in unison, then I continued, 'Thank you again for saving our lives'.

'I'm pleased I was able to. You take care now and try to stay out of trouble!', he smiled. So without further ado we slowly make our way out of the tunnel and back to our apartment. Mike getting some very odd looks on the tube due to his strange head apparel!

18th November 2018

SARAH

Having spent several hours at a very poorly Bradley's hospital bedside yesterday evening, I went back in to see him today. I didn't know quite what to expect, but I was somewhat surprised to find him in good spirits. He greeted me in his usual manner, 'Hello dear girl, it's lovely to see you'

'Hello Bradley', I leant over to kiss him, 'I'm pleased to see you looking so well'

'Yes you can't keep a good man down', he chuckled

'How are you feeling today?'

'Not too bad at all thanks. They gave me something for the pain, so I had a fairly comfortable night'

'Have the doctors told you what is wrong with you and what the treatment plan is?'

'Yes they confirmed it was a heart attack. I need a stent or something'. They are going to operate, probably Monday, but until then it's bedrest for me'

'So you're going to be alright then?'

'Yes nothing to worry about dear girl', he smiled

We carried on chatting for about an hour when Bradley said, 'I've had an idea'

'Yes? What is it?'

'Well when I've had the op, I will need to take it easy and I won't be allowed to drive for quite a while. So you take the Cayenne, I can't leave it at the Copthorne and you would be welcome to use it until I need it back again'

'Are you sure? I mean, thank you very much, it would be really useful, especially as I no longer have the Audi'

'Right, that's settled then. I'll phone the insurance company and get you added to the policy. Happy?'

'Yes, thank you so much!'

'No problem, in fact you will be doing me a big favour', he smiled. Just then the consultant turned up and a nurse started drawing the curtains around the bed. Bradley spoke, 'Look no need for you to hang around any longer. Here take the keys and promise that you'll phone me when you get home?'

'Of course darling', and I planted a big kiss on his lips, 'We'll speak later'.

19th November 2018

MIKE

'You two had bit of a close shave, didn't you', DCI Biggins postulated, as Connie and I sat the other side of his large cluttered desk. 'Yes, we most certainly did!', I replied.

'Well it's a good job I had one of my men tail the man hanging about outside your apartment', Biggins smiled in a kindly fashion. Absentmindedly he picked up an unlit briar smoking pipe and put it to his lips. There was some movement of his mouth before he suddenly became aware, snatching the pipe out and in one swift action hid it in his desk slamming the drawer shut. Biggins continued, 'You are both ok? None the worse I hope. It must have been a big shock to your system, eh?'. I was beginning to think Biggins was being far too casual in his attitude to this incident, when Connie spoke, 'Yes, it was stressful, especially after a long week worrying that Kylo Garcia was stalking us. Thankfully we don't need to worry about that anymore, now he's dead'.

Biggins looked directly at us, 'He's not dead', he said bluntly.

'What, what do you mean?', I asked, not understanding.

'The dead man, it isn't Garcia, it's one of his henchmen'

Connie exclaimed, 'So you're telling me that Kylo Garcia is still out there?'

'I'm afraid so. So for the time being I'm going to keep your apartment under observation'

'God! I thought we'd put all this behind us!'

'Not yet, so I need you two to stay on your guard'. Connie and I nod in agreement, Biggins continues, 'You might like to have this photo of Garcia', he pushes it across the desk. 'Now I do need statements from you, so if one of you would like to follow me please, I'll escort you to the interview room'

'I'll go first if you like Connie'

'Yes, that's fine Mike', she smiles, 'It gives me a bit more time to collect my thoughts'.

Back at the apartment I make sandwiches for lunch, plus two strong coffees. I exclaim, 'Well that was quite a shock!'

'Yes, you're not kidding'

'I don't like it, I don't like it at all'

'It's the uncertainty, this could really drag on'

'And we are still at risk apparently. How do we live our lives now?'

Connie frowns, pushes her plate away and says, 'I think we just have to carry on as we were. Trying to do normal things, but being ultra-cautious at the same time. It's a far from ideal situation'

'State the bleeding obvious, why don't you', I say impatiently.

'No need to take that tone with me Mike'

'Sorry Connie, it's getting a bit on top of me'

'That's OK. Try and relax. Why don't you read a book, it will take your mind off things?'

'Good idea, although I'm not sure that it will'

'Well you won't know unless you try it'.

With that I got up from my chair and selected a book from the bookcase. 'Catch-22 by Joseph Heller, I've always meant to read it but never quite got round to it'.

Connie smiled and said, 'Once my sandwich has sunk I'll go for a run, that's my escape!'

Feeling concerned I say, 'Just be careful, keep in public areas'

'Don't worry I will', Connie replied smiling.

CONNIE

While Mike buried his head in his book, once again I pondered the current situation. These thoughts playing on my mind, 'Had Kylo Garcia and his gang been scared off? Would we be left alone now? Are we still in danger? Almost certainly, oh it is all so very stressful. I wish the uncertainty was over. I need a break, Mike needs a break.' I have a lightbulb moment, 'Mike I've had an idea, next weekend, how about you and I have a weekend away in Snowdonia. The fresh air and change of scenery will do us both good, what do you think?'

Mike looks up from his book, 'Mmm, sounds like a great idea. I'd like to go up Snowdon, I hear the views are stunning'

'Good, that's settled, I'll book a B&B for us'

'Sounds like a plan'.

21st November 2018

MIKE

I'm at work when I take a call from DCI Biggins, 'Good afternoon Mr. Dean. Now I don't want to worry you, but my operative observed a man behaving suspiciously near to your apartment last night'. Shocked, I exclaim, 'Good grief! So Kylo or one of his gang is still sneaking around then?'

'Well we can't be sure about that, but there is a fair chance they are. Whoever it was appeared to drop something by Miss Crawford's car. My man made his move but was unable to question the person because they ran off'

'So we are none the wiser?'

'No, I'm afraid not. Do you have anything that you would like to report?'

'No except just to mention that Connie and I are spending the weekend in Snowdonia. We felt we needed a break'

'OK, thanks for letting me know Mr. Dean. I'm sure I don't need to remind you to stay vigilant. Well if that's all, I'll wish you good day'

'Thank you DCI Biggins and good day to you too'.

23rd November 2018

MIKE

Thursday night we had packed our going away bags in readiness for a quick getaway today. Connie and I had both engineered to finish work by 3pm, so we were comfortably away in Connie's car by ten to four, bracing ourselves for the five-hour drive to Betws-y-Coed. The Friday afternoon exodus from London is always slow and congested, but once we hit the M40 the other side of the M25, it wasn't too bad. I decided to pull into Warwick Services for an early evening supper, when I noticed the silver Mercedes that had been behind us for most of the journey, doing the same. 'Connie', I said, 'It is probably mere coincidence but the silver Merc that is pulling in behind us, has been in my rear-view mirror most of the way'

'Oh come off it Mike, you are just being paranoid don't you think'

'Maybe, but it is definitely the same car'

'But how would they possibly know where we are heading'. Connie's tone changed to one of "believable", 'Unless they placed a tracker on the car!' We glanced at one another.

I said, 'Well let's stop anyway, we don't want to raise their suspicions. Then we'll see if they follow us on the way out'

'Good idea Mike'. We went into the services, had something to eat, used their facilities and filled up with petrol before re-joining the M40. We made our way around Birmingham, the traffic particularly heavy at Spaghetti junction, then the M54 before it turns into the A5. All this way I didn't once catch a glimpse of the silver Merc. As we motored deep into the countryside, urban sprawl was replaced by rolling hills. I breathed a sigh of relief, and, looking across to Connie, could see she had nodded off. As we drew within sight of the magnificent mountains of the Snowdonia National Park, I roused Connie and we both enjoyed the scenery picked out by the headlights. Finally we arrived at our destination, approximately six hours after leaving Bermondsey, Tyn-Y-Fron Country House in Betws-y-Coed. It was everything that we had imagined, in daylight its elevated position providing stunning views overlooking the village and the beautiful Conwy Valley. We were warmly welcomed by our hosts and soon had settled into a very comfortable room, both very tired but content.

24th November 2018

MIKE

Connie and I both slept very well, enjoying a hearty breakfast before gathering our walking gear together. It was a gloriously sunny day but with low cloud occasionally obscuring the mountain tops. We had an uneventful half-hour drive to Llanberis and the start of our walk to Snowden's summit. We had packed everything we needed for the walk up Snowdon, or Yr Wyddfa using its proper Welsh name, rucksack, map, compass, torch, whistle, water, sandwiches, walking boots and waterproofs! No need for midge repellent or sun cream at this time of year! Soon we were striding past the ticket office of the Snowdon Mountain Railway, not required in our case, heading for the Llanberis Path to the top 1,085 metres above sea level. We expected the ascent to take about two and a half hours, with occasional stops to take in the scenery. About a third of the way up, Connie turned to me, 'What fabulous scenery Mike!'

'Yes, the lack of trees cause it to look a bit bleak, but the impressive mountains, valleys and lakes more than make up for it'

'Oooh, look at that dilapidated cottage. What a pity!'

'Fancy living there do you?', I winked

'Not likely, there's no Broadband!', Connie laughingly replied

'Hey, that's odd! I thought I saw someone lurking by the cottage and as soon as they saw me looking in their direction they ducked out of sight!'

'Come on Mike, you're seeing things or else it's terminal paranoia setting in!'

'No, I'm sure I saw someone. It must be a farmer or...', Connie cut in, '...or perhaps a walker caught short!', she chuckled. I laughed too and instantly alleviated my own concerns.

Connie declared, 'Anyway I'm sure we are safe here as there really isn't anywhere much where you could hide'

'You're right, I'm going to forget all about Kylo Garcia, relax and enjoy the walk'

'That's the spirit!'

However I couldn't help but think that if anyone was following us, then they would probably take the train.

The late autumn sunshine beat down on us and I could see super-fit Connie was really enjoying herself. It didn't seem any time at all until we were passing the Halfway House rail stop and ahead of us Clogwyn. The views were getting better and better the higher we went. Soon we had panoramic views of spectacular scenery in all directions. The cloud cover was thickening, but where the sunlight cut-through, the shafts highlighted the ground to provide a patchwork quilt effect. The wilderness a riot of shades of browns, greens and yellows. Dramatically, under the cloud the rockface darkened ominously but we carried on oblivious to any possible warning.

CONNIE

As we approach the summit the clouds are rolling in, heavier now, they seem to promise rain. Mike and I have donned our wet weather gear. I turn to give Mike some encouragement, he has dropped back a little. 'Come on Mike, only a few more steps to go', I shout at a point close to the summit railway station. Mike looks up and I can see he is struggling slightly, but he catches up and together we make our way up the last few steps to the summit. The views are spectacular, although they keep disappearing and then reappearing as the cloud rushes over the mountain ridge, with almost a 'liquid' feel to it. It is windy too, in gusts that buffet and tear at our clothing. We shouldn't stay here too long. 'Mike, I think we should start heading down again, the weather is closing in'
'Yes, you're right. Let's go'. Mike sounds relieved. We retrace our steps, very cautiously now. The railway station has disappeared from view, but thankfully the path is still

discernible. Mike stumbles and almost falls. 'Are you OK Mike?', I say giving him a hand up. 'Yes I'm fine', he replies. 'I'll lead, but stay close', I say loudly competing with the roar of the wind. I must concentrate myself, it is tricky, I need to keep looking down at the ground to ensure that I stay on the path. The cloud has completely enveloped us now, we are both wet from head to toe. Tiny drops of water hang off my eyelashes and the temperature has plummeted. It's much darker now and I can't see more than one or two metres ahead. As the conditions worsen, I turn in order to tell Mike that we need to hurry down, but he's not there! I shout, 'Mike, Mike, this way!' Then turning back, suddenly a face appears in front of mine, it hovers there a moment, but it's not Mike's! Abruptly recognition kicks in, to my horror I see it's Kylo Garcia! What's more, he is wielding a knife! Instinct takes over, I parry the knife with my arm against his arm. He snarls with rage and lunges again, but I step aside. I trip him as he hurtles past. He turns again and tries to swipe at my neck, but I duck inside, his arm going over my shoulder. I bring my knee up sharply into his groin, his eyes bulge. He shoves me hard, I try to keep my balance but my heel meets a rock and I tumble backwards. I can see a manic glint in his eyes as he charges, but extend my right leg under his torso and send him hurtling over me. This buys me time to regain my footing, which is difficult because we are now off the path. The ground is uneven and strewn with rocks. Garcia bristles with anger and gathers himself to rush at me once more, but I am ready for him. I execute a perfect kick to his arm and the knife goes flying out of his hand. He looks astonished, but then with a roar of hatred, comes at me again. I grab his arm and use his own bodyweight to send him soaring through the air, but he doesn't hit the ground. To my astonishment I realise he has gone over the edge. An anguished cry fades away to nothing amongst the fog of the cloud as Garcia tumbles to oblivion! I stand still a moment, unable to grasp the enormity of what has just occurred, then all of a sudden think about Mike. Where is he? What if he has already encountered Garcia? I carefully pick my way over the rocks and back onto the path. I shout, 'Mike, Mike!' No reply, then I remember my whistle. I put the whistle to my lips and issue three loud blasts. Complete silence, the sound seemingly lost in the fog, then a distance away, a whistle in answer. I guess that when I went off the path, Mike must have passed by me. So I follow the downward path and very soon I am reunited with Mike. 'Where on earth have you been?', Mike exclaims. I recount my shocking and deadly encounter to an incredulous Mike as we slowly make our way back down to Llanberis. To our relief, as we descend we come out of the cloud which makes the walk much more bearable. Once at the car we dry off with towels and change our footwear, before visiting a small café for a very welcome black coffee. Having restored some sense of normality, I call the police and tell them about my mountain top encounter. I think they thought I was making it up, until I told them to check out my story with DCI Biggins. Within half-an-hour the police arrive at the café requesting us to accompany them down to the police station in order to provide a statement. Which, of course, we do without hesitation.

25th November 2018

CONNIE

Over the course of the next few days Mike and I were interviewed, separately, several times by the police, before signing formal statements. Then the press got hold of the story and became a real nuisance, door-stepping us at every opportunity. However we declined to engage with the press as everything was still so raw and we didn't want any publicity. Somewhat surprisingly we had a call from DCI Biggins checking up that we were okay, he had of course already received copies of our statements. Obviously we were shaken and upset by events on Snowden. We just hoped that things would get back to normal and all the surrounding 'fuss' would disappear. Upon our return to work, initially there were questions from colleagues instigated by their curiosity, but that soon subsided. Immersing ourselves in work proved to be quite cathartic.

A couple of weeks went by and we were beginning to feel more relaxed. I had resumed training and Mike had joined a rifle shooting club. I was very pleased that he had found a new interest and seemingly continues to put his life back together again with the help of a few more counselling sessions.

Chapter 13 – Bradley Wilson-Smythe

26th November 2018

SARAH

It's just over a week since Bradley first went into hospital and I'm driving his Cayenne down to London to visit him following a 9 a.m. appointment in Sonning. I ease the SUV smoothly onto the M4 and am pleasantly surprised how light the traffic is. I think to myself, 'I wonder how quick this baby goes'. I floor it and she takes off with an assertive roar as the turbo kicks in. Wow! In no time at all I'm doing 70, 80, 90, 100, 110! What a beauty! However much I'm enjoying myself I ease off the pedal and cruise at just over 100 mph. Then I slow as I encounter a knot of traffic ahead. I glance in the rear-view mirror and my heart leaps in my chest, oh my God! There is a police car behind me with his blue light on and flashing headlights! He wants me to pull over. I slow and move over to the hard shoulder. The Cayenne comes to a standstill and I switch the engine off. I can feel my heart racing as I experience a hot flush. One of the two policemen walks up to my door and indicates for me to wind the window down.

'Madam', he says, 'Do you realise that you were travelling at over 100mph for approximately two miles?'

'Um, yes', came my faltering response

 'Well then, I want you to come and sit in my car while we take a few details'

The skies darkened ominously as high black clouds stack overhead, it looks like a storm is coming. I have a sense of foreboding as I alight from the car. The policeman gives me a direct look and says, ' I'll take those keys for now, thank you'. We sit in the back of his car while he goes through my particulars routinely. Meanwhile his colleague has gone to the Cayenne and is checking it over, I can't think why? He sits in the passenger seat and sifts through the glovebox. Ah, he's finished, he's walking back to the police car and to my absolute horror, is holding up a small clear plastic bag containing a white powder. I can guess what that is. 'Its not mine!', I gasp, 'I've borrowed the car', a wave of panic sweeps over me. This is serious! The police office says sternly, 'I'm placing you under arrest on suspicion of possession of Class A drugs. You do not have to say anything. But, it may harm your defence if you do not mention when questioned something which you later rely on in court. Anything you do say may be given in evidence'. He looks at me piercingly and asks, 'Do you understand?'

'Yes officer', I reply

'In that case you will accompany us to the police station where you will be held in custody in a cell and then questioned'. At that moment the heavens opened and torrential rain rattled down on the roof of the police car. Could this day get any worse?

At the police station the officers were very polite, but very formal. They explained my rights and I asked for legal representation. I also requested a message to be passed on to Bradley in the hospital, even though I felt really awful about this as I'd clearly implicated Bradley. I was then taken to a cell, searched by a female police woman and all my possessions, including my mobile phone, taken away. I was then locked in a cell, awaiting further questioning in the presence of my legal advisor.

It was several hours later when a solicitor from my local law firm, Cleverly, Briggs and Mathis appeared. She introduced herself as Gaynor Briggs, a senior partner in the firm. She questioned me in detail, stressing that I needed to be honest with her. Once she seemed satisfied that she fully understood the case, she advised me to answer 'no comment' to any subsequent questions from the police. Then it was time to be interrogated!

I was led to the interview room and DI Simon Jones introduced himself and explained the procedure. He then switched on the audio recorder, 'For the benefit of the tape, I am DI Jones, accompanied by WPC Susan Fletcher, Ms Sarah Lovage is the defendant and Ms Gaynor Briggs her legal advisor. Ms Lovage is being held in custody under suspicion of possession of a Class A drug. Is that understood Ms Lovage?'

'Yes sir'

'In that case I will begin questioning. At approximately 10:20 a.m. on the 26th November 2018 you were driving a Porsche Cayenne at more than 100mph down the M4 towards London. Is that correct?'

'Yes sir'

'The traffic officers who stopped you subsequently found a packet of white powder in the glove box of the car. Is that correct?'

'Yes sir, but I had no knowledge of its existence', I bleated

'I'll come to that in a moment. Upon analysis the white powder has been confirmed as being cocaine, a Class A substance. Now you said that you had no knowledge of its existence, have you ever taken cocaine?'

'No comment', I replied, desperately trying not to shake, not to give anything away

'Given that the Cayenne had been in your possession for over a week, I put it to you that you placed the packet of cocaine in the glove box. Am I right?'

'No comment'

'Furthermore, I suspect that you are a habitual user. Is this the case?'

'No comment?'

'Have you ever supplied Class A substances to other people? Surprised, I reacted with a vehement denial, 'What? Are you accusing me of being a drug dealer?' At this point my brief interjected, 'DI Jones, that question is out of order. Ms Lovage has only been arrested on suspicion of possession. Please withdrawn that question'

'My apologies, I withdraw the question'. He pauses, quickly glances over the papers in front of him and then continues,

'Ms Lovage I have here a search warrant for your apartment. The drugs team will enter your premises later today and I will schedule a further interview with you for tomorrow morning. In the meantime you will remain in custody. Is that understood?'

'Y-yes sir', I stammered

Looking across the table at DI Jones, Ms Briggs spoke coldly, 'You don't seem to have a lot to go on so you can expect my application for bail tomorrow'

DI Jones chose to ignore the remark, instead said, 'Interview terminated at 14:20 hours', and switched off the recorder.

27th November 2018

SARAH

I have had plenty of time to mull over my predicament. I wasn't so concerned about the speeding offence, no, it is the drugs related offence or offences, that scared the living daylights out of me. I felt fairly sure that the police would discover traces of cocaine in my apartment, but certainly not in any great quantity. My solicitor had made it abundantly clear, up to seven years in prison, an unlimited fine or both for 'possession' of a Class A drug. However for 'supply and production', up to life in prison, an unlimited fine or both! The latter offence was my greatest fear, whether my close association with Bradley would furnish the prosecution with sufficient grounds to convict me remains to be seen. Hopefully not, and then again I don't want to spend any time at all in prison. It was all just too horrible to contemplate!

At 11a.m. the four of us reconvened in the police interview room. DI Jones looked very stern, signalling that he wasn't going to go easy on me today. The formalities over, DI Jones recommenced the interview, 'Ms Lovage you are aware of the serious nature of the charges being brought against you, aren't you?'

'Yes sir'

'I have to advise you that the drugs team did find conclusive evidence of cocaine in your apartment. The only conclusion I can draw is that cocaine has been consumed there. What do you say to that Ms Lovage?'

'No comment'. At this response DI Jones' face flushed red, I had clearly angered him.

'Ms Lovage the team also conducted an extensive search of the vehicle using sniffer dogs. They discovered an extensive quantity of cocaine hidden behind panelling at the rear of the vehicle. What do you say to that?'

I gasped, this is what I dreaded! I managed a weak, 'No comment'. I felt sure that he knew he had me against the ropes.

'Ms Lovage I will lay the facts out straight before you. We have found cocaine in your apartment. We have found a small quantity of cocaine, indicative of personal use, in the glovebox of the vehicle in your possession, but more importantly a serious quantity of cocaine in the rear', he raised his voice, 'a quantity sufficient to ensure a conviction for supply!' For a moment there was complete silence in the room, then Gaynor Briggs said, 'Can we take a break please, I would like to talk with my client'

DI Jones replied curtly, 'Yes, OK. Interview suspended at 11:12 a.m.'

In private Gaynor Briggs spoke with some urgency, 'We are in a very serious position. The police finding a large quantity of cocaine in the car has elevated this case and risks a very long prison sentence. Do you understand the implications Sarah?'

'Yes I do', I reply quietly. Gaynor, looking me directly in the eye, continued, 'Well then answer me this, is it at all likely that Bradley is a dealer? I must have a honest answer'

'Yes, probably. He has supplied me, but only small quantities at a time, just for personal use'

'Good. In that case I think we can plea bargain, but this is only likely to be successful if you agree to be a witness for the prosecution. Against Mr Wilson-Smythe that is'.

I hesitated, I really don't want Bradley to go to jail, but on the other hand I don't want to go to prison myself. It's him or me!

'Yes, ok I'll do it, whatever it takes'

'Very wise. I'll speak to DI Jones to say this is what we are planning to do. In that way, hopefully, he won't 'waste' too much of his time on you!'

And so it transpired, the prosecution accepted a plea-bargaining arrangement and dropped all the charges, especially as this was a first-time offence. However I was prosecuted for speeding and received a thousand pound fine and banned from driving for 30 days.

30th November 2018

SARAH

I was relaxing in my apartment when the phone rang, it was Bradley. He said, 'Hello Sarah, it's Bradley here'

'Hello Bradley, how are you?'

'I'm feeling much better thanks and I'm out of hospital thank goodness. I don't think I could stand another hospital dinner!' He chuckled.

'Oh that is good news'

'I'd like to see you Sarah'

I hadn't told Bradley all that had transpired as originally I wanted to do this face-to-face. This was going to be a difficult conversation, one I didn't really want to have but I forced myself to. 'Bradley I have something to tell you and I'm afraid that it isn't good news'

'I'm all ears dear girl, fire away'

'I was stopped by the police for speeding and unfortunately they searched your Cayenne and found a hidden quantity of coke'

For a moment there was silence, then Bradley responded in a slow, measured manner. 'I was coming round for the Cayenne, do you still have it?'

'No, the police have impounded it. They won't release it to me, you will need to apply for it'

'Damn, and what have they said about the snow?'

'Well, they interviewed me under caution because they found a small quantity in the glove box and it was this discovery that led to a thorough search of the vehicle. They're on to you Bradley. I've been told in no uncertain terms not to have any further contact with you or I risk going to prison!'

'Fuck, fuck, fuck', came the panicked reply.

This was the first time that I'd heard Bradley lose his cool. Pulling himself together, Bradley continued, 'I don't understand, the police haven't been round to see me'

'I'm guessing that they have got you under observation then. I'm sure it will only be a matter of time'

'Dear girl, we have got ourselves in a pickle haven't we?', he resumed his normal persona

'I don't know how you can stay so calm. I've been worried sick'

'What will be, will be. I'm going to have to say 'cheerio' now as I need to clean my apartment,' he paused, 'thoroughly!'

'Oh, Bradley you are such a gentleman. I didn't really know what to expect'

'No need to worry about me dear girl, but a word of warning, the people who supply me won't be happy. They will come looking for answers. I sincerely hope that they won't trouble you. Please be assured that I won't mention your name, but I'm sure they have their sources'.

I didn't want to hear this! 'Thanks for the warning and I'm truly sorry that I've got you into trouble with the police. Especially when we were only just getting to know each other. Unfortunately for now I'm afraid it is 'au revoir''

'Yes, goodbye Sarah until we meet again, do take care of yourself'

'Goodbye Bradley', with that, and much sadness in my heart, I ended the call.

1st December 2018

SARAH

It's 10:30 a.m. on Saturday and I'd decided to have a lie-in. I was still in my dressing gown as I busied about the kitchen making coffee, and toast with marmalade, before sitting down in the lounge to enjoy them in front of the TV. Having mulled things over in my mind, I found myself beginning to come to terms with recent events. So I was startled when my phone started ringing. Hmm! 'Unknown number', shall I ignore it? No I better pick up the call. 'Hello Sarah here, who's speaking please?' There was no reply! Silence, but I had a creepy feeling that someone was on the other end, listening and perhaps talking but I couldn't hear them. 'Hello, hello! Who is that please?' Still no answer, I wait about another forty seconds until I heard a loud click on the line. Whoever it was has just hung up! I wonder who on earth that was and then decide to forget about it. I return to my coffee and toast. I settle back into my very comfortable settee. There is a debate on TV about the benefits of vaccination against flu. Suddenly the door bell rings, I think, 'Who on earth can that be at this early hour? Perhaps it's the post lady with a package?' I go to the door and open it. Oh my god! It's two men, dressed mostly in black and with balaclava style hoods pulled down over their heads. Before I could scream or do anything they have bundled me back inside my apartment and slammed the door behind themselves. Roughly they push me down onto the settee. The taller one speaks, 'Don't scream or call out or it will be worse for you!'

'No-o, I won't', I stutter. All the colour has drained from my cheeks.

The tall one continues in a mocking tone, 'A little bird tells us that you have been talking to the police. Is that correct?'

'Yes, they interviewed me'

'We understand that the little bird sang, sang far too loudly' His eyes intensely drilled into mine as though seeking answers there.

The smaller of the two chimes in, 'I've been told that the little bird sings too much', he spoke with a Thames Estuary accent.

The taller one continues, 'We've come to stop the little bird from singing', and he pulls out a gun. I recoil in horror! 'No, no, don't shoot me!'

'Well then perhaps we can come to an arrangement?', he says in a sly tone

'Yes, what?', I am shaking like a jelly

'Well, all you need to do is stop singing. No more helping the coppers, no more grassing up your mates, no more police witness. You understand?' Simultaneously he shoves the barrel of the gun into my ribcage. 'Ouch!', I exclaim.

'Well, do you understand?', He shoves the gun even harder into my ribs. I respond, 'Yes, yes, I understand!' He pulls back the pistol. 'Make sure you do lady or it'll be worse for you. This is your only warning!' He turns to his mate, 'Come on then, let's get out of here', indicating the door with a nod of the gun. Then as suddenly as they had appeared, they were gone. All that was left was a faint smell of cheap aftershave and me a quivering wreck on the sofa!

After a few minutes I got up and poured myself a large G & T, then sat down again to re-run what had just occurred in my own home! I can't quite believe it, it seemed unreal, like it was happening to someone else, something that you would read about in the papers or see in a movie! So what do I do? If I go to the police, these gangsters are sure to find out. Would they then come back to kill me? If I get called as a witness and don't turn up at court then the police will come looking for me. I'm doomed if I do and doomed if don't. Either way my prospects for survival don't look very good at all!

2nd December 2018

SARAH

I didn't sleep at all well, tossing and turning all night, racked with worry. I mulled over my dilemma, going over it again and again, until I reached a decision. A decision that I really didn't want to take. I got out of bed, had a quick shower, slipped on my dressing gown and made myself a mug of strong coffee. I took this into the lounge, steeling myself against whatever was to come. Finally I plucked up enough courage to pick up the phone. I made the call to the police station on DI Jones number, 'Ms Sarah Lovage here, could I speak to DI Jones please?'

'Oh I am sorry, DI Jones is on paternity leave. I'm DI Helen Sharp, can I help?'

I briefly explain who I am and that I'm being pressured by the drug dealers. DI Sharp doesn't ask for more details, but says she will come to my home to discuss the matter. I suggest an appointment in one hour's time, giving me ample time to prepare.

An hour later the doorbell rings, it's DI Sharp. She is mid thirties, smartly dressed with fiery red hair. She introduces herself with a pleasant smile, 'I'm DI Sharp, but please call me Helen'

'Pleased to meet you Helen and please call me Sarah', we shake hands. I continue, 'Please come in. Would you like a coffee before we get started?'

'Yes please, white, one sugar please'.

I show her into the lounge, 'Please make yourself comfortable', before I retreat into the kitchen. Returning a few minutes later with two steaming mugs of coffee, 'I'm going to need this', I smile.

'Thank you', smiles Helen taking the mug, 'Please don't stress too much. Sit down and tell me the whole story right from the beginning'

So I did, only skimping over parts that might incriminate me! Strangely I felt I could trust Helen. She had a sympathetic ear and quickly put me at my ease. As I drew to a conclusion I told Helen verbatim what the thugs had threatened with their pistols drawn. She looked quite shocked and exclaimed, 'Oh, that is serious, you must have been terrified?'

'Yes I was, I couldn't stop shaking. Even after they had gone.'

'Based upon everything you have told me, I think we need to get you into our Witness Protection scheme as soon as possible. I fear that your life is in danger'

'Oh', I hadn't expected this, 'Of course I've heard of Witness Protection, but what does it entail?'

'Well, first of all we will place you in a safe house. Then we will provide you with a new identity and living accommodation in another part of the country'

'But what will I do to earn a living?'

'Equipped with a new identity, there is no reason why you couldn't find another job as an estate agent'

'I see', I pondered, 'But what about the trial? Won't I be at risk there?'

'Not at all, we will arrange for you to give evidence by video link. Neither the criminals nor the public will see your face'

'That's very reassuring'

'Do you have any more questions?'

'Not at the moment, thanks'

'I'm sure you will think of other questions and there will be plenty of opportunity to ask them later'

'Understood'

'So shall I go ahead and start the ball rolling?'

'Yes please, I don't think I have much choice in the matter', I answered pensively

'No, I don't think you do, but please don't be too downhearted. I realise that this will mean a major upheaval in your life, but you are definitely at risk right now. Also, having met you, I think that you are a strong, resilient, resourceful person and you will get through this'

'Thank you Helen, I hope you are right!', I reply a bit more brightly

'Obviously it will take a little while to make the necessary arrangements. I'll get back to the station and make a few phone calls. In the meantime please pack your suitcases, you'll probably be leaving tomorrow!'

'Wow, as soon as that! It has all come as a bit of a shock!'

'We do take these matters very seriously'

'Yes, of course and thank you again Helen'

'Okay then, I'll make my way back to the station. It's been nice meeting you Sarah. So for now it's goodbye and good luck!'

We shook hands and I showed DI Helen Sharp to the door.

I went back to the lounge and contemplated how, in the course of just 24 hours, my life had been turned upside down. Absolutely nothing remained the same! New location, new house, new job, new friends, I could go on! Gosh, I would miss so much that I take for granted here. The familiar surroundings, my house, my local, my friends. That's a point, what will Mike and Connie think? I will really miss them both and especially Mike, I'm very fond of him. There's certainly a lot to think about! Anyway it's lunchtime, so I'll make myself a sandwich and have another coffee. Come to think of it, I'll need to empty the fridge and the freezer!

After lunch the phone rings, 'Hello Sarah, it's Bradley'. I didn't expect that! 'Hello Bradley, you do realise that I'm not allowed any contact with you?'

'Yes of course, dear girl, but something urgent has come up'

'Well what is it then?', I ask impatiently

'Can't say on the phone, but it's imperative that we speak. We must meet up'

'Well I can't, I simply have so much on at the moment'

'But you must, your life is in danger!'

I take a breath, 'What? How?'

'I really don't want to say over the phone. We have to meet please Sarah'

Bradley was very insistent, so based on our previous good relationship I said, 'Alright then. Where?'

'Thank goodness Sarah', Bradley sighed with relief. 'Number 20 Railway Cottages, Middenthorpe, near Slough. Can you get here, in say, an hour?'

'Yes, I suppose so', I answered somewhat reluctantly. Was I doing the right thing? I wondered.

'I'll see you later then old girl'. The call ended abruptly. I had some misgivings about this meeting, especially as I had been told in no uncertain terms to have no contact. However it is Bradley and he has always been very considerate towards me.

Three fifteen in the afternoon I arrived at number 20 Railway Cottages. It was a rather rundown narrow street, with two rows of Victorian terraced houses facing one another. Several of the houses were boarded up and a few older model cars bearing battle scars were parked, seemingly at random, down the road. One or two plastic wrappers caught the breeze and turned over lazily, otherwise nothing appeared to be happening. I wondered why Bradley had chosen such a place to meet up? Perhaps just to get away from prying eyes and CCTV? I knocked on the door and within a few moments Bradley was there. 'Come in dear girl', he beckoned. I walked across the threshold and a musty smell, a cross between rotten cabbage and damp, assaulted my senses. I'd already decided that this isn't a nice place! I followed Bradley down the dank hall towards a dark room that would be flattered to be called a sitting room. Dark green floral wallpaper was starting to peel off the walls. The curtains looked like they had never been washed, ever! As I entered the room I immediately became aware of two other people, we weren't alone! In these circumstances these two looked the most scariest people that

I've ever seen in my life and by their stature I think they are the two goons that paid me a visit yesterday! 'Bradley!', I shouted, 'What the hell is going on?' Before Bradley could say anything the taller one snarled, 'Sit down and shut up!', pushing me down into one of the dilapidated chairs. Then Bradley spoke softly, 'I am so sorry Sarah but they said they would kill me if I didn't persuade you to come here. I am so, so, sorry'.

'That's enough', Barked the tall one looking directly at Bradley, 'Your job is done, now get out before I change my mind!'

'What are you going to do with her?', Bradley asked

'None of your business. Just go!', he commanded threateningly. Bradley glanced in my direction and silently mouthed, 'Sorry', before beating a hasty retreat to the door. The tall one addressed me, 'We did warn you, but the little bird continued to sing'. Shorty echoed, 'We warned you we did', an element of almost joy in his voice. Thoughts flashed through my mind, 'They seem to know I've been in contact with the police again, but how? Were they watching my house? Or is there a corrupt copper in the force? If the latter, then they reacted very quickly!'

Tall continued, 'We have plans for you, but first I'm sure you'd like to see your accommodation', a cruel smile crossed his face. Once again a gun appeared in his hand, 'Shorty you lead the way', and nodding the gun in my direction, 'You, follow Shorty'. So up the creaking stairs we went and into a small,

197

what would have been once, a bedroom. However there is no bed, only an old mattress pushed against the wall and in the other corner a potty. Worse still the window was barred and boarded. The only light being a single incandescent bulb with no lampshade. Tall spoke again, a sinister inflection in his voice, 'Everything you need is here', he sneered, 'Now lie down on the mattress'

'No I will not!', I exclaimed fearing the worst

'Shorty, help the lady to lie down'

Shorty pushed me down and I screamed as loud as I could muster

Tall angrily hit me across the head with the gun butt, 'Scream as loud as you like bitch, we don't have any neighbours, so no one will hear you. Now do as you're told!'

So between them they held me down. My head throbbed and I could feel a trickle of blood going down my cheek.

Tall commanded, 'Now do your stuff Shorty'. Shorty opened a small zipped bag and produced a hypodermic syringe and several glass vials. He proceeded to load the syringe with a colourless liquid before injecting my arm. I tried to wriggle away, but they were too strong for me. I heard Shorty say, 'A shot of heroin will keep her quiet'. Tall retorted, 'Just as long as we can keep this going until after the trial', and then I passed out.

3rd December 2018

DI HELEN SHARP

Early this morning I'd been round to Ms Lovage's apartment but was shocked and surprised to find her absent. I immediately alerted DCI Biggins to my concerns. He requested me to urgently return to the station, where he briefed his team. Given the circumstances they quickly deployed their expertise in finding missing persons. They obtained Ms Lovage's mobile phone call records and that showed them that Bradley had made the last call to her number before her disappearance. Immediately an alert was sent out to all officers to report any sightings of either Bradley or his vehicle. Her apartment was thoroughly searched for clues but unfortunately the search was in vain. However when Bradley's registered address was visited his vehicle was found parked on the drive and, surprisingly, Bradley was at home.

BRADLEY

It was about three o'clock in the afternoon and I'd just sat down with a strong cup of coffee for a break from some rather tedious paperwork, when the doorbell rang along with some urgent knocking. 'Just coming, don't get your knickers in a twist', I muttered under my breath. When I opened the door I was startled to see two strangers on the doorstep. A male and a female, at first impression I wondered, 'Are they Jehovah Witnesses?'

'Are you Mr Bradley Wilson-Smythe?', asked the stocky male in a light mac.

'Yes, who's asking?', I replied.

'DI Jones and DI Sharp', as they brandished their police warrant cards. 'We would like you to accompany us to the police station to help us with our inquiries'

I was quite taken aback, surely there was nothing to connect me to yesterday's events? 'Can you tell me what this is about officer?'

'It is in connection with the suspected kidnapping of Ms Sarah Lovage'

Oh my god! They are on to me! I thought as the implications started to sink in. I must buy myself some time to think, get my story straight. 'What? What you mean she has been kidnapped?'

'Yes sir'

'Surely you can't think I had anything to do with it?'

'That's what we intend to find out, down at the station'

'This is ridiculous', I feigned outrage, 'I'm sorry I'm right in the middle of some important work, so I'm unable to attend today'

'I'm sorry you feel that way sir. We'd hoped you would fully cooperate, but this being the situation you have left me with no choice but to arrest you'. The policeman's tone had suddenly become much more authoritative. 'Mr Bradley Wilson-Smythe I am arresting you on suspicion of kidnapping', and proceeded with the caution in full. His colleague then applied handcuffs, asking, 'Do you understand this?'

'Yes', came my downhearted reply. I knew I had no option but to comply. 'Would you grab my keys and lockup the house please?

'Certainly sir'

A few minutes later we were on our way, speeding downtown in the police car.

At the police station they booked me in and asked if I wanted to contact my legal representative, which I did. Then I was shown to a holding cell, where I was made to 'stew' for more than three hours. Eventually my brief turned up and we discussed the situation in the privacy of the holding cell. I didn't disclose my involvement, I told my brief that the police must be mistaken. My brief called to the duty officer that we had had sufficient time and we were shown to the interview room. The audio recorder was switched on and formal introductions made. DI Jones led the questioning, 'Bradley Wilson-Smythe on Sunday 2nd December 2018 we have information that leads us to believe that you were involved in the kidnapping of Ms Sarah Lovage. What do you have to say on the matter?'

'My dear man, I don't know what on earth you are talking about!'

'So you deny any involvement then?'

'Yes sir, that is correct!'

'In that case why did you phone Ms Lovage at 1:37 pm on the same day?'

This question took me by surprise, I hesitated before replying, 'I simply phoned to see how she was'

'A complete coincidence then?'

'Yes sir'

'Your vehicle was picked up by several CCTV cameras that indicate a route into town. What do you say to that?'

I started to panic, I was sweating and could feel a hot flush sweeping across my face. 'I-I, I need to converse with my brief'

'How very convenient. Interview suspended at 19:22'

Back in the holding cell I felt that the game was up. I explained to my brief that I had been threatened by the drug dealers and forced to lure Sarah to the Railway Cottages. I wanted to carry on with the interview saying 'No comment', but my brief pointed out that Sarah's life could be in danger. He said if I cooperated with the police then the court would look upon that favourably and I could expect a more lenient sentence. So, with serious reservations regarding my own safety, I agreed.

We returned to the interview room and I explained everything that had transpired, including the address where Sarah was being held, 20 Railway Cottages. No sooner were the words

out of my mouth, than DI Sharp gasped and DI Jones sprang
to his feet, knocking his chair over backwards. He said,
'Interview terminated at 20:04', and looking at DI Sharp,
'Come on Helen, we have no time to loose!'. They both
dashed out of the room, sending in a regular police officer to
return me to my cell.

DI HELEN SHARP

DI Jones and myself hurried to the Ops Control room. We
needed to carefully plan the operation to release Sarah
Lovage. Failure to do so safely was not an option. We couldn't
risk putting Ms Lovage's life in danger. Simultaneously we
needed to obtain her release as soon as is practically
possible. Firstly we dispatched a small surveillance team to
park up nearby to number 20 Railway Cottages, they would
monitor any comings and goings, also feeding back
information regarding access to the property, front and back.
Then we called in the commander of the specialist team of
armed police officers who are well versed in forced entry to
premises. Although we didn't want to delay matters, the
commander cautioned us against being too hasty. A five thirty
in the morning raid would provide the best chance of success,
hopefully the kidnappers would be asleep and the element of
surprise would be on our side. So it was settled, the plan was
in place! There was nothing more we could do tonight. For the
first time today I could relax, and as I did, a giant wave of

tiredness washed over me. I looked at my watch, it was past ten o'clock at night! If I'm to be up again at three thirty a.m. I need my bed!

I arrive home at a little after ten thirty pm. In my current state I'm not expecting the onslaught from Joe, my partner. 'Where the bloody hell have you been? I've been worried sick!'

'You know where I've been, I've been at work!', I glare back at him

'Why didn't you call me to say that you were working late?'

'Because sometimes things happen so quickly that I don't get the opportunity. Especially when I'm working on a challenging case for the boss!'

'Excuses, excuses! It doesn't make things any easier for me Helen!'

'OK, I'm sorry, but please try and understand that when I'm working on a live incident it may become impossible to even message you'

'Yeh, whatever', Joe replied sarcastically.

I ignore his comment, walk to the fridge, grab a bottle of Chablis and wave this roughly in his direction, 'Do you want a glass Joe?'

'No thanks', he mutters

I pour myself a glass and sink into my favourite chair, to unwind at the end of a very full day. I re-engage with Joe, 'Oh by the way, I have to be up by three thirty a.m.'

'Well that just about takes the biscuit!'

'Oh Joe please don't go on about it, unsociable hours go with the job'

'Well I'm going off to bed now. You're not the only one who has work responsibilities!', He adds, 'So don't disturb me will you'

'Well if that's how it is, I'll sleep in the spare room tonight'

'Yes, do that', Joe replies and stomps off in the direction of the bathroom.

4th December 2018

DI HELEN SHARP

At four thirty I met DI Jones at the station and together we drove to the Railway Cottages in an unmarked police car. Our role is as observers and to provide any initial support for Ms Lovage, assuming everything goes according to plan that is!

We parked outside number twelve and, in the gloom, could just about make out the bodies assembling in the road in preparation for the assault. They are dressed all in black, with balaclavas, night vision and bullet-proof vests. Several were armed with standard issue guns. DI Jones and I quietly exited the car, ensuring the door closed silently behind us. We walked down the road towards number twenty, but halted opposite number sixteen. It was approaching five thirty, the assembled crew are in their positions. A few more minutes elapsed and then the commander's sweeping arm movement gave the signal for the operation to commence. Two officers led the way with a battering ram, which they swung between them. It hit the front door with a terrific crack and the door burst open. Immediately the armed officers rushed in shouting, 'Armed police! Put your hands in the air!' There was no immediate response, so the officers began sweeping the house, room by room. Into the darkened front room, suddenly a shot rang out, just missing the leading officer, who immediately returned fire. An anguished cry was accompanied by the sound of a pistol clattering across the floorboards. 'Hands in the air!', commanded the officer, this time his instruction was obeyed. Another officer, who had been making his way up the stairs, upon reaching the landing, turned and shouted, 'The window is wide open, I think the suspect has climbed out!'

'He won't get very far, just listen', replied another officer. I listened intently and could easily make out the 'whump, whump, whump' of a police helicopter getting nearer. Equipped with infra-red vision it would soon be in a position to spot any warm body trying to escape. Upstairs the officer encountered a locked bedroom door, turned the key and cautiously entered. There, lying asleep on a mattress, was Sarah Lovage, apparently unharmed. Satisfied that no one else was in the house, the commander called for myself and DI Jones to take charge of Ms Lovage. However when we attempted to rouse her, we struggled to get any reaction. Thankfully she was still breathing, so we immediately called for an ambulance. Upon their arrival one paramedic looked after the kidnapper who had been shot in his arm, whilst the other attended to Sarah. After carrying out twenty minutes of observations the paramedic told us that he suspected a heroin induced coma, but otherwise Sarah appeared unharmed. Sarah was carefully moved onto a stretcher and taken to the nearest hospital.

6th December 2018

SARAH

Very slowly I regain consciousness, my eyes flicker open. I can hear unfamiliar noises and there is a murmur of voices, but I can't make out what they are saying. Oh my head hurts! My eyes start to focus, I think 'Where am I?' Then, looking around, it's obvious, it's a hospital ward. I try to cry out, but no sound comes out. I feel dreadful. I spot a big red button and give it a squeeze. Moments later a nurse is at my bedside asking how I feel. My voice starts to come back with a croak, God I feel thirsty! The nurse helps me take sips of water. She then proceeds to ask me my name, this I get right! Next, 'Do you know what day it is?'

I take a moment to think about this, surely it's the 2nd December? 'Sunday', I reply.

'No my lovely, Thursday 6th December. You have been out of it for quite a while!'

I'm taken aback. What has happened to me? Have I been in an accident? Slowly some memories float back into my consciousness, I remember Bradley and going to Railway Cottages, but what then? 'Tell me nurse, what happened to me?', I ask, desperately wanting answers.

'I don't know my lovely. You need to ask the doctor when he comes round. In the meantime I'll be checking on you and, if you feel up to it, maybe you can manage lunch. I'll pop back with today's menu a bit later. Is that ok?'

'Yes thank you nurse'

'That's alright dear, and please call me Cynthia'

'Thank you Cynthia'

'Is there anything else you need right now?'

'No, I don't think so'

'Ok, but if you do need anything, just press the red button', said Cynthia smiling warmly, before walking out of the room. I closed my eyes again, trying to fathom out what could have transpired in those 'missing' days? It made no sense at all, but I would just have to be patient and wait for the doctor doing his rounds.

In due course Doctor Reynolds arrived at my bedside. He was in his early forties, handsome, with a dark beard and a smile that flashed a full set of whitened teeth. 'Hello Ms Lovage. I'm Doctor Reynolds. How are you today?'

'Hello doctor. I feel bloody awful to be quite honest'

'Ah well, I'm not surprised. You have been through quite an ordeal'

'Yes, so what exactly has happened to me?'

'I'm sorry to say that you were kidnapped and worse still your kidnappers injected you with heroin to keep you quiet. Part of the reason that you feel so unwell is that you are suffering withdrawal symptoms'

'Oh!', I exclaimed, shocked. A feeling of dread grows as the news began to sink in. 'For how long will I feel like this doctor?'

'Well it all depends, some people's bodies recover more quickly than others. It might be a week or it might take considerably longer. There could also be longer term mental health issues due to the trauma you have suffered'

I looked downcast. This wasn't what I wanted to hear.

'Please don't worry too much, you are in the best place here, where we can closely monitor your progress and attend to all your needs'

'Thank you doctor', I managed a weak smile

'Right then, I'll leave you to get some more rest and see you tomorrow', again the smile flashed across his face. He was incredibly handsome and he knew it!

Later that afternoon, after I had managed some soup and a soft bread roll for lunch, I had an unexpected visitor, DI Helen Sharp!

'Hello Sarah, how are you feeling today?'

'Rough!'

'That isn't surprising since you have been through quite an ordeal!'

DI Sharp then proceeded to take me through the recent events that I hadn't been able to recollect. I then asked another question, 'So did you get the kidnappers?'

'One of them, the one that was winged, after treatment is now in our custody. Unfortunately the other one eluded us and we are still looking for him'. An anxious frown bore witness to my concern as DI Sharp continued, 'Don't worry you're perfectly safe here. We have posted a PC just outside your door. Once you have been discharged from hospital we will take you directly to the safe house. Does that reassure you?'

'Yes thank you', relieved, I manage a smile

'Is there anything I can get you? Some grapes or a magazine perhaps?'

'That's very decent of you to offer, but not at the moment thanks. The staff here are looking after me very well'

'Good. I can see that you are very tired. So I'll come back to see how you are tomorrow as I do have a few more questions for you'

'Yes, hopefully I will be a bit more with it'

'I hope you are feeling better soon. See you tomorrow'

'Thanks, bye for now'.

I felt really tired and found myself drifting off to sleep again.

When I woke again it was early evening and Cynthia asked if I was hungry. I wasn't but I thought I ought to have something, so I opted for the lamb stew on the basis that it would slither down with minimal effort on my part. Dinner came and went, followed by a shaky trip to the bathroom. It actually felt good to clean my teeth and enjoy the fresh mint taste in my mouth. Back in bed and looking towards the door I could see the head and shoulders of the constable which helped me relax. It was gone nine o'clock, I closed my eyes and very soon a deep sleep claimed me once again.

I woke and glanced across at the clock, two thirty-five. Oh way too early! I turned over to try to go back to sleep. Have you ever sensed that someone else is in the room? Even though it was darkened, I felt another's presence. A dark shape came more into focus as it loomed towards my bed. Suddenly I recognised the shape, it was Shorty and he was carrying a knife! I went rigid with fear, my heart thumped in my chest. Then the adrenaline kicked in and I let out an almighty scream, 'Aahhhhhhhhhhhhhhhhh!' For a moment I don't think Shorty knew whether to run or not, he hesitated, which was sufficient time for the constable to reappear. 'Put the knife down', he said calmly in a loud, authoritative voice.

'Never!', came Shorty's answer and then he charged at the policeman who immediately tasered him! The knife clattered harmlessly onto the floor and Shorty fell to the ground, his body rhythmically convulsing. With one deft movement the constable kicked the knife across the room and then applied the handcuffs. At this stage I think Shorty realised the game was up! Recovering my composure I asked the constable, 'Where were you when this thug entered my room?'

'I'm terribly sorry Ms Lovage, I'd only popped out for a minute to use the bathroom. The perpetrator must have been biding his time, waiting for me to leave my post'.

'I dread to think what would have happened if I hadn't woken up when I did'

'Once again I can't apologise enough. Now we can add attempted murder to the longlist of charges he's going to face. He will be sent down for a long, long time, he's probably facing a life sentence!'

'He deserves it! The nasty little weasel!', I said with venom as my emotions got the better of me.

'Well I'll get this scum out of your sight, call the station and get him picked up. Good night Ms Lovage'

'Good night officer'

The officer unceremoniously grabbed Shorty by his arm and directed him towards the door, before disappearing down the corridor. A short while later the officer returned reassuring me a colleague had collected the prisoner.

7th December 2018

SARAH

An hour or so after breakfast DI Helen Sharp arrived at my bedside. She smiled and asked, 'How are you today Sarah?'

'I'm fine thanks Helen, although I had a nasty shock last night'

'Yes, I heard about that. That must have shaken you up!'

'It did, but thankfully no one was hurt, apart from the kidnapper that is!'

'Yes I think my colleague did a good job there'

'So, what happens next? Where do we go from here?'

'Well I need to ask you some questions about the lead up to your being kidnapped and the time you were imprisoned. Also about what happened last night. Then I will go away and prepare your statements. You will of course have an opportunity to validate them before signing'

'Yes, yes, as I expected, but what happens to me then?', I replied anxiously

'If everything goes according to plan, you'll sign the statements tomorrow morning. Then in the afternoon, you will be safely transported to your new residence in Weston-Super-Mare, where you will assume your new identity and make a new life for yourself'

'What! That soon?'

'Yes, we figured the sooner we can get you out from under the spotlight, press etc, the better'

'Wow! I assumed I'd remain in hospital a lot longer'

'Ideally that would have been the case, but while you remain here there is a not insignificant risk that someone may make another attempt on your life'

I looked down at the bed for a moment whilst the impact of these words fully hit home. I'm not out of the woods yet!

'Obviously you know best, I can only follow your advice'

Helen smiled and said, 'Don't look so worried. You won't be on your own. It's a two bedroom flat in Weston and a WPC has volunteered to live with you for the time being while you find your feet. She will provide help and advice, plus she knows the locality really well. Is there anything else that you want to ask me?'

'What's her name?'

'Tracey Johnson. She is twenty-nine years old and currently unattached'

'Does she smoke?'

'No, she is a non-smoker'

'What if I don't get on with her?'

'Well we will have to cross that bridge if we come to it, but fingers crossed eh?', Helen smiled again

'Yes, of course. I'm probably overthinking it at this stage, but it is a lot to take in!'

'I understand', Helen again radiated a comforting smile

'Oh, and what will I do for finance?'

'You will initially be on benefits, however armed with your new identity there is absolutely no reason why you shouldn't start looking for a job. Be that as an Estate Agent or anything else that you fancy'

'Thank you Helen, you seem to have thought of everything'

Helen smiled, 'We try our best! Now I'd like to ask some questions about recent events in preparation of your statements, if that's ok?'

'Yes that's fine. Perhaps you would like to help yourself to a coffee before we start? There's a machine in the corridor'

'That's a good idea!', Helen replied brightly, 'Would you like one too?'

'Yes please, black no sugar'

Helen turns and disappears in search of that precious commodity!

8th December 2018

SARAH

True to her word DI Helen Sharp was back in the morning with my statements. I carefully read through them and signed them off. 'Thank you Sarah', Helen declared, 'That's the end of that chapter hopefully. Have you any further questions for me?'

'What happens next? I mean with the court case and everything. How does it affect me?'

'It will take several months before the case comes to court. You almost certainly will be required to answer questions on the statements by the defence barrister'

'Cross examination you mean?'

'Yes that's right, but don't worry about your identity or exposure in court. You will be able to give your evidence by video link, from behind a screen'

'That's a relief!', I exclaim

'Now, about the Witness Protection scheme. We have arranged for you to have a new passport and driving licence in order to confirm your identity.'

'That's a point, what is my new name, you haven't told me yet?'

'Sarah Smith. We thought it would be much easier for you if we stuck to the same first name'

'Thank you. Although Smith is kind of boring!'

'Boring is good, it means that you won't stand out in a crowd, that is a good thing'

'Alright. What time am I leaving today?'

'One o'clock, straight after lunch that is. You'll be driven in an unmarked police car and I'll see you safely off myself'

'Thank you, that is very much appreciated'.

Another couple of hours went by and I found myself sitting in the back of a police Jaguar, hurtling down the M4 towards the West Country. It gave me time to think. 'What is Weston-Super-Mare like? Would I like it? Would I like my flat? Would I get on with my new flatmate? Would I be able to find work? Most importantly would I remain undiscovered?' Round and round my head these questions circulated, but unfortunately no answers came forth. It was all rather daunting!

Finally we pulled up in a cul-de-sac, in front of a small block of flats, typically seventies style. There was one main entrance, a hallway and stairs to a further two floors. My flat was on the second floor, number 12A. The police driver came up the stairs behind me, panting as he carried two enormous suitcases. I smiled to myself as I had just a rucksack and my handbag to contend with! As instructed I rang the doorbell and waited. The door was opened by a fresh-faced brunette, smartly dressed even though she was clearly off-duty. 'Hello, you must be Sarah?', she said with a West Country accent.
'Yes, and you must be Tracey?'
'Yes, spot on'
'Pleased to meet you Tracey'
'Mint. Come on in and I'll show you around'
'Thank you'
The hall was painted in a very light pastel green. Leading to a lounge, in magnolia that was adorned dramatically with bright red velvet curtains. The two chairs and settee were covered in a floral pattern, dated but they looked comfortable. I indicated to the driver to leave the suitcases there and thanked him. Next Tracey and I headed into the galley kitchen. The walls

217

were decorated in a pale blue, the units in an Egyptian Blue with a slate-grey worktop. The whole 'look' finished off with a blue floral design on a chintz fabric roller-blind. 'While we are here I'll put the kettle on. Would you like a tea of coffee? It's only instant, I'm afraid'

'Yes please, coffee, black no sugar. Instant is fine thanks', I think to myself I'll soon change a few things around here!

'Lush, I haven't had time to do a proper shop yet'

Ah! Maybe Tracey has only just moved in too. I mustn't be too judgemental!

'How long have you been in the police force Tracey?'

'Seven years, although sometimes it feels forever. I did a degree in Criminology at the University of Manchester, but came back to Weston my home town and joined the force. I decided to make it my career. A job where I can make a real difference. What about you Sarah?

'Estate Agent, especially on upmarket properties. I like to think I'm a fairly good one too, certainly above the average. Like your occupation, it is key that you get on well with people and stay calm in stressful situations', I chuckle ironically given what I have been through recently. Tracey gives me a slightly quizzical look, but refrains from questioning me further.

'Let me show you to your bedroom', Tracey offers

'Yes please'

Tracey leads the way to a small but functional room, decorated in a very neutral style, mostly magnolia. There is a bed, a wardrobe, a desk and office chair. This is ideal for me when I'm working from home. 'This is fine thanks Tracey. I'll drag my suitcases in out of your way'

'No rush, have you coffee first'

'Thanks', I return the smile. Yes, I think we will get along just fine!

About three hours later I had found homes for most of the contents of my suitcases. Tracey had shown me where everything is kept in the kitchen and how the bathroom shower operates. What else does a girl need to know? Tracey knocks lightly on my bedroom door, I respond, 'Come in'

'I hope I'm not disturbing you, but it's getting late. As I said earlier I've not had a chance to go shopping, so there is little to no food in the flat. However Papa's, the best fish and chip shop in Weston, is only a ten-minute walk from here. Do you fancy that?'

'Oh yes please. I am feeling rather famished!'

'Mint. We could go now if you're ready?'

'Yes, that sounds good to me!'

So we put our coats and boots on and made our way to the fish and chip shop, it wasn't far. And yes, the fish and chips were superb!

Later that evening I tell Tracey that I feel exhausted and will turn in for an early night. I lay on the bed unable to go to sleep, my head buzzing with all that had transpired over the recent weeks. I wondered how Bradley is doing. I surprised myself in that I still have feelings for him, even though he has deceived me, which had almost cost me dearly. However I realise that he was coerced into doing what he did. Now of course, with my new identity, I could never contact him ever again. The same is true for all my old friends such as Connie and Mike. Suddenly it hits me, I feel so alone, so empty and drained. Tears start to stream down my face. What have I got to look forward to? I feel I've lost everything. Except my life. I try to be more positive, but the negative thoughts go round and round inside my head. I replay all that has happened, somehow trying to change the ending, but to no avail. I'm kidding myself, of course you can't change the past. Only the future. Thankfully sleep, at last, embraces me.

10th December 2018

BRADLEY

Another Monday, another interview down at the cop shop. Good news and bad news. The good news is that, based upon Sarah's testimony, all charges in relation to Sarah's abduction have been dropped! The bad news is that I've been charged with both possession and the supply of Class A drugs. However I'm now out on bail provided I don't attempt to contact Sarah, continue living in my rented house in Walton-on-Thames and report to the police station once a week.

Obviously I've stopped having anything to do with the drugs trade, as I'm sure the police will have their beady eyes on me. As far as my job is concerned I haven't told them anything yet. Usually I go in to work two or three times a week and work from home one or two times a week. I've been living in a large four-bedroom house in Kenwood Drive which is very convenient for the train station as it's only an hour from town. Also it takes less than twenty minutes to walk to the station, which is great in summer! The house is also very convenient for the Conservative Club, which is where I often go for something to eat, chat and relax. In fact I'm off there now, it is only eight minutes in the car.

It's quiet in here today, ah there's Charlie over there, I'll go and have a chat with him. 'Good afternoon Charlie. How are you today?'

'Hello Bradley. Well I mustn't grumble, although my sciatica is giving me a bit of jip!'

'Sorry to hear that old fruit. I'm sure a tipple will improve things, what're you having?'

'That's jolly good of you, a Scotch-on-the-Rocks for me please'

I go over to the bar where Katie is serving. 'Good afternoon dear girl. How are you today?'

'I'm very well thanks Mr Wilson-Smythe. How about yourself?'

'I'm just tickety-boo thanks. But please call me Bradley, I don't know how many times I've told you', he grins

Katie, blushing, replies, 'So sorry Mr, err, Bradley. What can I get for you?'

'A Scotch-on-the-Rocks and a G-and-T please'

'Any particular Scotch?'

'Oh just Charlie's usual please'

'That's a Glenfiddich then and the gin?'

'Bombay Sapphire, double please'

'And the tonic?'

'Indian dear girl'

Katie dispenses the drinks, 'Anything else sir?'

'No, that's all for the moment'

'That's eleven pounds please'

I pay by card, collect the drinks and re-join Charlie at the table.

Charlie raises his glass, 'Cheers Bradley, your good health'

'And yours, cheers Charlie'

'Well what have you been up to Bradley? I haven't seen you for a while'

'Quite a lot actually, but you'll wish you hadn't asked', I chuckle

'Oh, do tell'

Straight faced I answer, 'I've robbed a bank!'

Charlie, who had just been taking a sip of his Scotch, splutters, 'Good heavens!'

I burst out laughing and Charlie realises I'm kidding, cueing laughter all round. I continue, 'Seriously I'm afraid I've been in all sorts of trouble. It's too complicated to go into too much detail, but it reminds me of my boarding school days when I was up before the beak'

'I think we all did things at school at we came to regret', enjoined Charlie

'Gosh yes, when I think about the time I got up on the school roof and hung matrons rather generous under garments from the weathervane!', I retold smiling at the memory

'You didn't?'

'I certainly did and I got caned for it too!'

'Bradley you're a dark horse!'

'Neigh!', I chortled

We both took a swig of our drinks, then Charlie continued, 'I did a funny trick, I super-glued a pound coin to the floor and then watched to see other kids trying to pick it up! It was hilarious!'

'It sounds it! Although it didn't endanger anyone, unlike this prank that could have been disastrous! It was in the metalwork class, we had the forge coals glowing red-hot. The master had just popped out of the workshop for something. There was one pupil, Jack, who was a real maverick. He threw a handful of live two-two bullets into the fire. None of us could believe that he'd actually done it, but we quickly ducked down behind really substantial work benches as the bullets started to go off, sending bits of metal in all directions! It was a really stupid, dangerous thing to do and we were lucky that no one was hurt!'

'Oh my god! I'm glad I didn't go to your school!'

'That was the worst prank ever, but the funny thing is, when the master returned he was oblivious to what had transpired only minutes before. He didn't have a clue!'

'Teachers are a curious lot, they are all so different. Our PE teacher was nicknamed Togs, because he always said, "Right get your togs on lads!" He could be quite callous at times. For one exercise that I feel he must have invented, he laid flat on the floor swinging a large lead weight on a steel cable around and around, about one foot off the ground. We had to jump over it, God it really hurt if it caught you on the ankles!'

'At least one or two teachers had a sense of humour. We had a new Physics teacher start at the school. A couple of the established teachers told him about the ancient school custom of beating the bounds with, wait for it, sticks of rhubarb! So off went the little party and beat the bounds of the extensive playing fields. Only on their return was the truth revealed to the newbie that no such ancient custom existed!'

'Oh I like that one, very good!'

'How about another drink Charlie?'

'Certainly, my shout'

With that Charlie went to the bar, calling at the loo on the way'

Charlie returns, 'There you go sir, cheers!'

'Bottoms up!'

Charlie groans softly as he tries to get comfortable in his chair.

I ask, 'What's up? Are you in pain?'

'Just a bit. Didn't I tell you I was invalided out of the army?'

'No you didn't, but I knew you are ex-army of course. So what happened?'

'It was 2004 during the second Iraq War. I was leading a reconnaissance mission to observe a small settlement. We'd had intel that there was a group of insurgents using it as their base. There were no more than twenty very basic dwellings surrounded by scrubby desert. Very little cover on the approach, so we went on a dark night using night-vision goggles. We got within about two miles in a truck and then made our way on foot. It was a slog, our kit isn't that light. Anyway we got within about three-quarters of a mile of the settlement when Smudger Smith trod on a landmine. Poor sod, he died instantly', Charlie paused, taking a deep breath before continuing, 'Unfortunately for me, a piece of shrapnel went straight through my knee, but worse still the explosion had alerted the insurgents. They still couldn't see us, but that didn't stop them firing randomly into the darkness! It was pretty hairy I can tell you! So we abandoned our mission and got the hell out of there as fast as we could. I was supported by two of my men, it was agony, never known pain like it. Smudger's body had to be carried, God rest his soul. Eventually we made it back to the truck. We were lucky that the insurgents didn't come after us, but I think they realised that if they left the shelter of the buildings, then they would be easy targets. Of course I've had surgery, a new knee and further treatment, plus a long convalescence but I was adjudged unfit for active service. So here I am!'

'Wow, you certainly have been through the mill!'

'Yes, but at least I'm still here to tell the tale'

For a few minutes we are lost in our thoughts. I'm sure Charlie is remembering his fallen comrades.

'What about you then Bradley? What brought you to this part of the world on a Monday lunchtime? Tell me about your career.'

'Overall my job, I studied economics at college and didn't really know what to do with my degree. Then I went to one of those "Job Fairs" and I liked the look of the young lady on one particular stand, went over and started chatting. She persuaded me to come in for an interview, which went reasonably well and so I ended up a stockbroker. I discovered I have a natural aptitude for it, so I was able to move between companies and made a lot of money. However things change and I suffered "burn out" and sadly had a breakdown. It was a long recovery but eventually I went back to work, but very much on my own terms, hence I only work about three days a week now. Though I still make sufficient money to keep the wolf from my door', I wink and smile at Charlie

'Crikey, so we both have had our share of troubles', reflected Charlie

'Yes, I think this calls for another drink. My turn', I say as I get out of my chair

'Thanks Bradley. We should perhaps eat something too?'

'Certainly, I'll bring the menu over'

Sometime later Charlie and myself sank back into our chairs, feeling very satisfied with our mains, deserts and now coffees. Charlie spoke, 'There is something very pleasing about good food, good wine and good company', and he patted his paunch.

'Yes, a very pleasant way to spend the afternoon. Especially on a Monday!', I returned.

'I come down to the club most week days for my lunch and the company, but I don't see you that often Bradley. So what are those "troubles" that brought you down here today?'

'I'm afraid I got mixed up with a nice young woman and one thing led to another. A bit of bother with the police. Then a heart attack and hospital. See I told you it was complicated!'

'Sounds like it. Would you care to expand?'

'No, not really. Sorry, but it will spoil the mood'

Charlie looked a bit disappointed, but then looking out the window he brightened up, 'Oh look the sun has just come out'

'Marvellous! Perfect timing, as I really should get back'

'Must you?'

'Yes I'm afraid so. Things to do'

'Oh well, it's been pleasure to have your company'

'Thank you, and the same goes for me. See you again soon'

'Yes, bye for now!'

I leave the club and for a few seconds contemplate calling a taxi. 'No, it's only a eight minute drive', I tell myself as I ease myself into the comfy Cayenne's driving seat.

Arriving back home I park on the gravel drive in front of the property. Inside I make myself a strong cup of coffee before settling into my armchair in front of the TV. Before I know it I've nodded off, the after effects of a good lunch and a few drinks. Eventually I wake to an untouched cold coffee! It's dark now and I decide to retire early, but first a quick shower to freshen up. I lie in bed thinking about Sarah, I really liked her a lot, she was great fun. How I wish things could have turned out differently. I ponder my past mistakes, throughout life we are all faced with choices, unfortunately I made a few wrong ones. I drift off into an uncomfortable, fitful sleep.

In the middle of the night I find myself awake, not for the first time. However this time the outside security light is on, it illuminates my curtains. Initially I ignore it, probably a cat or an urban fox perhaps, but no, I hear a crunch on the gravel. Slightly dazed through sleep, I manage to get out of bed and make my way to the window. Looking out I see nothing unusual, but I definitely heard something. Oh well, best get back to bed.

11th December 2018

BRADLEY

Another day, another dollar! It's a day in the office for me today, a bit mundane I realise but one must keep the wolf from the door you know! I carry out my ablutions and enjoy a breakfast of fresh orange juice, marmalade toast and fresh ground coffee. Then I grab my car keys and dash out of the door. I jump into the Cayenne, keys into the ignition, turn the key....

DI HELEN SHARP

I drive onto the property on Kenwood Drive, Walton-on-Thames where Mr Wilson-Smythe resides. Forensics are already here, everything is cordoned off and a white tent hides the scene of the explosion. I walk over to the tent and tentatively open the flap. Nothing prepares me for the sight that meets my eyes. The still smoking Cayenne is a mangled wreck, all the windows blown out, the doors and bodywork distorted almost beyond recognition. Worse still, there are various body parts strewn around, blackened and burnt. I recoil in horror, rush out of the tent and throw-up onto the grass!

A short while later I'm sitting in Mr Wilson-Smythe's kitchen sipping a strong black coffee that one of the forensics officers has kindly made for me. I'm well and truly shaken. So what's gone on here? A bomb has exploded, that's for sure and Bradley is dead. Who would go to such lengths? As far as I know the only people with anything to gain are the drug dealers, this would stop Bradley testifying and also prevent him from divulging whatever he knows of the upward supply chain. I phone my boss and request a search team to conduct a forensic examination of the whole house in the hope of finding any evidence or clues to who the perpetrators might be.

12th December 2018

DI HELEN SHARP

Exciting news! The forensics team discovered a burner phone in Bradley's bedroom drawer. Back in the laboratory they removed the SIM card and successfully recovered all the information from the card, including previously deleted data. The only contact listed was Pablo. Then they managed to get into the phone and discovered a series of incriminating text message exchanges between Bradley and Pablo. The mobile phone network provider was contacted and asked to provide data identifying the area where the recipients phone was used by triangulation between the transceiver towers. I can't wait for the results!

13th December 2018

DI HELEN SHARP

The network provider pulled out all the stops and has identified an area in Lambeth North that is a mix of commercial premises and flats. My colleagues are working hard to obtain a list of the tenants.

This afternoon an initial list was emailed across to me and I could hardly believe my luck, one Pablo Ortiz appears as a possible candidate! No time to loose, we must start planning a dawn raid for tomorrow morning!

14th December 2018

DI HELEN SHARP

It's 4:30 a.m. and I'm sitting in an unmarked police car in Lambeth North and it's bloody freezing! I'm feeling knackered after another row with Joe about my antisocial hours. As a result I didn't get much sleep last night. However two strong coffees have put some life back into the old gal!

All around me there is plenty of activity as armed police officers disembark from a number of vehicles and prepare themselves for what is to come. Two of the men manhandle a large metal weight that swings between two sets of ropes.

They all look very fit and up for it, as they say. One particular officer stands out from the rest, he is obviously in charge and giving out the orders. Then as one, silently, they all move off towards the entrance to the flats.

The large metal 'torpedo' weight swings and the flat door disintegrates. Ten officers hurry through the opening not knowing what sort of reception they will get and by how many. They open the door to one bedroom, no one in there and it appears to be an office. Then to the other bedroom, upon opening the door their flashlights pick out some movement amongst the bed covers. Dressed in just a T-shirt and boxer shorts a bleary-eyed little man with weasel-like features sits up in the bed, open mouthed. 'Que carajo!', he swears.

'Police. Hands in the air where we can see them'. Another of the officers goes over and pulls the cover off the bed. No weapons are revealed. The little Spaniard starts to protest in a strong Spanish accent, 'What is happening? Why are you here? I've done nothing!'

'Are you Pablo Ortiz?', the leading officer asks

'Yes'

'Pablo Ortiz I am arresting you on suspicion of drug trafficking. You do not have to say anything, but anything you do say may be taken down and used in evidence against you'

'Hah! You will find nothing, I am clean', he said smiling sardonically

'Take him away'. Pablo was cuffed and led away to the waiting police car.

An exhaustive search of Pablo's flat ensued. Nothing was left to chance, the whole place was turned upside down, even the balcony was thoroughly examined. A sniffer dog was used to locate any drugs, but not one grain of cocaine powder or any other drug was found. It was as if Pablo knew that the premises would be searched. Perhaps it was just a necessary precaution on his part? Who knows. However two useful pieces of evidence did come to light, firstly his burner, the one that he had been using to communicate to Bradley with. Secondly, a small notebook was retrieved from inside his mattress. It was pure gold, containing a record of his drug transactions, dates, quantity, drug, cost and supplier/buyer name in code. Armed with all this information I felt sure that this would result in a conviction and possibly to uncovering a major drug supply network.

Chapter 14 – The Noose Tightens

MIKE

It's Friday afternoon and I've managed to engineer an early finish. I've just made myself a coffee and sink into my favourite chair, when the phone rings. I pick up, 'Unknown Caller' pops up on the display, cheerfully I say, 'Mike Dean speaking'. No response from the other end, just a faint hum and crackling. Then a loud click and the line goes dead. It must be a wrong number I suppose. I start reading the newspaper but don't get very far when the phone rings again. I pick up, this time more hesitantly saying, 'Mike Dean speaking. Who's calling please?' For a long moment there remains silence, I am just about to put the phone down when I hear an intake of breath before a deep man's voice with a Spanish accent slowly drips down the line, 'I will kill you, kill you both. És una qüestió d'honor'. The line goes dead and a cold shiver runs down my spine. A thousand questions cascade through my mind, 'Are we in danger? Who is the mystery caller? Is he connected to recent events in Spain? Or even perhaps Snowden? If so, how? How did he get my number? Could this be a prank call in light of all the publicity? Do I take this seriously? How will Connie react? Do I contact the police?' Severely shaken, I decide to do nothing until I've had the chance to discuss with Connie.

Around seven pm Connie arrives from work, I make her a coffee and ask her to sit down as I have something important to discuss with her. Immediately her eyebrows are raised in a look of surprise mixed with concern. 'What is it Mike?', she exclaims with a hard edge to her voice. I describe the earlier goings-on in detail. 'Oh my god Mike! I don't want to believe the whole Spanish thing is starting up again, we are cursed!'

'Maybe it isn't', I interject

'You have got to be joking? The Spanish accent, the threat, the implication that someone is out for revenge. It can mean only one thing, that Los Ghouls aren't finished with us yet!'

'Of course you're right Connie, I see that now', I respond. 'So what do we do? Report this to the police?'

'Yes, I think so, it is our only option. Better do it now, sooner rather than later'.

'OK, I'll do it straightaway'. I have kept DCI Biggins mobile number in my phone, so I'm able to tap the 'Call' button. I can hear the phone ringing three times before someone picks up. 'Biggins here', comes the familiar dulcet west country accent, accompanied by a somewhat raucous background noise. I surmise that Biggins is enjoying after work drinks with his colleagues before replying, 'DCI Biggins, Mike Dean here. Sorry to bother you, but something has come up. Is now a convenient time to talk?'

'Hello Mike, yes that's fine. Let me move to somewhere a bit less noisy, just give me a minute please'. A couple of minutes go by. 'Mike are you still there?'

'Yes. I'll put you on the speaker so Connie can hear you too'

235

'Good, that's better, now I can hear myself think! So what do you want to talk about?'

I explain the situation including Connie and my notion that this was connected in some way to what occurred in Barcelona and possibly on Snowden.

DCI Biggins pondered before replying, 'Well that does sound plausible. Let me sleep on it and I'll call you in the morning to discuss further. In the meantime I suggest you stay in your apartment. Is that clear?'

'Yes thanks. About what time tomorrow?'

'Shall we say eleven? That will give me time to make an initial enquiry of my Spanish friends'.

'Fine. We look forward to speaking to you then'. I put the phone down.

Connie states dourly, 'Well at least it's Friday Mike. I don't think we can take any more time off work just yet'.

15th December 2018

MIKE

At eleven on the dot my phone rings and I pick-up. 'Good morning, Mike Dean speaking'

'Good morning Mike, DCI Biggins here. How are you today?'

'I didn't sleep very well but mustn't grumble'

'Sorry to hear that, about the sleep that is. I'm sure it is quite a worry for you'

'I certainly could have done without it'

'I can understand that. So straight to the point. I have found out that Kylo Garcia, former leader of the Los Ghouls, has a brother Carlos. The Spanish authorities think that it is highly likely that it was Carlos who called you. Unfortunately there isn't much that we can do about it unless we have some hard evidence. On that point, I have asked for a full trace to be put on your phone line. This will automatically record time, date, caller ID and trace the originator'.

'So what you're implying is that Connie and I just sit tight?'

'Well, essentially, yes that's correct'

'Like sitting ducks?'

'Now steady on! I'll reinstate the surveillance outside your apartment, but unfortunately I am unable to offer any guarantees. That is the reality of the situation'

Connie and I exchange looks. I respond for both of us, 'We have no option, we have to accept it. However I can't say we are over the moon'

'I entirely understand Mike and Connie. Well that's all from me. Do you have any further questions?'

'No, thank you DCI Biggins'

'In that case I'll drop off the call, but remember if you do have any further queries then please don't hesitate to get back in touch'

'Noted, many thanks again. Bye for now'

'Take care you two, goodbye'.

I let DCI Biggins views sink in, then looked directly at Connie, who appeared to be digesting the information too. With a serious tone I speak, 'I don't like this situation at all. Once again we are sitting ducks. Once again it puts our whole life on hold!'

'I agree Mike, it is far from ideal. I'm already feeling stressed out!'

'Can't we do something about it?'

Connie doesn't respond immediately, I can almost hear the cogs whirring! Then, 'I think we should bite the bullet. The best form of defence is to attack. I think we should go back to Barcelona.'

'What?', I exclaim. 'You can't be serious?'

'Yes I am. Just think about it Mike. If we stay here we are at risk, predictable and our enemies can plan accordingly. However if we go back to Spain we have the element of surprise on our side, we dictate the agenda. We take the attack to them!'

I'm not altogether convinced, although I trust Connie's judgment. 'OK, but what do we do when we get there? What's the plan?'

'Well we will require to keep under cover, so as not to alert them. However we will need help. Who do you think is closest to their underworld?'

'I don't know'

'Maria López, leader of Los Silenciosos, my doppelganger! She will have her informants, she will know who is leading Los Ghouls and what the relationship is to Carlos Garcia.'

'Now I see where you are coming from. So based upon a conversation with Maria, we formulate a plan?'

'Yes. So shall we do it?'

'I'm in, but what about work? You said yourself last night we can't have more time off. I've already had a lot of time off what with my past troubles and everything'

'That is going to be tricky. It could scupper our plans. We will both need to approach our managers and request additional time off. They already know about the exceptional circumstances and your mental health. I think they will be sympathetic. Anyway all we can do is ask, we must at least try!'

'Agreed. First thing Monday morning I'll approach my manager, maybe buy him a coffee and a doughnut first. That always helps!', I smile for the first time this morning, pleased that we are being proactive.

17th December 2018

MIKE

The meeting with my manager went better than could have been expected. I think when I explained the conversations with the police inspector, it made them sit-up and take me seriously. Connie also was given the green light. We managed to book tickets to fly out to Barcelona the very next day, so with some trepidation we packed our rucksacks, had an early night and were ready for whatever was waiting for us in Spain.

DI HELEN SHARP

This morning I'm interviewing Pablo Ortiz, accompanied by his brief. My boss is alongside me. He switches on the audio recorder, 'For the benefit of the tape, I am DCI Charlie Biggins, accompanied by DI Helen Sharp, Mr Pablo Ortiz is the defendant and Ms Penelope Williams his legal advisor. Mr Ortiz is being held in custody under suspicion of the supply of a Class A drug. Is that understood Mr Ortiz?'

'Yes'

'Good, then I'll hand over to DI Sharp who was the arresting officer'

I look directly into Ortiz's cold eyes, he doesn't flinch, his face gives nothing away. My first question is intended to shake him into giving a response, 'Mr Ortiz I believe that you are a key individual in the import and distribution of Class A drugs. Is that correct?'

'No comment'

'We have charged Mr Bradley Wilson-Smythe with possession of Class A drugs that he claims were supplied by yourself. What do you say to that?'

Ortiz glances at his brief and responds, 'No comment'

'A mobile phone was found in your possession. Upon examination this links you to Mr Bradley Wilson-Smythe. You can't deny that?'

'No comment'

'Furthermore we have established beyond doubt that you are in regular contact with a Carlos Garcia, a known criminal, who resides in Spain. What do you say to that?

'No comment'

'I have obtained copies of your bank statements. These show considerable sums coming in and going out of your account, yet we can't find any evidence of your employment. How do you explain that?'

'No comment'

At this point I produce the notebook, contained within a clear plastic pouch. 'Is this your notebook Mr Ortiz?'

For the first time Ortiz shifts uneasily in his chair and glances towards his brief, then answers, 'No comment'

'Well that is very strange, because Mr Ortiz, the handwriting in the notebook exactly matches your handwriting! What is more, the entries appear to be a complete record of your drug dealing transactions. Surely you can't deny that?'

There is a long pause, but once again the answer comes back, 'No comment'

At this point in the interview DCI Biggins patience appears exhausted. I can tell that he is getting stressed because he is fiddling with that damn pipe in his pocket again. Suddenly he picks up the notebook and slams it down on the desk in front of Ortiz. 'In the face of overwhelming evidence you still insist upon 'no comment'. Don't you understand that you face possibly a lifetime in prison?'

Ortiz's brief interjects, 'You're out of order DCI Biggins. My client remains innocent until proven otherwise in a court of law. I insist that you withdraw your last comment'.

Reluctantly DCI Biggins, 'I withdraw my last comment', and feeling frustrated, 'Terminating the interview at 10:27 a.m.', switches off the recorder. The tension relieved, the brief starts to rise from her chair but Biggins cuts in, 'Just a moment please'. 'Off the record I am considering contacting Carlos Garcia. I might even tell him that Pablo Ortiz says that he knows you in connection with the drugs trade. There, what do you say to that?'

An unexpectedly very pale Ortiz looks terrified, immediately grasping the consequences of such an action. This could lead to his life being put in immediate danger through the elimination of a key witness. His brief takes charge, 'Would you let me have a few minutes with my client please?'

'Certainly Ms Williams. We can reconvene at eleven if that suits you?'

'Yes, thank you'. We leave the interview room for a welcome break and a strong black coffee. Well, that was an unexpected turn of events!

At precisely eleven o'clock we reconvened in the interview room. 'Well?', DCI Biggins inquired. Ms Williams replied, 'My client intends to fully cooperate. Would you like to resume the interview on the understanding that no word gets back to Spain, in particular nothing to link my client to Carlos Garcia and his associates?'

'Yes, I think we can manage that', and turning to me added, 'Please continue with your questions DI Sharp'

'Yes sir'

DCI Biggins switched on the voice recorder, 'Interview resumed at eleven ten'

Straight to the point I started with, 'Mr Ortiz, do you recognise this notebook?'

'Yes it is mine', Ortiz responded downheartedly, his eyes never leaving the notebook

'Do the entries contained within the notebook relate to transactions of Class A drugs?'

A pause then, 'Yes Ma'am'

'Have you ever supplied Mr Bradley Wilson-Smythe with cocaine?'

Again hesitation before uttering, 'Yes Ma'am'

I turn to DCI Biggins, 'That's all I need for now sir'

'Good. Terminating the interview at, um, eleven fourteen'

Ten minutes later I'm summoned to DCI Biggins office. As I enter Biggins looks up and says, 'Ah Helen, good job in there. Well done!'

'Thank you sir'

'Take a seat. The investigative work you have done on this drugs case has been superb. Not only have we apprehended a low-level dealer, but we have nabbed an important middle tier importer and supplier. There is an opportunity here to crackdown on an international supply chain'

'Thank you sir. But how do you know the Pablo Ortiz is part of an international drugs network?'

'Well now, it's a hunch really. I have a nose for these things', he smiles and continues, 'As soon as the name Carlos Garcia came up I had my suspicions, the Garcia family has been on my radar for some time. They seem to have their fingers in a lot of pies. To my certain knowledge they are involved in all sorts of criminal activities including drugs, kidnapping and attempted murder!'

'Now that we have the main coordinator in England behind bars, what else can we do?'

'I have a police contact in Barcelona, Inspector Martin, whom I have had conversations with in respect of the Garcia family. I'll give him a call right now and I thought that you might like to be present'

'Oh yes please sir!'

'Right then', Biggins picks up the phone and dials Inspector Martin's direct line.

After several rings the distinctive voice of Martin's answers, 'Inspector Martin, cómo puedo ayudarte?'

'Good day Inspector Martin. DCI Biggins calling from England'

'Good day to you DCI Biggins. It is good to hear from you. I hope all is well'

'Yes thank you. I trust things are going well for you too'

'Yes indeed thanks. Now how can I be of assistance?'

'I am pleased to say that we have apprehended one of your countrymen, one Pablo Ortiz. From all the evidence we have gathered it appears that he is a key drugs dealer in an international network, importing the drugs and then distributing them in the UK. Now listen to this, his main supplier is Carlos Garcia! We have spoken many times about the Garcia family. I felt sure that this intel would be very useful to you'

'Most certainly, we have been trying to nail this gang for many years. The problem is that they seem very adept at covering their tracks!'

'Well this time, thanks to the sterling efforts of DI Sharp, we recovered a notebook detailing all Ortiz's transactions. I will arrange for a copy to made and sent to you'

'Thank you so much. I feel that the net is perhaps closing at last on Los Ghouls gang'

'My pleasure, well I must go, but we will speak again very soon I'm sure'

'Yes, buenas tardes, until next time señor Biggins'

'Buenas tardes Inspector Martin', and Biggins ends the call.

He looks across at me, smiles and says, 'Yes sterling work DI
Sharp. Finish your shift and get off home. Time to take a well-
earned rest!'

'Thank you sir, I'll do that', I return his smile and feel quite
elated as I bounce out of his office.

I arrive home and Joe greets me with, 'Aha, home on time for
a change. To what do I owe this honour?'

'Ha, ha, very funny!'

'Sorry love', Joe puts his arm around me, 'I do understand that
you have been under a lot of pressure lately'. I nod in
agreement. Joe continues, 'How would you like me to make
you a nice cuppa?'

'That would be grand Joe, thanks'. He kisses me gently, then
releases his arm and makes his way to the kitchen.

Later we had a real heart to heart talk, Joe has acknowledged
that my career is important to me and will support me more. In
return I have promised to let him know if I'm going to be
working late. We've discussed starting a family too with Joe
being a stay at home dad if and when the time comes. I'm
hoping that's enough to keep Joe happy as I'm determined to
make Detective Superintendent one day.

Chapter 15 – Grasping the Nettle

18th December 2018

MIKE

We arrived in Barcelona and immediately sought out a camping shop to purchase a tent, three season sleeping bags plus various bits and pieces of equipment. We thought that camping was the best way to stay under the radar, so to speak. We had identified a suitable site, Camping Estrella De Mar, about a fifteen-minute drive from the centre of Barcelona. Before we headed off to the campsite we left a note for Maria López at the ARTiSA café, it said, 'Maria, we need to meet you urgently. Please call as soon as possible. Connie & Mike', followed by Connie's mobile number. We decide to avoid car rental because it requires production of official documents and we want to remain anonymous as possible, so we take the bus, a forty-minute journey.

CONNIE

The Camping Estrella De Mar site is very pleasant, with good facilities and only 400 metres from the beach. By 3pm we had booked in, set up the tent and grabbed coffees from the snack bar. It had all been bit of a rush, but we had made it, we are here and I was beginning to feel more settled. Then my phone rang! I didn't recognise the number, 'Hello Connie here, who is calling please?'

'Buenos días Connie, it is Maria, you left a message for me'

'Buenos días Maria. Yes, thank you for calling back. Mike and I are back in Barcelona'

'Què!', a shocked Maria exclaimed, 'Why are you back here? You put yourself in danger!'

I explain recent events and the rationale for returning to Barcelona.

Maria inhales deeply, 'I see. So you think Carlos Garcia is the problem? How do you think I can help?'

'As I explained our lives are threatened, which means yours is too. I was rather hoping, that between us, we could come up with a plan to remove this threat. Ideally one that would result in Carlos being held behind bars for many, many years'

'I understand. I will give it much thought, but I can't promise anything. We should meet tomorrow at 10 a.m. at the ARTiSA café and then we shall see.'

'That's brilliant!', said a delighted Connie, pleased that Maria was at least entertaining the idea. 'Thank you so much. We look forward to meeting you tomorrow at ten. Bona tarda'

'Until tomorrow. Bona tarda'.

Mike had heard every word and he too looked pleased. 'That's a good start. At least Maria didn't reject the idea out of hand. I can't wait to see what tomorrow brings!'

'Me too, but until then I suggest we just chill. In fact I'm going to go for a swim in the sea!'

Late that afternoon as evening approached, having had an energetic swim, I felt much more relaxed. Mike had taken charge of cooking on the charcoal barbecue. I sat back and enjoyed a large glass of Rioja. Little lights came on everywhere as dusk gathered, providing a magical backdrop. For the moment I put thoughts of our troubles to the back of my mind and watched Mike busy himself with the barbecue, 'He does have a good physique now', the thought runs across my mind, but I don't have any romantic notions, that ship has well and truly sailed!

Dusk became night and the temperature plummeted. The hustle and bustle noises of the day subsided, leaving a vacuum of silence in its stead, only punctuated by the occasional sound of a door closing or the scream of an urban fox. I decided to turn in, my sleeping bag providing welcome respite from the cool air. Very soon I was soundly asleep, oblivious to the troubles of the world....

Suddenly I was transported back to La Mercè Festival and the night of Correfoc where devils dance in the streets. I was being pushed along by the crowd, unable to choose my direction of travel, swimming against the human tide. Brightly painted devils leered at me from all directions. A sense of panic and confusion swept over me. Fireworks seemingly exploded in my head, the deafening noise adding to my angst. The faces of the devils now loomed large in my face, one after another as if to crush and subdue me. Now I had just one thought, I must get out of here, escape from the madness of this crowd. I turned, then reeled in shock as I looked directly into the eyes of Kylo Garcia! He glared back at me, his eyes turning red, full of hate and anger. His face came closer still until I could feel his hot breath on my skin. He hissed at me, 'I will kill you, revenge is mine!' Then I woke, shaking, my brow wet with beads of perspiration. For a moment confusion reigned, where am I? Slowly the fog cleared and I reached out to touch the reassuring form of Mike, who had remained fast asleep, oblivious to my trauma. It was sometime before my brain quietened down sufficiently for sleep to come once again. Much to my relief, the next time I woke dawn was breaking.

19th December 2018

CONNIE

Mike and I take the bus to Barcelona, making our way to the ARTiSA café for about 9:40 am. Mike ordered coffees and pastries for us both while we waited for Maria to arrive. We didn't have to wait very long before Maria, again dressed all in black swept into view. Once again I examine her features that so closely resemble my own. I never cease to be amazed at just how closely they match. 'Buenos días Maria. Thank you for meeting us. Would you like to join us for coffee and pastries?'

'Buenos dias Mike y Connie. Un cafè negre si us plau. Sorry, I'll speak in English'. Maria speaks clearly but with a strong accent.

'Thank you', I nod acknowledging that Maria had lapsed into Catalan.

Maria warns, 'I don't think you realise how dangerous it is, returning to Barcelona. Carlos Garcia has taken over from Kylo as the leader of Los Ghouls. They have eyes and ears everywhere. Even though you are taking precautions, it won't be long before your presence is discovered.'

I reply, 'Yes, of course we realise that, but better to resolve this on our terms than remain as sitting ducks in England.'

'So how do you intend to progress this?'

'Perhaps by setting a trap, similar to last time?'

'Hmmm, the problem with that is Carlos will be on his guard. No, we need to come up with something quite subtle. Do you have any suggestions?'

Mike suggests, 'Lure him onto a boat, then the police surround it.'

Maria responds, 'That would be very difficult to arrange. What would we use as bait?'

Mike looks down at his feet before quietly saying, 'Connie'

I look aghast, 'No, I don't think so Mike!'

Maria calmly articulates what we are all thinking, 'This isn't going to be easy. I need to go away and have a good think about this. Perhaps you too?'

'Yes, of course you're right. Mike and I will discuss at length. When shall we meet up again?'

'I'm busy all day tomorrow, but would here 10 a.m. on Friday work for you two?'

'Yes that's great. Thank you so much for trying to help us.', I speak for both of us.

'Fins demà bon dia', and with that Maria swept out of the café.

'Well that's that for now', said an exasperated Mike

'Don't worry, we will think of something I'm sure. In the meantime I think we should let Inspector Martin know that we are back in Barcelona'

'Yes, if only out of courtesy'

'OK I'll phone him now', I pick up my phone and select the number from 'Contacts'.

'Inspector Martin, cómo puedo ayudarte?'

'Good morning Inspector Martin. Connie Crawford here, with Mike Dean.'

'Ah, good morning to you. How can I help you?'

'We wanted to let you know that we are in Barcelona'

'What! Are you crazy?', Inspector Martin sounded quite angry.

'Apologies, but you are taking an enormous risk'.

'Not really. We are 'undercover' so to speak. Staying at the Camping Estrella De Mar site, to avoid detection'

'So why have you come back to Barcelona?'

'We are hoping to flush out Carlos Garcia. We know he has a vendetta against us'.

'In my opinion you are playing a very dangerous game'

'Maybe', I reply blushing with embarrassment.

'My advice to you, is leave Barcelona as soon as possible and don't come back. For your own safety'.

'Thank you for your advice Inspector. However we have some business that we want to resolve first'

'That is your call, but you know where I stand on the matter'

'I do and thank you once again'

'I wish you well. You know where we are if you need us'

'Yes thank you Inspector. Buenos días'

'Buenos días'

'Well Mike, that's all we can do for now'

'Yes it appears so. Does that mean that we have a day-off tomorrow?'

'Perhaps. We still need to think about how we can entrap Carlos Garcia.'

'Of course, but we could do that anywhere. On a train for example.'

'Good point. Now you've got me thinking. Madrid's art galleries are internationally recognised. I've always wanted to visit them'.

'Great, I'm all for a trip to Madrid. For one thing it would ensure that we are out of Carlos' reach. So how do we get there?'

'The AVE train from Barcelona to Madrid. The highspeed train does the journey in two and a half hours!'

Mike, enthuses, 'Let's do it! We could go today, stay the night in a cheap hotel and return tomorrow late afternoon.'

'But we haven't got our toiletries with us.'

'Never mind, we can buy a cheap kit and anyway the hotel will provide something.'

'You're on! Just a moment, let me look up the train times…… ah, right here we are, departs Barcelona Sants station at 12:50 arrives Madrid Atocha at 15:45. If we hurry we could make it.'

'Let's go then', said Mike beckoning the waiter over for the bill.

MIKE

Outside ARTiSA I hailed a cab and 20 minutes later we arrived at Sants station. Purchased our tickets and didn't have long to wait for the train. A sleek AVE, what a beauty she is! The journey is smoothly uneventful, I sit there watching the landscape flash by at speeds of up to 298 km/h! Upon arrival in Madrid we buy a few essentials and book into a boutique hotel. Some of the art galleries stay open to 8pm, so we are able to visit a couple and drink in the culture. I was transported, I suddenly found my worries had melted away like snowflakes in April sunshine. The marvellous Museo Del Prado has works by, among many others, Velázquez, Goya and Rubens. Then back to the hotel for dinner and then to bed.

CONNIE

No sooner had my head hit the pillow than I went into a deep sleep. Suddenly I was back on the AVE, but a darkened version. No sign of Mike anywhere, nor any other passengers. Then a ticket inspector came into view, lurching down the aisle. As he loomed closer I could make out his features, it was….it was a ghoulish Kylo Garcia! I wanted to run, but I was fixated, rooted to the spot, shivers running down my spine, for where his eyes should be were two empty black sockets! Terrified, I presented my ticket for inspection. A deep, heavily accented voice spoke these words with devilish delight, 'Where you are going you won't need the return ticket'. He glowered down at the petrified me, and then, just as suddenly as the vision had appeared, the nightmare faded away. I woke shaking and sweating profusely. I wondered, is this a premonition? I'm having regular nightmares now. We need to end this once and for all. Eventually sleep returned to ease away my fears.

20th December 2018

CONNIE

We visited a few more art galleries until midday when we spotted a nice-looking restaurant for lunch. Mike and I chose a delicious selection of tapas, together with a bottle of the house Rioja. Followed by a melt-in-the-mouth Crema Cremada for dessert. We sat back and relaxed over our coffees. Mike mused, 'Madrid, what a wonderful city. A place to be in love'

'Well don't get any ideas about that in my direction', I chuckle

'No I wouldn't', Mike responded, 'I know how much I hurt you. I wouldn't expect for you to have me back. In any case I think we have both moved on'

Me, more seriously now, 'Yes indeed, but I'm sure we will remain good friends. Especially after all that we have been through together'

'I'd like that', Mike paused, then continued, 'There seems to be phases in the process of love and attraction. Phase one, physical attraction, some would call it 'lust'', he laughs. 'Phase two, passionate love, where every characteristic is important including physical, intelligence and personality. Phase three, friendship and long-term commitment, usually developing while the couple are living together. Unfortunately we didn't get through Phase three. My fault entirely'.

I smile, 'No, more's the pity. However I've learnt from our experiences too. While I'm not in a hurry to fall in love again, I realise that some of the characteristics that are important to me are; honesty, commitment and kindness. Of course not forgetting that this is underpinned by personal health and wellbeing!'

'You're right of course', Mike laughs, 'Hark at us going on, we do sound like an old married couple!'

I join in the laughter. 'On that happy note I think we should ask for the bill'.

After lunch we walk around Madrid admiring the architecture, before catching the 16:00 hrs AVE back to Barcelona arriving as scheduled, 18:30 at Sants station. It's dark as we exit the station, which when you aren't too familiar with your surroundings, is a tad disconcerting. At that moment the 'taxi for hire' light illuminates on a stationary cab. Mike and I rush over and jump in. The rear doors lock and then, bizarrely, another man jumps into the front seat alongside the driver. Immediately suspicious, I shout through the glass partition, 'What's going on?' Not a word in response, instead the passenger swivels in his seat brandishing a firearm! The taxi pulls away with 'Don't you want me baby' music blasting through the speakers. For a second I ask myself, 'Is this another nightmare?' In despair I try the door again but no joy to be had there. The taxi doesn't hang about, Mike and I get thrown from side to side. After what seems to be an age, the taxi pulls up in a darkened street. 'Oh my god Mike! I recognise this, it was where I was held before!' Both heavies marshal us out of the cab and into the building, with cold steel thrust into our backs. Then down into the dingy cellar with its single light bulb. 'Who are you? What do you want?' I try communicating once more, but not a word is spoken and the door closes, locks turning providing the only answer I am likely to get!

Hardly daring to believe what has just happened, Mike and I sit in the gloomy room as clouds of depression descend upon our shoulders. Silence pervades apart from the distant sound of a dripping tap. The dank cellar smells awful, a mixture of mouldy damp and urine. Mike clearly can't accept it, as he starts kicking the door, but to no avail. 'Mike', I say, 'Calm down. Remember I've been here before, there is nothing we can do, or at least attempt to do, until our captors visit us.' 'How can I accept this? They haven't even provided any water!'
'At least we are still alive'
'For the moment yes but Connie we've been really stupid thinking we could outwit this gang. This could be the end of us', Mike responds darkly.

So we sit and wait for what seems an eternity. This time without the cheery services of Juan. Nobody brings food, drink or empties the filthy bucket in the corner! It feels like evening when there are noises outside the cellar door, shortly followed by unlocking sounds. The door swings open and two heavies enter, the second one carrying a firearm. The first, a confident, thickset individual speaks. 'Are you enjoying your stay in our establishment? No? Well too bad! Let me introduce myself, I am Carlos and your meddling is responsible for the death of my brother Kylo'. I interject, 'That isn't true! He...' 'Shut up!', Carlos angrily cuts me off, 'Did I say you could speak? No! Your fate has been decided. I understand you like jumping out of planes? Tomorrow we shall be going on a short flight over the Med and there you shall be leaving us, but this time without parachutes! He glares at Mike and I, then affects a false laugh, 'You like my erm little joke eh? No parachutes! Ha, ha, hah!' With that he turns and makes for the door, with his henchman in close attendance.

Mike and I stare at each other. 'Well that doesn't sound too good, does it?', I observe. Mike replies, 'No, it doesn't. We're doomed!'
'We aren't done for yet. There is still some hope'.
'How do you work that out?'
'Maybe we can get the jump on them tomorrow'
'Fat chance!'
We lapse back into silence.

The paillasse is painfully uncomfortable so neither of us get much sleep. The time drags, seconds turn into minutes, minutes into hours. Still we await Carlos' return with dread and much trepidation. Our desperate situation swirls round and round inside my head. Getting the jump on Juan was relatively easy, these heavies are a different matter entirely! The outlook is bleak.

Suddenly the interminable silence is broken by several raised voices outside. Then, from just the other side of the door, 'Inspector Martin here. Keep clear of the door. We are coming in'. With that warning his men break the door down.

'Thank goodness you came', said a very relieved Mike.

'How did you know we were here?', I ask.

'Your associate, Maria, contacted me when you didn't show up for your meeting. We didn't know that you would be here, but it seemed a logical place to start looking. Are you both unhurt?'

'Yes, we are hungry and lacking sleep, but otherwise ok'

'In that case, I'd like you to accompany me to my offices, in order to provide statements please. Is that OK?'

'Yes, that's the least we can do', I respond full of gratitude.

21st December 2018

CONNIE

Later that morning we leave the police station exhausted and make our way back to the Camping Estrella De Mar site. I just want to sleep! However I have one more thing I must do, I must thank Maria for alerting the police. I call her number and she picks up, 'Maria López'. I reply, 'Buenos días Maria, Connie Crawford here'

'Buenos días Connie. I am very relieved that you are safe'

'Thank you and thank you for your intervention. If you hadn't I dread to think what would have happened to us'

'Yes, Carlos seems obsessed with revenge. He is not a very nice person. Maybe a touch loco'

'Yes and I can imagine how angry he will be, knowing that we were within his grasp'

'It continues to be very dangerous for you. We should talk. I suggest we meet tomorrow morning, the same arrangements as previously'

'Yes please, I'd like that. We need to figure out what our next moves are'

'That's settled then. Until tomorrow. Buenos días'

'Buenos días and thank you once again'.

22nd December 2018

CONNIE

Arriving slightly early at the ARTiSA café, Mike and I order coffee and await Maria. At precisely 10 o'clock she enters and greets us with a warm smile and a cheerful, 'Buenos días'. Alights on a chair and snaps her fingers to get the waiters attention, 'Un cafè negre si us plau'. Then looking directly at Mike and I she asks, 'How are you two? Well rested I hope?'

'Yes thank you, we certainly needed the sleep', I reply and Mike nods in agreement.

'Good, then it's straight down to business', Maria states firmly, 'It is so very dangerous for you here and in England, I think your best course of action is a pre-emptive strike'.

Mike, looking doubtful, says, 'OK, but what on earth can we do?'

Maria continues, 'The good news is that I have found an angle, or rather one of my sources has provided some useful intelligence. The bad news is that it will involve you in travelling to Algeria, and even then it may prove to be a fruitless mission'.

I'm taken aback and Mike's jaw has dropped, he splutters, 'But that sounds crazy, please explain'

Maria slightly impatiently, 'Of course, if you give me half a chance!' She continues, 'My source reports that Los Ghouls continue to traffic people, they have opened a new route from Mostaganem in Algeria to Carboneras in Spain. If you could infiltrate the people smugglers and then alert the authorities then all the bad people would be locked away for a very long time'

'You mean for the authorities to catch them in the act?'

'Yes, of course'

Mike interjects, 'This sounds a very risky endeavour!'

'Well yes, but then tell me what other options do you have?'

'Maria has a point Mike', I answer, and turning to Maria, 'If, and it is a very big 'If', if we take this course of action, then what are our next steps?'

'There is a flight from Barcelona to Algiers tomorrow, then a flight from Algiers to Oran. From Oran it is about one hour by road to Mostaganem. You will need to find Cafeteria L'adresse near the harbour, Port de Mostaganem and ask for Farook. They will get a message to him. The rest will be up to you.

I look at Mike, 'It sounds like a massive undertaking but what else can we do?'

Mike replied, 'There are so many unknowns, we will be taking a massive risk, but I agree, we have run out of options and are fast running out of time! So yes, let's do it! After all, what is the worst that can happen?', he laughs.

Keeping a straight face I turn to Maria, 'We'll do it, but what about the money to pay the people smugglers?'

Maria replies, 'Don't worry, I will provide the funds. If we can eliminate my rivals it will be worth it! I don't think you have a choice, but it has to be your decision. Please keep in touch. Good luck!' She passes a package across the table.

'Yes, I think we will need all the luck that we can muster!', I peer into the package and see a bundle of US dollar notes. 'Thank you for all your help and we hope to see you on our return. Please keep us in your prayers!'

'Yes of course! Thank you and adiós por ahora.', with that Maria stands up and leaves the café.

'Well Mike, we have a lot to think about. Firstly we need to book air travel, hopefully we can get on a flight. Then we need to pack some things, we need to work through our plans in detail. We will need some suitable 'local' clothing, so that we blend in in Algeria. We will need a credible back story too. I think the currency is the Dinar, we will need some of that too'

'OK Connie, I suggest that you book the flights online while I obtain the currency'

'Sounds good to me. We can develop our strategy whilst travelling. Oh my god, there is so much to think about!'

23rd December 2018

MIKE

After a hectic 24 hours Connie and I found ourselves on an Air Algérie Airbus A330 on our way, with just a change at Algiers onto a flight to Oran. With some trepidation we fleshed out our plans to infiltrate the human traffickers. We would pose as asylum seekers trying to escape a corrupt political system, where we are 'wanted' by the authorities.

After touching down at Oran we made our way out of the airport terminal and headed for the taxi rank. 'Do you speak English?', I asked the driver. 'A little', he replied. 'Can you take us to the shops please?' 'Yes, Medina Jdida, OK?' 'OK', we jump in and are on our way. Marche Medina Jedida is a massive, chaotic market that sells everything. Colourful stalls set up in a haphazard way and some traders with no stall at all, simply laying their wares on the ground! We soon find what we are looking for amongst the bargain clothes, I found a long robe or Thobe in a drab brown, Connie looked me up and down smirking.

'What?', I exclaimed, 'When in robes do what the robes-men do'.

'How droll', replied Connie dryly, before bursting out laughing. Connie chose a Chador or Burka that covered her head-to-toe. We both bought sandals too, disposing of the cheap plimsols that we had been wearing knowing that we would need to travel as light as possible. Having done our shopping we sampled the local delicacy, Kerentica, a cake made from chickpea flower and eggs, accompanied by a glass of mint tea. Suitably refreshed we found another taxi to transport us on to Mostaganem, approximately an hours ride away.

The taxi dropped us off on the Boulevard de la Salamandre, close to the ramshackle harbour, where we soon located the Cafeteria L'adresse. It had been a long day and the late sun warmed us as we seated ourselves at one of the outside tables. The waiter came over and I ordered coffees for both of us, trusting that the French influence would mean that they were half-decent. I added, 'And please tell Farook we are here'. At this the waiter looked startled and hesitated, then recovering he said, 'Oui Monsieur', turned and walked back inside. Two minutes later I could hear his muffled tones on the telephone.

Twenty minutes later a dusky individual with a scar across his left cheek arrived at our table. 'Hello. You prefer we speak English?', he asked in a heavy French accent. 'Yes please', I replied, we had already agreed that the man would do all the talking as is the custom in much of the Arab world. Farook sat down and asked, 'Where did you hear my name?'

'One of the camps', I replied, 'I understand that you can arrange our passage to Spain. We have our own reasons for not being able to go via official routes'.

'Do you have money?'

'Yes we can pay'

'OK, ten thousand US dollars each'

I had to stifle a gasp.

'You pay half now and half when we in Spain'

We had been expecting this, 'OK' I replied and put my hand in my bag.

In a hushed voice Farook quickly jumped in, 'Not here, not now. I give you directions'. He pulled out a biro and drew a crude map on a napkin. Farook continued, 'See we are here. The harbour is here. We meet in fishing hut, near fishing boats. See?'

'Yes thank you'

'We meet in two hours time, it will be dark then. OK?'

'OK'

'I go now. Au revoir'. With those few parting words Farook took off again.

Connie and I looked at each other, 'We don't seem any closer to our intended targets, do we?', I said. 'No', Connie replied, 'hopefully once in Spain we will be approached by the gang members and learn a lot more'. We ordered another coffee, knowing that it would be our last for several hours and then proceeded to the seafront to discuss various possible scenarios upon our arrival in Spain. 'They may simply want the money and leave us to our own devices', Connie articulated.

'Or try and extort even more money from us. I've heard of instances where they take your passport and force you to work for them to pay off the debt'

'Or they traffic us to another gang and we become their prisoners'

'Worse still, someone recognises us and, well, the end result isn't something to dwell upon!'

'No'. I felt I couldn't sit here any longer mulling over dark thoughts. So more brightly urged, 'Come on, times getting on, let's find that hut'.

So we made our way back towards the harbour and located the hut as per the napkin map.

Chapter 16 – Saharan Ordeal

MIKE

It was quite a large wooden hut, we entered to see about fifteen people huddled together looking decidedly apprehensive, all eyes turned in our direction. 'Hello', Connie said in a gentle tone, 'we are here to do the crossing'. The group visibly relaxed, 'Welcome', replied a wizened old man draped in robes and leaning on his staff. A young boy, around 13 or 14 years old, took a step forward and enquired, 'Are you English?' Is it that obvious? I thought. 'Yes and where are you from?', Connie answered

'Mali', the boy replied

'What is your name?, Connie continued the conversation

'Amadou'

'Are your parents here Amadou?' He looked crestfallen, for a moment he looked at the ground before replying, 'No, my parents are both dead. I will tell you my story'. Amadou commences with the tragic events that led up to the violent death of his parents. Connie and I listened with heavy hearts as Amadou continued.

AMADOU

'My brain was still trying to comprehend what had just happened, but slowly I realised that this was about survival. I quietly moved forward and scouted around to ensure that all the robbers had gone. Satisfied that the coast was clear I made my way to the henhouse and collected a few eggs, carefully stowing these in my rucksack. I also found a discarded plastic bottle and filled this with water from the well. Our house was still smouldering, but completely burnt out. One thought dominated my mind, I have to get away, as far as possible, these robbers could return at any time. So I started walking, I knew not where but in a northerly direction. I walked and I walked and I walked until I could walk no more even though the temperature was a comfortable twenty degrees. I dropped to the ground and cried myself to sleep.

When I came to, the sun was up and it already felt hot as I looked across the parched landscape. A few trees were dotted here and there, but otherwise it was parched grass, dirt and dust. In the distance I spotted a group of typical mud huts, complete with funny looking conical thatched roofs. Tentatively I made my way towards them. As I approached a child pointed at me and a shout went up. More children and two adults appeared, they were dressed in colourful tops, the boys in shorts, girls in skirts – and they were smiling. Phew! I was so relieved that they were friendly. They welcomed me and I explained my situation. I shared some of my eggs, while my hosts provided fufu and a thin vegetable soup. I stayed the rest of the day and night with them. It gave me a chance to think, to plan. I decided that there was nothing here for me, I would go to Europe, Spain, France and possibly even England! The next day I said goodbye to the charitable family and walked towards the main road. I was very apprehensive because the main road, as well as my escape route, would also be a highway for bandits. The villagers had told me to follow the river valley to Moribila. I wasn't too sure about the direction but I knew the main road was somewhere to the east. The river valley led me to the small town and the RN13 trunk road. I had decided to head to the Saharan city of Gao as I thought that this would provide the best chance of finding work. I desperately needed money for food and the journey. I had scrawled Gao on a scrap of cardboard and stood at the side of the road for what seemed an age, but eventually a car stopped and I was in luck. The driver was a middle-aged gentleman who introduced himself as Youssouf, a school teacher in Gao. He asked me my name and I replied,

'Amadou'

'Where are you from Amadou?'

'Sorobasso, near Koutiala'

'Why are you going to Gao?'

So I felt I had to explain what had happened.

Youssouf turned his head and said, 'That is truly awful! Why didn't you go to the authorities for help?'

'There is nothing left for me here', I replied with a heavy heart, 'I have made my decision, I am moving on. I hope to find work in Gao'

Youssouf went silent for a few minutes as he digested my words. Then, 'Where are you staying tonight?'

'I don't know but I'll find something', I lied knowing full well that without any money I would be sleeping on the streets.

'You could stay at my place, just while you sort things out. I have a spare room'

'That's very generous of you. Yes please, thank you'

'Well I couldn't allow you to fend for yourself. By the way, this is a long journey, about twelve and a half hours. So we'll stop for lunch and break up the journey. I'll buy you lunch as I guess that you haven't got much money'

'Thank you I am very grateful!'

It was dark when we drove into Gao. First impressions weren't good; dusty and dirty, with industrial debris strewn against the side of commercial buildings. There were lots of single storey flat roofed dwellings. Also the very poor living in makeshift shelters. Surprisingly there were street lights down the main roads. I could see a few trees dotted here and there. Eventually we pulled up outside a larger than average building built from concrete blocks and with its own courtyard. 'We're here!', said Youssouf smiling. We got out of his car and entered the building. Inside it was surprisingly bright and cheerful. Once Youssouf had unpacked the car he poured two glasses of water. This was most welcome after such a long drive in the heat of the day. I suddenly felt very tired and pleased when Youssouf showed me to my room. I lay on the bed and wondered what tomorrow might have in store for me, before a deep sleep claimed me.

The next morning I woke up feeling totally refreshed and went into the next room where Youssouf was sitting at the table eating his breakfast. 'Amadou come and join me', he said. I pulled up a chair and helped myself.

'Amadou I've been thinking about where you might find work. Your best bet is the Hotel Village Tizi-Mizi, which is the best hotel in Gao. They may have something; reception, cleaning or helping in the kitchen. How does that sound?'

'If I could get work there, that would be brilliant!'

'Would you like me to drop you off there on my way into school?'

'Yes please, but how do I get back?'

'I'll give you a street map. It will be about a forty-minute walk, but only about ten minutes in the car', he smiled

Youssouf stands, goes over to a chest of drawers and pulls out the street map. 'Look this is where we are now and this is Tizi-Mizi'. He marks both points.

'Yes I can find my way I'm sure, thank you'

'In that case it's time we set off'.

Ten minutes later I'm standing in a busy, dusty street opposite the hotel. Bicycles, mopeds and motorcycles are speeding past plus the occasional car or truck. I wait for a gap in the traffic and then make a dash across the road. The hotel is behind a high white wall, TIZIMIZI is written along the wall in large blue capital letters. Not knowing what sort of welcome I will receive, I enter the compound tentatively.

That evening I am pleased to announce to Youssouf that I've got a job! The owner was a nice man and offered me the nominal position of porter, but he stressed that I could expect to be called upon to do many duties! I said to Youssouf, 'The only thing is that I'm doing an evening shift five to eleven' Youssouf smiled, a big broad smile, 'Well that's perfect then because I asked the headteacher if he would allow you to attend lessons and he said "yes". I do think it is important that you continue with your education while you are here. What do you think?'
'I'm a bit surprised everything is falling into place for me, but yes please!'
'Super! I have spare pencils and a notebook you can have'
'Thank you again Youssouf, that is good of you'.

And that was that, my life was organised around school, work and sleep! Over the coming months that I stayed at Youssouf's I enjoyed his company. I paid for my keep and managed to make regular savings. In fact I stayed there for fourteen months before I was ready to move on. This was helped by the fact that the hotel had internet access and I was able to plan my route.

I'm leaving Gao, heading North towards Algeria and deeper into the Sahara Desert. Youssouf has kindly dropped me off at a service station on the RN18 highway, close to the Ferry Port. We hugged, I thanked Youssouf again and he wished me luck. He had previously lectured me on the possible dangers that I would be facing! He had even bought me a leaving present, a desert scarf, also known as a keffiyeh. This is worn around the head and neck to provide protection from the heat and sun in desert environments. It is also used to keep the head and face protected from dust and sandstorms. I stood on the service station forecourt with my cardboard inscribed 'Tessalit R18/R19', looking like a seasoned desert traveller. Nobody I approached would give me a lift, either they weren't going that far or they were suspicious of my motives. It was hot and dusty, I had been waiting for over an hour, then a large white pickup truck pulled in for fuel. I walked over to the two men and asked for a lift, they responded in Tamasheq, fortunately I knew a smattering and I was able to converse after a fashion. They asked me where I was going and why. When I replied in broken speech they seemed to find this funny, I don't know why, but anyway they offered me a lift. It was a four-seater, so I climbed into the back seat. As I settled down for the journey I spotted the passenger in the front of the vehicle had an AK-47 assault rifle with him! Should I be worried? I hope not, it's probably for his own protection, I thought trying to convince myself. There wasn't a lot I could do about it now as we were on the R18 heading North. The men said that they were going to Tessalit 'on business', but didn't divulge what sort of business. They planned to take two days, with a camping stop about halfway. They told me that Tessalit was a village commune built around an oasis, mostly populated by Tuaregs. They are Tuaregs too, a traditionally nomadic Berber people. So, thankfully, very at home in the Sahara Desert! Conversation was limited, so we fell silent, with just the constant drone of the engine for company for mile after mile after mile. I hadn't realised just how vast the Sahara Desert is, dust and sand giving way to a more mountainous region comprised mostly of sandstone. Often it seemed as though we were the only ones on the planet!

Finally we stopped to set up camp for the night. I then began to realise just how prepared the men were. In the back of the pickup they had very large cans of fuel and some of water. Also a stack of dry wood and kindling. They soon had a fire going, making unleavened bread and herbal tea. We sat around the fire and I felt a shared appreciation of the experience, although I did notice that the AK-47 was kept well within reach! It was quite dark now and the night sky was a mass of stars, as though someone had stitched a million diamonds onto a cosmic tapestry. I was thrown a heavy blanket and nodded my thanks, it was time to get my head down.

Just as dawn was breaking I woke full of sleep, but suddenly was aware of something moving under the blanket next to me. 'Snake! Snake! Snake!', the Tuareg shouted urgently. I shot out from under the blanket and then I saw it, a large, black rubber hosepipe being waggled by the other Tuareg. My face must have been a picture, as the Tuaregs doubled-up with laughter! However I soon forgave them as a mug of tea was thrust into my hand. Ground millet and water was made into a paste and heated. I was so hungry I gratefully ate every last morsel!

I noticed the wind had got up, whipping the dust into miniature tornadoes. I stood fascinated, watching them twist and grow or simply disappear. One of the Tuaregs nudged me and indicated me to hurry. So I quickly gathered my things together and headed for the truck. As I stepped up to get in, I glanced across the vast expanse of desert and that is when I first noticed it. In the distance, but fast approaching, was a sandy brown wall of dust, a tsunami of boiling sand particles! The Tuaregs had seen it too and indicated for me to immediately get in the truck. We wound up the windows and in a few minutes were completely enveloped in the dark cloud, the sun seemingly blotted out of existence. So we sat there, in semi-darkness and waited and waited for several hours for the dust storm to pass, although it seemed a lot longer as the time really dragged.

Eventually our journey resumed, mile after mile of unforgiving desert. I wouldn't want to be stranded out here! The monotonous sound of the engine in contrast to the silent vastness that surrounded us. My compatriots occasionally engaging in conversation with each other, but not involving me. Dusty and hot, hour after hour we made our way across the relentless landscape. So it was a relief when we stopped for a late lunch at a small oasis. Again they quickly made a small fire for unleavened bread and herbal tea. This was accompanied by tinned sweetcorn and tomatoes. To my surprise there were a few birds and insects at the oasis, as well as some very welcome shade from a few palm trees. Lunch over, I needed the toilet, one of the men produced a toilet roll and a lighter. He indicated that I should go behind a convenient rock a short distance away. Having completed my toilet I set fire to the toilet paper as the desert code is not to leave any rubbish behind. The pickup was refuelled from one of the large jerry cans and then we were on our way.

It was getting dark when we entered Tessalit. The pickup coming to a halt in a dusty square. I eased myself out of the truck as my limbs had stiffened up as a result of sitting so long in the confines of the vehicle. Looking around I could see crude sandy coloured walls and the occasional tree. A woman emerged from a nearby dwelling and embraced one of the men, then casting a glance in my direction, struck up a conversation with him. She then approached me speaking in a Berber dialect and shook my hand. She indicated for me to follow her into the dwelling and, despite the language barrier, made me feel most welcome. Ample food and tea were provided, which I consumed with the men only as they explained it is considered very rude to eat in front of a woman who is not your partner.

I had already decided on the next part of my route, across the border into Algeria to the city of Bordj Badji Mokhtar, named after the Algerian independence activist Badji Mokhtar. So I wrote this name down and showed it to the men, who nodded in recognition. 'Tomorrow', came back their single word reply. I was in luck! The next day we embarked upon a four-and-a-half-hour journey north. It was a testing journey in the heat of the day, a roasting forty-two degrees! After approximately four hours we passed over the border crossing at El Khalil, announced by a large sign that proclaimed 'Republique Algerienne, Democratique et Populaire'. A further half-an-hour saw us entering Bordj Badji Mokhtar. Again my travelling companions ensured that I was warmly welcomed and I spent a fairly comfortable night.

I woke early and decided to explore Bordj Badji Mokhtar. With a population of around twenty thousand it is considered a large town. I headed towards the centre as I wanted to purchase some sandals. I soon found the shops and made my purchase. Next I went into the Mokhtar Habib café and sat down with an espresso, my mind turning to a tricky problem, 'How do I get to Reggane? Six hundred and thirty kilometres away! At that moment a dusty, somewhat bedraggled, figure entered the café. His brown robes covered him head to toe, his weather-beaten face all that was showing. He ordered a coffee and then, turning to me, asked in French, 'Would you mind if I sat at your table?'. 'No, of course not', I replied in French.

'Thank you', he smiled revealing a mouth short of three front teeth, but his dark brown eyes sparkled. He introduced himself as Jarrah. He proceeded to question me on what was I doing in Mokhtar? Where is my family? Where was I going? Seemingly satisfied with my answers he proceeded to tell me that he was a trader who frequently crossed the border between Algeria and Mali. 'What do you trade?', I enquired. 'Oh this and that. Goods mainly', he grinned. 'So you are going to Reggane?'

'Yes, that's right'

'It's a good road to Reggane. And after Reggane?'

'Well, eventually I want to cross to Spain'

'I see', Jarrah scratched his chin as he pondered this news, before continuing, 'Maybe I can help you', he smiled, 'I have passengers I am transporting to the coast who are catching boat to Spain. They are migrants, like yourself, they make new life for themselves. Perhaps you would like to join them?'

'I don't know', I replied, 'How much would it cost?'

'You only little. I transport you to coast for free. Then you negotiate boat to Spain'

'Wow! What an offer!', I thought, 'Too good to turn down!' I couldn't believe my luck. 'I don't know what to say. I mean, thank you so much!' Little did I know then that Jarrah would earn a commission on my crossing fee!

'Come with me', Jarrah said, 'I show you transport'. We went outside and walked about one hundred metres down the street to the square where a well-worn Mercedes-Benz Zetros stood. An ex-military lorry, it had obviously taken a few knocks, however this four-by-four is extremely rugged and ideally suited to the Sahara. 'High kilometrage, so I got it at the right price. Very reliable, you can't afford to breakdown in the desert!'

I stood silent in awe for a moment. Suddenly the thought flashed across my mind, 'How on earth could this scruffy little man afford a vehicle like this? Even given that it was in quite a state! It was much later on that I discovered that Bordj Badji Mokhtar was renowned for banditry, drug smuggling and people trafficking!' Putting aside any last-minute reservations, 'Count me in!', I enthused

Jarrah grinned, a big ear-to-ear grin, 'Good choice'. Then, with a more serious face, 'We leave at nine a.m. sharp. It is a nine-hour journey to Reggane. 'Don't be late!'.

At nine prompt I was back at the square. I was surprised to see about twelve people climbing on board the back of the truck. I guess it showed in my face, because a still dusty Jarrah swept towards me, 'Don't worry my friend, you will ride up front in the cab with me. I like your company'. So with no further hesitation I too climbed onboard.

The six-cylinder, 428hp engine growled into life and we were off. In no time at all we had left civilisation behind and were steadily eating up the kilometres across a largely empty desert. I have to admit, I did nod off to sleep a couple of times. The desert can be quite monotonous at times!

We had been going for around five hours, when suddenly two white pick-up trucks appeared, seemingly out of nowhere. As they drew closer I could make out gunmen sitting in the back. The trucks closed in and the lead truck positioned itself immediately in front of us and started to slow. Simultaneously the other truck drew alongside our drivers window and gestured for us to stop. Despite the heat a cold shiver of fear swept over me. What did these gunmen want with us?

Perspiration peppered my brow and festered there as multiple scenarios raced through my mind. With AK47's pointed at us, we had no option but to do as we were told! Our transport quickly came to a halt. At this juncture I was shaking with fear. One of the gunmen, who I assumed was their leader, conversed with Jarrah. They argued, about what exactly I don't know, but the upshot was that we all had to disembark. They indicated that we move away from the vehicle. They seemed impatient, as I felt the hard nozzle of the gun thrust into the side of my ribs. Our little group quickly moved to where they wanted us. The gunmen attempted to converse with each person in turn, mostly with little success. They wanted to see our documents, or at least for those of us who had documents. Eventually they had finished 'processing' us and then surrounded Jarrah. Somewhat surprisingly Jarrah didn't appear at all intimidated. A further argument ensued, and then I observed Jarrah handing some money over. This seemed to satisfy the gunmen, who with no more ado, jumped back into their trucks and disappeared into the desert. Once again our party boarded and we are on our way, severely shaken but thankful that we are still alive!

It was dark when, approximately five hours later, we arrived in Reggane, pulling up outside a rundown looking building. We soon learnt that this was to be our accommodation for the night and we had to pay, of course. Exhausted from the journey I gratefully accepted a mattress on the floor and was soon enveloped by a deep sleep.

At 6 a.m. the next day an agitated Jarrah was rousing the party. He seemed to be in a bad mood. Once we had commenced our journey, I spoke to him, 'Jarrah you seem out of sorts today. Has something upset you?'

'Yes, the French', he replied

'Please explain'

'In the 1960s the French conducted nuclear tests in Reggane. The tests contaminated the Saharan desert with plutonium, as well as exposing more than ten thousand people to radioactive fallout. I believe France conducted sixteen tests in Algeria with an estimated 27,000 to 60,000 people affected'

'That is horrific!', I exclaimed with dismay.

'Yes, in my view it is a crime against humanity. Even today I understand only one Algerian has received any compensation from the French government. Now do you see why I am angry?'

'Yes, it is understandable. I hadn't heard about this before'

'So not on your precious BBC World Service then?', Jarrah said sarcastically

I looked at my feet. I couldn't think of an appropriate reply. After a moment or two Jarrah spoke more kindly, 'I'm sorry, I shouldn't take my feelings out on you. None of this is your doing.' Another pause and then, 'I will be glad to see the back of this place. Too many bad memories.' I wanted to know what Jarrah was eluding too, but felt I had better let the matter drop for now. It was obviously a very sensitive subject for him.

The journey continued, sometimes the terrain was more mountainous, which although slower, was at least more interesting. Occasionally we would pass through a small town on the N6 such as Adrar, Tsabit and Kerzaz. It was still rather monotonous, but I'd had an interesting conversation with Jarrah telling him about my home and the tragic loss of my parents. He'd reciprocated, telling me that he grew up in Reggane. His father had been a soldier in the French army but had died from the effects of the radioactive fallout. His mother had been rendered infertile for the same reason and later died from leukaemia. Consequently Jarrah doesn't have any brothers or sisters. These conversations were all rather depressing and so we lapsed back into silence.

Another four hours and we arrived in the city of Béchar. Wow! With a population approaching 200,000 I've never been to a city this large! Mains sewage, drinking water, electricity and a university – all mod cons! Jarrah says we are staying here for a whole day in order to break up the journey and take on supplies. Although there are ten hotels, we have put up a large tent for our sleeping quarters and to provide some relief from the hot sun. The Oued Béchar river runs through the city, helping to ensure that there is plenty of greenery around. I'm really looking forward to exploring the city tomorrow.

I wake and for a moment struggle to remember where I am. I rub my eyes and the sleeping dust falls away. The dust, the dust! It gets everywhere and into everything! The sun is up, I can't wait to get out and explore Béchar. I rise and put my robes on, not forgetting the keffiyeh that Youssouf had given me. I start the long walk into town and am surprised to see row upon row of date palms. I look around and further afield I can see the rocky highlands of Djebel Béchar. I walk briskly as the temperature is a very chilly 10 degrees centigrade, although this is likely to climb to 17 or beyond on this December day. As I get closer to town I pass fig and almond trees plus a farm with sheep and goats. I enter the outskirts and pass by housing, a clinic and school. Further on I marvel at La Grande Mosquée de Béchar, its sweeping arch-like architecture complimented by its towering minaret. Eventually I make my way to the tourist area where I have lunch, do some people watching, before making my way to the river and then back to the tent. Arriving there late afternoon, Jarrah sought me out, 'We go early tomorrow, 08:00 hours, just before sunrise. Make sure you are up and ready, as we have a full day of travel ahead of us'.

'Don't worry, I'll be there. I have too much to lose to miss the ride'.

'OK, sleep well my friend'. With that he disappeared to finish his preparations for the journey.

Someone is shaking me awake, through the gloom I can just about recognise Jarrah. 'Wake up! Wake up! It is time we went', Jarrah urged.

'What time is it?', I managed to say, trying to shake off the vestiges of a deep slumber.

'About 7:20 sleepy head', Jarrah said finishing with a chuckle. A yawn was my only response. Once again I gathered my few belongings together and managed to grab a cup of hot herbal tea that some kind soul had warming on the fire outside the tent. By eight o'clock we were on the road again. Ahead of us was roughly a seven hundred-kilometre, nine-hour drive, including crossing the Saharan Atlas Mountains! So off we went up the N6 for over four hundred kilometres, thankfully we stopped for a short break at Aïn Séfra, then El Kheither for lunch. Then on the N109/N13 for one hundred and fifty-three kilometres to Sidi Bel Abbès. Although the journey really dragged at times, the Atlas Mountains made it much more interesting such that the remainder of our journey to Mostaganem, another one hundred and twenty-seven kilometres was picturesque, - if not a bit scary!

It was a little after sunset that Jarrah announced that we had arrived. We all disembarked close to the harbour where we were met by a somewhat furtive looking man who introduced himself as Farook. He seemed to be the organiser and handed over a brown paper bag to Jarrah. They had a brief conversation in French before shaking hands and parting company. Jarrah turned to the assembled group and with a smile bid us all, 'Bon voyage'. We thanked Jarrah and wished him a safe journey back. Farook then led us down to this harbourside hut, so here we are!'

23rd December 2018

CONNIE

Amadou sighed. 'So that is my story. Not a very happy one I'm afraid.'

'Oh! That's dreadful! I'm so sorry for your loss', I said

'Thank you. So now I plan to start a new life'

Smiling and meaning it, I hugged Amadou 'I wish you the very best of luck'.

For the first time a half smile played on Amadou's lips. 'Thank you, I am very determined'

'Your English is very good. Did you have a teacher?'

'No, I helped in the kitchen and listened to the BBC World Service on the radio. I learnt from that'

'Well that's amazing! You have done very well. You must have a natural aptitude for languages'

'I also speak French and Bambara, plus some Arabic'

'Wow! That is very impressive. Where are you heading to?'

'I'm hoping to reach London. I hear the streets are paved with gold!', Amadou replied with a wink and a cheesy grin. He continued, 'What's your story? What led you here?'

By now most of the group had lost interest in us, but we daren't disclose anything that would put us at risk, so I answered, 'It's a long story and one I'm afraid will have to wait for another day. However, I can assure you that we haven't done anything illegal'. I felt a bit awkward not being able to be open with Amadou. So I rummaged around in my bag and pulled out a small chocolate bar which I offered to Amadou. Amadou gratefully accepted it and dispatched in short-time!

Just at that moment, the door swung upon and Farook entered, he glanced around the room before asking, 'Is everyone ready?' in both English and French. Without waiting for an answer he continued, 'Have your money ready. Payment time'. He then proceeded to collect money from the assembled group.

Leaving the hut our group made its way to the quayside. Farook pointed at our designated craft, 'Be careful getting onto the RIB. One at a time please'. I whispered to Mike, 'What's a RIB?' Mike replied, 'Rubber Inflatable Boat'
'Oh'
'Not exactly an ocean-going craft!'
Already seated in the boat was a swarthy Arab with missing teeth and a crooked smile. His dirty hands grasping one end of the rope that wound round the quayside capstan before returning to a tying point on the boat. It was dark now and the

inadequate harbour lighting glimmered off the rippling water. One by one we cautiously boarded the boat and took a seat wherever possible – it was rather crowded!

The last person stepped aboard and found a small space to sit on the floor of the boat. Farook helped remove the tethered rope from the capstan, crossed himself and muttered, 'Bon voyage'. Our skipper gathered the rope in, grasped the tiller and the boat edged out into the harbour. Upon reaching the harbour entrance the noise from the engine increased and the boat sped forward, lurching up and over the swell. There were some unhappy faces around, I guess most people had never been to sea before.

Chapter 17 – Sea legs

MIKE

Some hours passed by and the monotony was only broken by the skipper refilling the fuel tank. It was decidedly uncomfortable, there was hardly any room to move our limbs, the constant drone of the motor and several people were now being sick over the side. In contrast to conditions in the harbour, a wind had got up and the swell intensified. The sound from the outboard motor decreased in volume as we climbed up a wave and increased as we accelerated down the other side. Spray was beginning to penetrate our clothes, adding to our discomfort. What had been a beautiful starry night, lit overhead by a multitude of twinkling jewels, had turned into a black darkness as storm clouds built overhead. Ominously, I could now hear the rumble of thunder! I squeezed Connie's hand to reassure her.

CONNIE

I was losing track of time because my very real concern was for our safety. Mike held my hand. The storm was now directly overhead, crashing thunder and lightning every few minutes. Suddenly another flash, striking the sea seemingly within metres of our position. The light illuminating the grimly terrified faces of all on board. The boat appears to be making very little headway as the waves are enormous. We are shipping water! Some of us are trying to bail out the water, using whatever comes to hand, boots, bags and even plastic sandwich boxes. Desperate measures indeed but all to no avail. For just then a colossal wave hit, flipping the RIB over. The motor cuts out. Everyone is in the water! A few manage to hold on to the boat. Mike and I have lifejackets but unfortunately there weren't quite enough to go round! Another flash of lightening and I spot Amadou metres away, his arms flailing as he desperately tries to stay afloat. Oh my god, he doesn't have a lifejacket! I'm a strong swimmer, I strike out in his direction. Try as I might I'm not making any progress, the sea is sucking me back! Another flash, 'Where is Amadou?', in the chaos I no longer have sight of him! I turn around, my eyes desperately searching in every direction, flashes permitting. I can see Mike and some of the others in the water holding on to the boat which they are attempting to turn upright. It's almost impossible in this wind, as they try to lift it the wind forces it back down. However they persevere with their attempts. 'Amadou! Amadou!', I call in desperation. 'Amadou! Amadou!', I call again, but the words become lost on the wind. Fearing the worst, but not wanting to acknowledge the sickening tragedy that is unfolding. I keep looking and hoping, for how long it is impossible to tell. Meanwhile the RIB has been righted, the skipper has the tiller and a flashlight. I can just about make out Mike with an oar in hand paddling his way towards me. Soon I am being pulled aboard, but several people are missing, so we search the immediate area as best

291

we can. We manage to retrieve three people, all wearing life jackets. With the deepest sorrow there is no sign of Amadou, my heart aches. 'We can't leave, we must keep looking!', I plead with the skipper. He looks at me blankly, I think he doesn't understand. I try again, this time in French, 'On ne peut pas partir, il nous manqué encore des gens'. I have his attention, his eyes lock onto mine, he shouts in order to be heard above the noise of the wind and the waves, 'Nous devons y aller ou nous allons manquer de carburant!' I gather that we could run out of fuel, the implications of which are unthinkable! A wave of despair sweeps through my body, I don't want to leave but we must leave! I shake all over from a mixture of shock and interminable sadness. Mike and I cling to each other, the tears pouring down our faces. If only I'd realised Amadou hadn't got a life jacket, I would have gladly surrendered mine.

Eventually the storm subsides and after giving the motor some attention, the skipper manages to get it started. All of us are wet and bedraggled, but with a heavy heart we are on our way.

24th December 2018

CONNIE

As dawn breaks we are approaching the Spanish coast. I'm grateful that we have survived, but feeling dreadful shivering with cold, in shock and mourning Amadou. Our skipper appears to know where he is and we simply track the coastline for an hour or so. Eventually he turns the boat towards a beach on the edge of a small village. We land, cold to the core and thoroughly exhausted. The skipper indicates for us all to follow him and we make our way to a small café. He wants us to wait outside, which is met with groans and under breath mutterings. The skipper reappears and gestures for us to go inside. Apparently he knows the proprietor as towels and blankets are provided. An electric fire is on and steaming hot cups of coffee are thrust into our shaking hands. Most of us have lost our few possessions but thank goodness for bum-bags, we have some cash, bank card and thankfully our passports. We are able to purchase some pastries! The skipper informs the group in French that a minibus is on its way to pick us up. With some trepidation Mike and I wonder what is in store for us now!

Chapter 18 – Out of the Frying Pan and into the Fire

CONNIE

The minibus has arrived, we climb onboard. The driver says, in Spanish, 'I am Paulo. Prepare for a long drive, we are going to Barcelona'. Mike and I look at each other, we hadn't expected this! Paulo resumes his seat, starts the engine and we're off down the dusty, windswept coastal road. Twenty minutes later we are on the autopista accompanied by the steady drone of the engine. 'Mike', I say, 'I'm really worried, we just don't know what is ahead of us. We are, effectively, Paulo's prisoners!'

Mike responds, 'I agree, you hear stories of refugees being tricked into 'owing' money to a gang and being made to work to pay off the debt. It is another form of extortion'.

'I hope that this isn't going to be our fate then! I don't know how much more of this I can take. I keep thinking about poor Amadou. Oh Mike it's so awful!' Tears start to run down my cheeks.

'Yes I've been thinking about him too. It's dreadful. Such a nice young man, and so intelligent too. What would the future have held for him? We will never know'.

'If only we could have done more for him. Found him a lifejacket from somewhere or grabbed hold of him when the RIB turned over'.

'Don't torture yourself. Unfortunately life is full of 'what ifs' and 'buts', but no one can turn the clock back. We must try not to dwell on it too much, we must stay positive'.

'You're right of course, yet I'm determined Amadou won't be forgotten. I will think of some way to commemorate his passing.'

For a while the conversation lapsed into silence, while Mike and I are lost in our thoughts. Then Mike started again, 'What are we going to do about our situation? We should have at least a semblance of a plan'.

'I've been thinking', I paused, 'The minibus is bound to stop somewhere on route, for fuel or a break. We could make a run for it perhaps?'

'Umm, that sounds a bit hit and miss. What would we do then? It doesn't get us any closer to our objective, which is seeing the demise of the Los Ghouls gang'.

'In that case we have no option other than to stay with the minibus and hope we can elude our captors somehow in Barcelona. Needless to say this will be very dangerous as someone is sure to recognise us!'.

'What do you suggest we do then Connie to negate the risk? After all you're the Project Manager!', Mike said with a smile.

'Oh shut up Mike. It may not seem like it, but we have got some significant resources available to us. We are fit, intelligent and we have the element of surprise. We are in disguise to some degree, what with our robes and you have several days beard growth'.

'OK, but what's the plan?'

'When we get to Barcelona, we must gather as much information about the gang's activities as we can and at the first opportunity take this to the police'.

'Hmm', Mike scratches his chin, 'Not much of a plan'.

'Well, I'm afraid it's all we've got!', I say abruptly, not taking any offence.

All our adrenaline had dissipated, replaced by utter exhaustion. The minibus eats up the miles to the constant buzz of the engine, which soon lulls us both into a fitful sleep.

It is early evening when we arrive in Barcelona. The minibus pulls up outside a large warehouse, immediately several sour-faced men appear and direct the minibus occupants into the warehouse. Mike and I ensured that our robes at least partially covered our faces, we did not want to be recognised! Once inside we could see just how large it is. Most of the floor area was a factory populated with sewing machines and packaging. At the far end there was an accommodation area, I use the term 'accommodation' lightly as it consists mainly of paillasses for sleeping on plus a few basic refectory tables. Against the wall is a food preparation area and four kitchen sinks. We later found out that these double up as washing facilities!

Thankfully there are separate toilet blocks. At the other end of the warehouse is a mezzanine floor that is accessed via an industrial metal staircase, this also provides access to an office with large windows that gives a good view of the whole area. Several men were moving around inside the office. With a sudden shock I recognised one in particular, one that had been haunting my recent nightmares, it was Carlos Garcia! I urgently grabbed Mike's arm and whispered, 'Don't look now but I've just seen Carlos through the office window! Whatever happens he mustn't recognise us'

'No, that's the last thing we need. We would be completely at his mercy!', came Mike's hushed reply.

We are directed to the 'accommodation area' and told to sit around the tables. One of the sour-faced men; big, burly, unshaven with a pistol shoved in his waistband, addressed us in Spanish, 'Bienvenidos,', he grinned displaying his black and missing teeth, 'son mis invitados, pero deben pagar por mi ayuda y alojamiento. Asi que mañana trabajas. Pero ahora cenamos.' His associate, a scrawny rat-faced individual translated in broken English 'Welcome. You are my guests, you pay for my help and accommodation. So tomorrow you work. Now we eat'. They cast their eyes over the assembled group, looking for any queries or dissent. A murmur went through the assembled group, but no questions were raised, everyone was too exhausted to argue. We guessed the big man was in charge and he barked out his orders before retreating to the office. Almost immediately two women appeared carrying plates of bread, cheese, salad and potato omelette. Plastic 'glasses' are also provided so that we can help ourselves to tap-water.

Upon seeing the food Mike and I discovered that we felt ravenously hungry. The food, although very basic, is adequate. 'Mike', I whispered, 'We appear to be captive'. 'Yes', he replied, 'But I don't think we can do anything about our situation right now'.
'I agree, we need to better understand the lie of the land. Let's see what tomorrow has in store for us'.
'It would be good to know how many people are involved and what their role is. Then perhaps we can plan our escape'.
'Shush! Keep your voice down Mike!', I urged as one or two of our group started looking in our direction. 'We can't be too careful!'
Finishing our meal, we then use the facilities before settling down for the night.

25th December 2018

CONNIE

I hadn't slept very well and awoke early shivering from the cold. I turn over to see if Mike is awake and he is. 'Mike, do you realise it's Christmas day?' Mike grinned, 'Happy Christmas!'

'Happy Christmas, but I'm afraid I haven't got you a present!'

Mike laughed, 'Well that's lucky because I haven't got you one either!'

Soon the others are stirring, some weighing up their situation and chatting with their neighbours. A few make their way to the facilities, such that they are, to carry out early morning ablutions. Half an hour later the two women appear carrying trays of pa amb tomàquet as it is known in Catalonia, or tomatoes on toast as we know it! I am thankful that steaming hot coffee is made available too. In fact it's when one of the women offer me a refill of coffee, that something strange occurred, she slips me a note and a finger to her lips indicates that I need to keep it secret! I drink my coffee, not too hurriedly as I didn't want to raise any suspicions and then make my way to the toilet. The note reads as follows:

"*Estimada Connie, we have been watching these premises and pleased you have made it. I have contacted the Policía and they will raid the premises at 5 pm. It will be very dangerous, so go out the fire escape on the harbourside of the building. I will be waiting. Maria*".

I flush the note down the toilet, then go back to where Mike is sitting and whisper the news. Mike gives me a puzzled look, 'What? Our escape will be fraught with difficulties! Look, the fire exit is on the mezzanine, near to the office. We'll be seen!'

'We'll have to take that risk, I don't think we have any other option', I replied

'It's not going to work Connie'

'We will have to make it work Mike. Hopefully there will be much confusion and nobody will notice us'

'Sorry, but I'm not convinced'

'I'm not going to argue with you Mike. I think the bigger risk is remaining down here, potentially sitting ducks!'

With a resigned look, Mike shrugs his shoulders, 'I suppose so'.

Just then the big man reappeared together with the scrawny one. They give out instructions, the 'workforce' is split into groups to do different jobs. The first group is shown how to cut out the material to make a rucksack. The second group how to operate sewing machines. As well as making the rucksack, their task is to sew drugs, in tablet form, into the rucksack straps. Mike and I were placed in the third group who put the finished rucksacks into individual plastic bags, then box up ten rucksacks at a time, ready for dispatch. Soon the warehouse reverberates to the sound of sewing machines whirring away. By lunchtime everyone has got the hang of things, apart from two people who are nursing injuries. Occasionally the big man would reappear and review the work, he seems quite pleased with the progress being made!

It is approaching five o'clock. Mike and I nervously wait, steeling ourselves for what is sure to come. Work has finished for the day as all the rucksack material has been used up. The others are sitting around chatting or resting on the paillasses. Without making it look too obvious, we wait expectantly with half an eye on the main door. Suddenly the main door bursts open with a loud clatter. Two figures, all in black, throw in smoke grenades. Confusion reigns! The two figures beckon the people by the main door to hurriedly exit that way, but before more than a handful could go through, several people rush out of the office firing pistols and one of them is Carlos! The figures in black retreat, whilst the pistol bearing gang members rapidly made their way down the stairs. By this time most people have moved away from the main door and fled to the far side of the accommodation area where they cower in terror. The smoke quickly blankets the whole warehouse, an acrid fog that catches in your throat. 'Move! Quickly now Mike, this is our chance', I urge, coughing and spluttering as we go. The smoke, punctuated by flashes, is now so dense that we can only just about see where the stairs are! We make our way to the stairs as bullets ricochet around, a few hitting the metalwork with a resounding 'zing'. A terrific firefight is getting underway. Up the stairs as fast as we can go, although it is getting hard to distinguish anything at all! 'Zing', another bullet ricochets off the stairs. 'I'm hit!', Mike shouts in alarm and stumbles onto the stairs. I stop dead in my tracks and turn back. I ask, 'Oh my god, are you ok?'

'Yes, I think so', replies Mike clutching his arm.

'Are you able to continue?'

'Yes', says Mike regaining his feet.

Finally we reach the fire exit and burst through, the welcoming fresh air hits my lungs. Mike right behind me, we descend the external fire escape as fast as we can. Mike spots it first, 'Look', he points at a sleek speedboat with Maria at the wheel that is heading directly towards our position on the quayside. The speedboat stops just below us, motor still running, 'Quick, get in the boat', Maria implores, gesturing with one arm. 'I'll go first', I say and with no hesitation jump into the boat. 'Now you Mike', Mike jumps and the boat rocks madly as he falls on the deck. Maria hit the throttle, the engine roars, and with a massive sense of relief, we are underway! I examine Mike's wound, apart from a lot of blood there doesn't seem to be too much damage. I tie Maria's scarf tightly around the arm to stem the bleeding.

Ten minutes later we are a good distance away from the action where the police, equipped with night-vision goggles, are winning the fight. 'Thank you so much Maria, you have saved our lives!' Mike enjoined, 'Yes thank you Maria, we'll be forever grateful'. Maria replied with a smile, 'My pleasure, but you have been very lucky!' She continues, 'I think that this is the end for Los Ghouls gang. Their enterprise is in pieces, key players arrested or dead. Of course the police will need statements from you both. I looked at Mike, 'I'm more than happy to provide a statement if it means that this nightmare is finally over!'

Mike exclaimed with feeling, 'I agree, one hundred percent!' Maria pronounced, 'My car is nearby. Mike let's move you to hospital straightaway to get your wound attended to. I can wait and take you to the police station later if you would like me to?'

'Yes please', Mike responded and sighed, 'What a way to spend Christmas!', adding, 'As the great bard once wrote, "All's well that ends well"'. I pulled Mike to me and hugged him. 'You idiot', I said laughingly. Mike and I had survived, and our future was looking much rosier than it had of late. Over the next couple of days we gave our statements and learnt that Carlos had been killed in the firefight. While we didn't want anyone else to lose their life, we couldn't help feeling a massive sense of relief! At last the nightmare is over!

Later we retrieved the few belongings we had left in Barcelona and booked a farewell dinner with Maria in order to thank her properly. On Maria's recommendation we went to a lavish restaurant. The food was delicious, especially when accompanied by some excellent Spanish wines! As we relax after the meal I ask Maria, 'How did you end up running your, er, enterprise?'

Maria replied, 'That is a long story. Maybe for another time'

'Oh no', Mike interjected, 'Please, there may not be another time. Please tell us about yourself'

'Yes please do!', I enthused

'Okay, since you insist', Maria smiled, 'I will start at the beginning'.

We listened with a mixture of horror and amazement as Maria relayed her story. She was a child, a thirteen year old when Kylo locked her in the cellar.

Chapter 19 – Maria's Trials and Tribulations

"I heard the key in the lock and the cellar door swung open. Kylo entered carrying a tray with a glass, jug of water and la pataqueta. He placed the tray on the floor. I cried out, 'You can't keep me here! Let me go!'. Kylo sternly replied, 'No chance. Think yourself lucky that I have brought you this. So stop your whining bitch!'. With that he turned and made his way back the way he had come. I'm sorry to say that was the pattern for the next few days. It was a horrible existence. However I didn't entirely waste my time, I kept fit by exercising and also planned my escape.

On the fifth day of my captivity I was standing in the corner when Kylo entered the cellar. The moment he bent down to put the tray on the floor, I seized the opportunity. I'd been hiding the rustic terracotta jug behind my back. In one venomous swift movement I raised it up above my shoulders and brought it crashing down on Kylo's head! He didn't stand a chance! He crashed to the floor, I'd knocked him out cold, the contents of the tray scattered across the floor. Kylo lay there unmoving, a trickle of blood emerging through his straggly hair. I held the glass close to his mouth, where much to my relief, faint condensation formed. Reassured that I hadn't killed him, I quickly escaped into the night. As I mentioned before I'd had time to plan my escape and decided to seek refuge in the abbey, Santa Maria de Vallbona de les

Monges. Marta had told me all about this famous institution run by Cistercian nuns and I hoped to be the grateful recipient of their compassion. The only problem then was that the abbey is about 115km away! With little money, I had decided to walk. Along the way I begged for food and slept in barns, it was very cold at night so I stole some extra clothing off washing lines.

It was dusk when four days later I found myself at the front door of the abbey, bedraggled, weak with hunger and on the point of collapse. I knocked upon the studded door, but no one came. I had a stout stick, a fallen branch, that I had picked up in the woods and I took it in both hands. As feeble as I felt I knocked the thickest end into the door, 'Bang, bang, bang!' After a minute or two I heard the bolts being drawn back and the heavy door swung open. 'Who is it that makes such a rumpus at this time in the evening?', scolded an elderly nun, 'You girl are interrupting Vespers!'
'I am very sorry but I have nowhere else to go. I have been abused and walked all the way from Barcelona to get here', I replied. The extra effort of which caused me to faint right there on the steps before the door. The elderly nun turned and called for help. Other Sisters came running. They carried me in and laid me on a very plain bed in the infermeria. I came to with smelling salts wafting up my nostrils. The Sisters, looking

very concerned, gathered around the bed. Mother Teresa was the first to speak, 'How do you feel now?'

'Better thanks, I don't want to be any trouble'

'What is your name girl?'

'Maria López Señorita'

'You may call me Mother Teresa', the nun said smiling kindly. She pointed in turn at each of the other nuns, 'This is Sister Flora, Sister Beatrice and Sister Carmen. They will help look after you. Are you hungry Maria?'

'Yes I'm famished', I answered

'Sister Carmen, get some soup and bread for our guest'

'Yes, I'm on my way', came the deferential reply from Sister Carmen, and she disappeared in the direction of the kitchen. Mother Teresa, who was obviously in charge, then addressed Sister Beatrice, 'Once Maria has had her supper, I'd like you to show her to the bathroom and run her a bath please'

'It would be my pleasure', Sister Beatrice answered

'Sister Flora, thank you for your assistance but please go about your usual duties'. 'Now Maria, please tell us what led you to find the path to our door?'

So I told her what had befallen me, while Mother Teresa looked very concerned and only occasionally interjected with a question. When I'd finished Mother Teresa looked thoughtful before saying, 'You obviously need a place of safety, some respite from the evils of this world. You are very welcome to stay here'

'Yes please that would be wonderful!', I gratefully enthused

'Well that's settled then', and Mother Teresa gave me a big hug.

Sister Carmen returned with a bowl of steaming vegetable broth which I consumed in double quick time. It felt so good to have something substantial in my stomach once more. After I'd had my bath I returned to the bed in the infermeria, it wasn't long before I was subsumed by a deep sleep.

The next day Sister Carmen roused me from my sleep, 'Good morning Maria'. 'Good morning Sister Carmen', I replied.

'I have found you some clean clothes', and she laid them across the foot of the bed

'Thank you', I smiled, then, 'What time is it please?'

'Just after seven. We thought it best to leave you sleeping awhile, although I have been up since five thirty'

'What do you do here?', I asked

'Mostly I work in the kitchen and the garden, that is when I'm not praying!', she giggled, 'I am a novice you see'

'How old are you then?'

'Seventeen. How old are you?'

'Fourteen. I had my birthday while I was walking here. No-one to wish me Happy Birthday but I had my freedom'.

'Only fourteen and already you have suffered so much. Mother Teresa told us. Sorry I don't mean to pry. I will help you to feel comfortable here'

'You're very kind, thank you'

'Now, I must go about my other duties. We'll talk again later', and she left the infermeria.

I got dressed, then unsure what else to do sat on the bed. I didn't have to wait very long before Sister Flora came bustling in, 'Good morning Maria', she said cheerfully, 'I'm glad to see you up and dressed. Everything here revolves around our prayers. Matins, Lauds and Vespers being the main ones, although often there are a few others to fit in. So you see, we have a very structured day!'

I asked, 'How do you know when to go to pray?'

'Oh that's easy, the bell is rung to alert us. We drop what we are doing immediately'

'So you don't need watches?'

'No', she laughed, 'just good hearing when I'm in the garden!' She paused, 'Right young lady, let me have a look at those bruises please'. Sister Flora rubbed a white ointment onto the bruises on my face, arm and legs. When she had finished she stood back and with a satisfied expression said, 'There, that will help. Now how would you like some breakfast?'

'Oh yes please, I'm feeling so hungry again'

'Well in that case you had better follow me sharpish'.

I followed her through a series of corridors until we reached a door with the word 'refectori' printed on it. 'In here', stated Sister Flora as she pushed open the door. We entered a large, well lit room, with a multi-arched ceiling in pale-yellow stone.

There were perhaps thirty trestle tables neatly arranged in the room. Many seats were occupied and the nuns looked up, curious to see who had thrust themselves upon them. At that moment Mother Teresa stood up and immediately complete silence enveloped the room, 'Allow me to introduce Maria López. She will be staying with us for some time. Please make her very welcome'. With that she sat down again. Most of the nuns nodded in agreement, before the murmur of conversation gently swelled once more. Sister Flora ushered me to the cafeteria style serving area where I was able to make my selection before taking a seat.

During the day I was shown all the facilities including the kitchen, laundry, sewing room, washing facilities and garden, not forgetting the monastic chapel! Later I was taken to the dormitory where a bed had been allocated to me, together with a bedside locker. It would all take a bit of getting used to!

The following morning Mother Teresa sat down with me.
'Maria how do you feel today?'
'Much better thank you. My bruises aren't troubling me either'
'Good. You are a brave girl. How are you settling in here?'
'Very well I think. Everyone has been most kind-hearted'
'Excellent. We would all like you to stay if that is what you want. You would work for the Sisters, mostly in the laundry, kitchen and garden. How does that sound?'

'I'd like that very much thank you'

'Well that's settled then', Mother Teresa smiled, 'I'll send Sister Carmen to fetch you. You can work alongside her and she'll show you the ropes. Happy?'

'Yes thank you. I like Sister Carmen'

'I'll speak with you again this evening just to see how things have gone today'. With no more ado Mother Teresa went about the business of the day.

From that day forward work, rest and play settled into a routine. To be honest there wasn't much time for play, but I'll not complain. All the Sisters were considerate towards me. Sister Carmen and I got on like a house on fire! Sometimes we were a bit naughty, making fun of or doing impressions of some of the nuns before dissolving into fits of laughter. Occasionally we were spotted by one of the Sisters, then a stern look and a raised eyebrow was sufficient to quell our revelry!

Unfortunately things took a turn for the worse after I'd been at the abbey for about five weeks. I woke up one morning feeling sick. In haste I rushed to the bathroom and only just made it in time! A deluge of vomit hit the white porcelain! Sister Flora was nearby and heard me. When I had finished being sick I washed my face and swilled my mouth out with water. Sister

Flora asked, 'Whatever is the matter Maria? Have you got an upset stomach?'

'No, well yes, maybe', I continued, 'I've never felt like this before'

'Oh, we had better get the doctor in to examine you'

'If you like', I said somewhat reluctantly.

The next day the doctor came in to examine me. I had been sick again. When he had finished he said, 'You don't have a temperature, no rashes, your stools are normal. No one else in the abbey is showing any signs of sickness. Do you think you could be pregnant?'

I looked at him shocked, 'What!', I thought, 'surely that is impossible!' Then the penny dropped, that nasty beast Kylo! I began to panic, would the nuns throw me out? I have very little and nowhere else to go! 'Doctor', I spoke quietly, my voice shaking, 'Yes it is possible, I have been raped!' The doctor raised his eyebrows, 'You poor thing', he sympathised and reached out to hold my hand. 'I will need to tell Mother Teresa, but I'm sure she will act kindly'. With that he left me wondering what the future had in store for me!

Ten minutes later Mother Teresa bustled into the room, 'You poor dear', she exclaimed, 'You should have told me before. You must be very distressed about what happened to you'

'It's not that simple', I said. Then I explained the circumstances and that I had been unconscious at the time. The evidence being circumstantial until now. 'Don't worry',

Mother Teresa articulated, 'We will look after you. You can stay here at least until the baby is born. It must be quite a shock, so I'll allow you some time to think about it and then we will talk again'

'Thank you Mother Teresa, you have been very compassionate towards me, I can't thank you enough'.

Later in the day we did discuss it. I had lots of questions because I had had no education on pregnancy. Mother Teresa said she would inform some of the other nuns and ensure that my duties weren't too strenuous. One good thing that came out of this was she assigned me to assist her with the abbey bookkeeping, because it entailed sitting down. The result, after some months, was that I gained a good understanding of finance. This would be very useful later on in my life.

So the days elapsed, I carried out my duties, attended prayers and as the morning sickness passed, my belly slowly grew until one day I could feel the baby kicking. Once more I sat down with Mother Teresa for a private conversation. 'Mother Teresa', I said nervously, 'You will think me a wicked child, but I don't want this baby!' Mother Teresa looked concerned as my words sank in, then she asked, 'Why not Maria?'

'This baby wasn't created out of love, it was wrought by an act of violence by an evil man!', I burst out.

'Oh Maria, please don't distress yourself. The baby isn't to blame for any of this. You must think about this very thoroughly. Maybe, in time, you will bring yourself to love baby or maybe we need to find a different solution, but please be assured that we will help you and support you in whatever decision you feel you need to take'

I let out a sigh of relief, I had dreaded telling Mother Teresa exactly how I felt. So with more confidence I proceeded, 'I have given this matter a lot of thought, I am adamant that I do not want this baby. I am prepared to give him or her away'

'Very well then, if that is your final decision, I will make the necessary arrangements', Mother Teresa stated resignedly

'Yes that is my final decision. Thank you for being so understanding', and I hugged her. However even then there were tears in my eyes at the enormity of the decision that I had made. The sense of loss almost overwhelmed me.

By and large the Sisters were understanding, although one or two were a bit standoffish with me, I don't think they agreed with my decision. However as time got nearer to my due date there seemed to be a general acceptance as to what would happen with the baby.

Then one sunny morning, yawning, I got out of bed, stretched and to my surprise my waters broke! I'm afraid I panicked and shouted for help. Sisters Flora, Beatrice and Carmen all came running. Sister Beatrice was first to arrive on the scene, she weighed up the situation and seemed to know exactly what to do. She barked an order at Carmen, 'Fetch a bowl of hot water and some towels'. 'Yes, right away', replied Carmen excitedly. Then Beatrice requested Flora, 'Flora please go and fetch Mother Teresa immediately'. Flora nodded her agreement, turned and hurried away. Beatrice helped me back onto the bed and told me not to worry. Soon a small throng gathered around my bed as the first waves of labour pulsed through my body. 'So this is it', I thought to myself.

As it turned out I was in labour for about eight hours. All the while the Sisters fussed around me, coming and going with advice, drinks and words of encouragement. It was a great comfort to have them around. So it was at about four o'clock in the afternoon that I delivered a very pink, but more importantly healthy, baby boy! He had a good set of lungs too!

Later, after I had had a little sleep and all the fuss had subsided, Mother Teresa sat with me. She asked, 'Have you decided what you are going to call him?'

'No, and I don't want to name him either. I mustn't get attached to him. I don't want him'

Mother Teresa pursed her lips before saying, 'Well my dear, that being the case, the sooner we find a good home for him the better. In the meantime I'll call him Mateo, meaning gift of god', adding, 'Poor little mite, he would feel a lost soul without a name'

I gave Mother Teresa a reproachful look. Hadn't I just said I didn't want a name for the baby? At that moment Carmen walked in and no more was said on the matter. Mother Teresa got up, patting down her robes, saying, 'I must go now, other duties to perform. Sister Carmen would you mind sitting with Maria for a while please?'

'I'd love to and can I hold the baby?', Sister Carmen asked with a broad smile on her face

'Of course you can', I said returning her smile.

Sister Carmen gingerly picked up Mateo, wrapped in a shawl, speaking to him softly. This obviously gave her great pleasure. Of course she doesn't have any of the painful memories and associations that I have!

It was three days later when I was told a couple offering a large donation to the nunnery had turned up and taken my baby away. Mother Teresa was surprised that they were willing to pay so much and they asked her for complete confidentiality. I assumed they must have wanted a son so much that they would give him the love that I myself could not. I never saw him again. Initially I thought that would be that but over the ensuing days I found myself wrestling with my conscience. As I lay on my bed I posed rhetorical questions. Surely there is no greater love than that between a mother and her child? Why didn't I have maternal feelings towards the baby? Should I have kept him? After all the Sisters would have supported me. Also mother's milk is supposed to give baby the best start. Conversely, every time I looked at baby he reminded me of the horror that I had been through and the revulsion that I felt for Kylo. I still have nightmares and wake up in a cold sweat. Will I ever come to terms with this? What a dreadful dichotomy! I revisited my internal struggle many times and the more I did, the more my hatred for Kylo burned inside me. I became adamant that, when the time was right, I would seek retribution!

Over the next couple of years I settled into a fairly comfortable routine, the nuns providing my continued education and in return I worked hard in the kitchens and the laundry. Also my bookkeeping skills improved further and I became quite competent to the extent that Mother Teresa trusted me. She even brought me in to the discussions with suppliers, although I mostly took a back seat. However not everything was plain sailing, I still had nightmares relating to Kylo and the baby. I would wake up in the middle of the night, shaking and in a cold sweat! I would then lie there fretting, the injustice gnawing away inside my head making it impossible for me to go back to sleep.

I got on well with most of the Sisters, they appeared to like me and I worked hard with particular diligence with my studies, they even taught me to speak English which is why I can converse with you now. I attended prayers and Religious Studies, although my heart wasn't in it. I think the Sisters

317

thought I might even graduate as a nun. However I began to have a greater longing for the outside world. I harboured ambitions to run my own business and, most importantly, to seek revenge on Kylo. So one day I said farewell to the Sisters and took a lift to Barcelona, where I managed to catch-up with some of my old contacts. Soon I was carrying out tasks for the criminal fraternity and for commercial enterprises to. Along the way I picked up various snippets of information that I was able to put to good use. These enabled me to take on discreet activities, grow my operation and take on additional staff. Soon I was earning good money and gaining a reputation. Unfortunately this meant stepping on other people's toes, and, much to my delight, one of these was Kylo's toes and the toes of his associates!

One day I was sitting in a café having a coffee with my good friend Pedro when he told me something very interesting. Now Pedro had worked for me for some time, but he also works for others. A freelance criminal I suppose you would say. Please don't look at me like that, with limited job opportunities, a person has to make a living somehow or other! Pedro had been working in Kylo's warehouse loading and unloading goods from trucks, when he overheard an argument between Kylo and one of his henchmen, Tomás. They were in the office but the door was open. Tomás was saying, 'I don't want to come in on Saturday it's my day off and I've got tickets for the

Barcelona versus Real Madrid match'. Kylo responded angrily, 'I don't care if you have a fucking audience with the Pope! You bloody well will be in on Saturday or else!'

'Or else what?', said Tomás petulantly

'Or else you won't work for me again and I'll see that no one else in Barcelona employs you'

Tomás looks at his boots and disgruntledly mutters, 'That's not fair'

'No? Well for your information, you'll soon learn that life isn't fair!'

'What's so frigging important about Saturday anyway?'

'There is a big consignment of brandy coming. A 16-ton container load'

'Wow!'

'So I need your help with the forklift unloading the beast. After all you are my most skilful driver', Kylo explained trying to lighten the conversation

'I suppose so', Tomás conceded and then with cunning, 'But I want double-time pay'

'You'll be lucky! Time and half is the best I can offer'

'OK then', Tomás replied and held out his hand which Kylo grasped firmly and they shook on it.

Maria continued, 'So I put two and two together and concluded that the consignment of brandy is either counterfeit or stolen goods. So then I pumped Pedro for details about the warehouse, what security measures were in place? Is there a guard or any regular patrols? How are the entrances and exits secured? Are the premises alarmed? Obviously Pedro guessed straightaway that I had designs on that cargo of brandy, so I had to cut him in. In return he'd assist in the execution of my plan. So on Saturday I had another of my men, Jorge, discreetly observe that the delivery actually happened. Then at one a.m. we went into action, we had to strike quickly because I guessed that Kylo would start distributing the bottles on Monday or as soon as he possibly could. I'd hired four trucks each with a four-ton load capacity, that way we could take the entire sixteen tons and move it a long way from Barcelona, in separate directions! My men had donned black trousers, jumpers and balaclava. There was a single guard, half asleep! Pedro crept up to him from behind, then held a wad of cotton soaked in chloroform over his mouth and nose until he had stopped struggling. The guard slumped to the ground and Pedro quickly fastened gaffer tape around his wrists, his legs and over his mouth. Jorge hurried over with a ladder and positioned it under a rather antique looking alarm box. Pedro climbed up the ladder and squirted quick-setting foam inside, there was now no chance this could be activated! The massive warehouse doors were secured by two large sliding bolts with padlocks. Jorge was quickly there again with a small oxy-acetylene set and rapidly burnt through the metalwork. The doors were pulled back and the first truck went in. The men worked diligently but as silently as possible, although the rest of the industrial estate seemed quiet enough. Soon the first truck was loaded and dispatched, followed in quick succession by a second, then a third and finally the fourth. I must admit I did breathe a sigh of relief as I stood there surveying the now empty warehouse. Then I did something rather rash, I took a white card out of my pocket and wrote, "Missing something?" together with a smiley face. Somehow I don't think Kylo saw the funny side! Oh, revenge is so sweet!'

Connie, looking rather shocked, asked, 'Wasn't that a bit risky? Surely Kylo would have guessed that it was you?'

'Yes, I am fairly certain he would have guessed, but I was buzzing with adrenaline and I got carried away in the moment!'

'So did you get away with it?'

'Yes and no. Of course Kylo couldn't go to the police, but I heard that he was making various enquiries within the criminal fraternity. However my team were all very tight lipped, so he had nothing concrete to go on. However I know that he tried to interfere in my business affairs on more than one occasion!"

'He must have guessed then'

'Yes, I presume so. Then again that was nothing compared with my next stunt!', Maria grinned

'Oh please do tell us more!', Connie quickly enjoined

'Yes please do', said Mike

'Let me order some coffees first'

Once the coffees had arrived, we settled back in our chairs and I commenced the next part of my story. 'It originated a few years ago, in July 2015 to be precise. Five artworks by Francis Bacon, together with a safe containing jewels and other precious items were stolen from the Madrid home of banker José Capelo Blanco. The five works were estimated to be worth in excess of $28m dollars, making this the biggest heist of contemporary art in Spain!

José Capelo was a close friend of Francis Bacon for four years until Bacon's death in Madrid in 1992 at the age of 82. Obviously the police worked very hard to identify the perpetrators of the crime, unfortunately with little success, until an extraordinary breakthrough. In February 2016 the investigators received an email from a London company that specialises in tracking stolen works of art. The company had been contacted by someone in Stiges near Barcelona, who wanted to verify the authenticity of one of the paintings. The inquirer sent the company photos of the work by email, which revealed Bacon's signature on the back of the painting. This led the company's specialists to suspect that the photos had been taken after the burglary. The photographs were forwarded to the Spanish investigators, they determined the model of camera used, where it had been rented from, and subsequently, who had rented it. The renter turned out to be one of the perpetrators! Then in May 2016 the police made seven arrests in Madrid. Well, you can imagine the gossip that ensued amongst the criminal fraternity! It was as though someone had taken a big stick and stirred it within a hornet's nest! How did all of this impact me? I hear you ask.'

Mike and Connie were listening intently. 'Yes, please go on', Connie enthused.

I continued, 'I was in ignorance about most of this, but on the grapevine I'd heard that Kylo was moving a valuable cargo. I couldn't find out what the cargo was, everything was being done very secretly. This of course indicated it was something of great value and caused me to take an even greater interest! However one of my informers was able to find out when and where the cargo was being moved from. So there I was, at ten in the morning sitting alongside Ricardo my driver, in a white Fiat Ducato van outside a property in Stiges. 'How much longer must we wait?', asked a bored Ricardo. 'Not much longer', I replied patiently. Sure enough at that moment a blue Iveco Daily appeared coming down the drive. 'Wait a moment before you start the engine', I cautioned Ricardo. 'Let's not make this too obvious'. I noted down the matricula - registration number - and read it out loud to Ricardo. We waited for the blue van to reach the corner of the road before I gave Ricardo the order to follow and we were away. Before long we were a respectful distance behind the blue van on the A-2 heading in the direction of Zaragoza. 'What's the plan then boss?', Ricardo asked.

'I don't really have one', I admitted, 'We need to find out what they are up to and where they are going. Also most importantly, what their precious cargo is'

'Huh!', a not too impressed Ricardo grunted, then, 'Like you instructed, I have a full tank of fuel and the tools of my trade', he laughed at this as the 'tools of his trade' are mostly for committing criminal acts.

'Just concentrate on your driving and whatever you do don't lose sight of that van!'

'OK boss'

The autopista wasn't terribly busy, so Ricardo had no problem following the blue van. 'Where are they going?', I wondered as the journey was becoming quite monotonous. After approximately three hours we found ourselves on the Zaragoza carretera de circumval. 'I could do with a coffee', hinted Ricardo

'Do your job, we'll have plenty of time for coffee later'

The blue van indicated and took the exit towards Madrid. A few minutes later it was pulling into a Repsol services and parking up. 'Park close by', I told Ricardo and he dutifully did. Two heavies got out of the van and swaggered into the building that contained a restaurant and other facilities. I waited for a few minutes until they had disappeared inside and then said, 'Ricardo bring your bolt-cutters and jemmy. We're going to take a look inside!' For a big chap Ricardo could move surprisingly quickly. He jumped out of our van and within seemingly seconds, had broken into the back of the blue van. I could see straightaway a collection of frames or doors wrapped in blankets and held against the inside of the van by retaining straps. I pulled one of the blankets back and saw immediately it was a painting. I guessed it must be valuable if Kylo was going to all this trouble, so with some urgency I said, 'Ricardo, help me grab this painting and let's get out of here!' Ricardo quickly loosened the retaining strap and freed the painting. Safely stowing it in our van, still wrapped in the blanket. Soon we were heading back towards Barcelona. I'd had no more than a glimpse of the painting and didn't really like what I saw. The subject was an ugly representation of a man, surely this couldn't be worth anything much? 'Did you see the painting Ricardo?', I asked

'Sí, I wouldn't pay a single euro for it', he shrugged

A short time later we stopped at the services for a short break and coffee. Then we didn't stop again until we entered the suburbs of Barcelona, where Ricardo changed the false number plates over for genuine ones. We then continued in a roundabout manner until we were back at our base. I asked Ricardo to carefully carry the painting into our warehouse and hide it on top of the internal roof of the small office. It was only much later that I found out exactly how valuable the painting was. I realised then that it was too hot to handle, so to me fairly well valueless. Although I did have the satisfaction in knowing that its disappearance must have been a great embarrassment to Kylo, who would probably be made to pay one way or another for losing such a valuable masterpiece. He may even have suspected me, as from that point onwards he seemed even more intent on wrecking my business, and me of course in wrecking his!

In July 2017 the police announced that they had recovered three of the five Francis Bacon paintings that were stolen in 2015. Seven people had been arrested in May 2016 and three more in January 2017. Unfortunately Kylo wasn't one of them! I still don't like the painting, so it remains where I put it', I chuckle.

'You don't mean above your office?', Connie asks

'Yes, I'm afraid it is!'

Mike spoke quietly, 'We'll just have to pretend we didn't hear that last part'

'What last part?', said Connie smiling

'Happy Christmas to you both', Maria raises her coffee cup

'A very Happy Christmas to you Maria and thanks again!'

'No problem. Now I will personally take you to the airport and make sure you get on the plane home before you can cause any more trouble!', she laughed.

EPILOGUE

A tall swarthy, almost handsome young man stood watching as Maria waved off the two English troublemakers. He clenched his fists so tight his nails dug into the flesh of his palms. Through gritted teeth he muttered, 'I will have my revenge one day you bitch Maria. You killed my father and my uncle. You will pay dearly for that!' With those scathing words Mateo turned his back and walked away....

The End

Printed in Dunstable, United Kingdom